ENIGMA

By the Author

Shadow Series

Moon Shadow

Shadows of Steel

Shadow Dancers

Enigma

Enigma

by

Suzie Clarke

2022

ENIGMA

ISBN 13: 978-1-63555-999-6

This Trade Paperback Original Is Published By
Bold Strokes Books, Inc.
P.O. Box 249
Valley Falls, NY 12185

First Edition: November 2022

Credits
Editors: Victoria Villaseñor and Shelley Thrasher
Production Design: Stacia Seaman
Cover Design by Tammy Seidick

Acknowledgments

This book would not be the quality it is without the sensitivity and expertise of my BSB editors, Victoria Villaseñor and Shelley Thrasher. Thank you for your care and guidance.

A special thank you to Jeannie, my fellow author and friend, for her willingness to talk and listen in the wee hours of the morning about my concerns for this book. Your insights were invaluable.

No historic fiction can be written well without significantly researching the time period. I will never be the same after researching for the story of Enigma. I stand in awe of the timing of events that happened prior to WWII to prepare the United States and our people to participate in a war we did not want to enter. From inventions in industry and farming, to government programs and political and military leadership, everything pointed us toward and prepared us to enter WWII. Although not all Americans agreed on going to war, we as a nation worked together and did what we had to do.

Thank you to the Barberton Library staff for their generosity and assistance.

I wish to express my deep appreciation and gratitude to all the organizations and individuals who have worked tirelessly to preserve historical documents, including radio broadcasts, recordings, and photographs of the time period. Those materials were critical in helping me get a sense of the culture, atmosphere, and concerns of our people here in the United States during the 1930s and early 1940s.

I'm proud to claim my heritage as an American citizen. I will be forever grateful to the noble men and women who currently serve and have served our country, both in the military and on the home front. Bravery is not limited to those who march into the battle, but also to those who stand and wait for their return.

It is not in the taking but in the giving that we can truly understand the meaning of Patriotism.

To Mom and Dad, Aunt Bette and Uncle Frank,
and all who paid the price for a world at war—
both across the seas and here at home.
Thank you for your courage, sacrifice, and magnificence.

CHAPTER ONE

Agent Polly Sylvester handed the dollar to the cab driver from the backseat. "Keep the change." She opened the door, then her umbrella, and slid from the dry cab into the cold, pelting DC rain. She shivered. The downpour was worse than yesterday, unusual for November. The sun hadn't made an appearance in five days, adding to the sense of foreboding hovering over the US capital.

Since the initiation of the draft in September of last year, President Roosevelt's State of the Union address on January sixth this year, and the increase in war-production materials, the mood of the country was beginning to change. Most everyone realized the United States was going to enter the war in Europe. It was just a matter of time. But many still believed America should remain neutral and isolated. Europe's plight, Japan's aggression, and pleas for peace and negotiations were the topic of discussion in every office, dinner party, country club, or social gathering in Washington.

Polly angled the umbrella for better protection and maneuvered between the double rows of near-identical black Fords, interspersed with an occasional eye-catching Plymouth or Buick along the curb. Mostly they were drab government vehicles with impatient drivers honking and jockeying for position to get their wards as close as possible to the entrance of the Lafayette Building. She dashed for the steps, regretting she couldn't run up them or, at least, take them two at a time. *Damned heels.* The bottom of her raincoat blew open, and by the time she reached the top, her silk stockings and the front of her black wool skirt were soaked. *Damned rain.*

In the lobby, she stepped to the side and shook the water from the umbrella, trying not to spray herself and others as they passed. She closed it and snapped the strap around the folds, then slipped off her drenched raincoat, draping it over her arm. She moved into one of the lines of people plodding toward the security desk, some with anxious expressions, others with a look of anticipation.

"Polly? Hey, Polly," a male voice called.

She turned, then smiled when she recognized Jimmy Pendergast farther back in the line next to hers. He looked like he'd just dragged himself and his brown leather satchel out of the Potomac. Evidently, he hadn't been able to get a cab from the office, which meant he'd missed the early train, which meant he and Eloise, his new bride, had stayed up late again. A twinge of emptiness pried its way into Polly's thoughts. She forced it back, reminding herself that relationships only got in the way and made her vulnerable.

Jimmy tipped his fedora and moved forward, now standing directly across from her. He pointed to her new felt bonnet hat. "Love it."

She laughed. "And I love what you've done to *your* wardrobe."

"Yes." He shrugged and grinned. "I look like a drowned rat. Good thing I have a change in my office." He glanced around as if checking to see who might be listening. "Did you hear?"

Intrigued, Polly shook her head.

He leaned in. "A German sub hit the HMS *Ark Royal* off Gibraltar and sank it," he said, his voice lowered.

Polly gasped. "No," she whispered. "If the United States doesn't get into the war soon, there won't be anything left of Great Britain."

Jimmy nodded, then eased away. "Going on another assignment?"

Her security clearance was far above his. He knew she couldn't answer his question, but he always tried. "Run along, Jimmy," she said, still lost in the ramifications of what he'd told her.

"Tell Agent Arrogant over there hello for me." He cringed, lifting his chin in the direction of the stairs that Henson, her security escort, was descending. "See you back at the office."

She waved him away as she moved to the soldier at the reception desk and handed him her credentials. She signed in under the date, Tuesday, November 18, 1941. Would she be home for Thanksgiving this year, or away on assignment? Not that it mattered. She didn't have any love interest, and no one would be waiting for her when she got back. A slight sigh escaped as she filled in her destination. "Assistant Director—Office of American Defense."

She met Agent Henson at the bottom of the stairs, and without greeting, they climbed the marble steps to the second floor, their footfalls echoing off the stark white walls—his a low-pitched swish-shuffle, hers the tap-tap of high heels. The sounds clashed, like their personalities.

It'd been weeks since she'd been to the Lafyette Building. Another special assignment was fine with her. She wanted to be in the field where the action was and where she could make a significant difference, not in the office doing the same searches and investigations day after day. Her last mission had been in Detroit, stuck in a dank basement with dim lighting for days, poring over reams of documents and what little evidence they had, trying to ferret out who stole the plans for the newly designed Sherman tank or, as the guys at the factory called it, "Easy 8." But she'd done it. The culprit ended up being one of the assembly-line workers. They were able to catch him at the Canadian border, the designs for the tank sewn into the lining of his jacket. He'd talked after some firm persuasion from Polly's colleagues and gave up the German contact who was meeting him in Windsor-Ontario.

She quickened her pace to keep up with Henson, then half-stepped to get out of stride with him.

He topped out at maybe six feet, about four inches taller than she was in her heels. He cast her a side glance as the muscles around his mouth tightened. He pushed his shoulders back and stiffened his arms against his sides. He didn't march. More like he tramped with an attitude stuck up his rear end. Just a glance probably helped him feel superior.

She got the message. He didn't approve of her being there. Lines were drawn once again.

She'd had her fill of lines, domineering males, attitudes, and needing to fight her way in. But it was ever thus. "Women can't do this type of work." "They aren't physically or mentally capable." "How will they be protected in the field?" She'd heard those comments over and over again. She'd scored just as high as any of the men on her proficiency tests, and in marksmanship. And she'd given her instructor a bloody nose when he decided to show *her* she couldn't handle herself in a physical altercation. She'd had to prove herself with every assignment. But they couldn't stop her. She'd angled and elbowed her way in, and she wasn't leaving. Especially now. Not after she'd fought so hard to get here. Her work spoke for itself, even if most of the men weren't listening.

Her last assignment in Detroit had been important for her career. After four long years, the men she worked with had finally accepted her. Well, at least *most* of them had, but not Henson. And he would most likely be her Washington contact on the next assignment. He could take his line and shove it where the sun didn't shine.

She stopped at an open doorway on her side of the hall and peered in. No reason, mostly just to irritate him.

The office was typical of all the federal offices now. They were filled with government employees in a state of heightened excitement and anxiety, or what Polly liked to call organized disorder. Typewriters clacked. Phones rang. Instructions were shouted. She watched, taking in the chaotic scene.

Three men hovered in the corner, gesticulating wildly. One pointed at the others, a lit cigarette clamped between his fingers. "It's not our job to police the world. Don't stand there and tell me Japan won't counter. We froze all their financial assets here in America this past summer. And with the oil embargo? Believe me, oil is life." He took a deep drag on the cigarette and blew the smoke at his colleagues. "And another thing, the Lend-Lease Act signed in March smells like yesterday's can of opened Spam. I'm telling you, *pudge boy* made some kind of a clandestine deal with President Roosevelt when they were in Newfoundland." The other men nodded, clearly hanging on every word.

"Come along, Miss Sylvester." Henson's tone was clipped as he grasped her elbow.

"Churchill will make any deal necessary to get the help he needs," she said.

"Hmm. I'm sure."

She slipped free of his hold. And his attitude.

Their footsteps were barely audible as they passed more bustling offices, but the noise level faded when they reached the rotunda that opened out at the end of the hallway. The curved wall to the left held more office doorways. The other side boasted an expanse of glass framing an impressive view of the White House.

President Roosevelt hadn't been in residence for three days. Polly kept tabs on his whereabouts. He was with Secretary of War Henry Stimson and several other members of his cabinet at the military base in Frederick County, Maryland, that the president called Shangri-la.

Henson led the way toward the ornately carved wooden door across the imposing space.

Instinctively, Polly straightened and tugged at the bottom of her gray wool gabardine suit coat, hoping there were no wrinkles. Her damp stockings clung to her calves, making her self-conscious.

Henson motioned her to a seat in one of the dark-purple, cushioned chairs outside the door. "One of the department heads, Mr. Williamson, will see you shortly, Miss Sylvester."

Like she didn't know who she was here to see. She bit back a retort. The games she had to play. "Thank you," she said as pleasantly as she could manage.

He nodded slightly and left.

Polly crossed her legs, checking to make sure the seams of her stockings were straight.

She surveyed the people through the open doorway in the office closest to her as they quietly chatted, passing one another, papers and folders in hand. Two men, nearest the entrance, stopped to greet each other. The taller one, with thinning light-brown hair and metal-rimmed glasses that slipped down his large, pronounced nose, reeked of accounting. Ink smudged his thumb and forefinger, and the sleeve of his jacket was rumpled from where he constantly dragged his arm over the ledger. His brown-leather wingtip shoestrings were parallel to the deck, and his tie was knotted so tightly it moved every time he swallowed. Definitely accounting. The shorter man with a crop of dark-brown hair was probably from the Office of Strategic Planning. An easy spot. Chalk dust on his suit coat and the tops of his black dress shoes, and dark circles under his eyes. The latter was the real giveaway. No one in the Office of Strategic Planning had slept more than four hours a night in ten months, not since the president's State of the Union address.

His words burned in Polly's mind. "There are those who would clip the wings of the American eagle in order to feather their own nests...The first phase of the invasion of this hemisphere would not be by the landing of regular troops. The necessary strategic points would be occupied by secret agents and their dupes. And great numbers of them are already here…"

She knew why she'd been summoned. She was sitting outside the office of the assistant director of OAD. It didn't take a genius to figure it out. She could hardly stay seated. Her mouth was dry, and she was sure her lipstick was no longer evident because she'd licked her lips so much. Would she go somewhere in the United States again? Or outside the country? Europe? She startled when the door opened.

Abigail, Williamson's secretary, greeted her with a smile. "Miss Sylvester, he'll see you now. May I take your raincoat and umbrella?"

Polly's heart rate accelerated. She inhaled slowly, trying to take in an unnoticed deep breath. "Yes. Thank you." She rose and gratefully surrendered the wet items. She adjusted her jacket one last time and positioned her clutch bag under her arm, then followed Abigail through the reception area to another heavy oak door.

Abigail knocked, then opened it. "She's here, sir." She motioned for Polly to enter, then closed the door behind her as she left.

Despite his disarming smile, Assistant Director Steven J. Williamson projected an intimidating figure. He topped at least six foot two inches, had a full head of blond hair, and bright-blue, penetrating eyes. And he was the one man in the United States government who'd given her a legitimate chance and believed in her.

When she first went to work for Assistant Director to the Secretary of War Halbrook P. Merriweather, she'd hoped she could use her skills, but she'd ended up being a glorified secretary. A year later, in the fall of 1937, the OAD was formed, and Steven J. Williamson was named as an assistant director. He'd worked with Polly on several projects for Mr. Merriweather and asked her to join the newly formed department. He'd taken a risk by including a woman.

The pungent odor of Abigail's gardenia perfume lingered and mingled with the heavy scent of Williamson's pipe tobacco. The mixture reminded Polly of the first time she'd met him. It was at a party she would never have been able to get into on her own.

She'd been in Washington DC for a year and couldn't get her foot in any of the government-agency doors. Then her cousin Edmond came to visit, and everything changed. He had strong political connections in his home state of New York and personally knew Charles Evans Hughes, the chief justice of the United States. He'd taken Polly to a political party fund-raiser, and a door had flown wide open for her. It began with a simple social conversation with Assistant Director Merriweather.

"So, what picture do you think will win the Academy Award?" asked Merriweather.

Polly didn't have a clue.

Edmond whispered in her ear, "The Informer *or* Mutiny on the Bounty. *Anyone's guess."*

Polly took a shot. She had a fifty-fifty chance, but Clark Gable was popular, so that weighted her decision. "Mutiny on the Bounty.*"*

"Oh, for God's sake. That picture's never going to win."

So much for making a good impression.

"And I suppose you think Hauptmann didn't kill the Lindberg baby?" Merriweather asked.

Polly was flabbergasted. Most everyone had judged him guilty, but she didn't have the information she needed to make an informed decision about guilt. The newspapers, the lawyers, the police's bungling of the evidence, even Lindberg himself had influenced the jury. She didn't know how to respond, but from the terse expression on Merriweather's face and the emotion in his question, whether he wanted to admit it or not, he had doubts.

Edmond stepped in for her. "Polly's an excellent analyst, and I'm sure she'd be a valuable asset to your staff. Why don't you give her a try?"

Merriweather looked Polly over from head to toe. "A female analyst, huh?"

Richard nudged her. "Do it, Polly."

She looked more closely at the man, discerning all she needed in a few seconds.

He reeked of the heavy odor from cigar smoke that clung to his formal dinner jacket. The strength of it meant he hadn't been alone, which meant he must have been meeting with other men prior to the dinner, which meant he hadn't spent much time with his wife tonight. "Well, you like Cuban cigars." She winced inwardly. It didn't take any skill to determine that fact.

"And..." he prompted her.

He wore a heavy dose of aftershave. A strong scent of peppermint dominated his breath. Was it an attempt to try to hide the liquor? Polly also noticed a faint, lingering whiff of perfume on his lapel, floral with a trace of musk. The same perfume Senator Randall's assistant was wearing. Another clue he probably wasn't with his wife. Was he having an affair? The way he looked at Senator Randall's assistant, it was most likely her. None of this would help impress him, though. If she said anything about it, she'd be kicked out the very door that might be opening. "You're a southpaw," she said instead. It was an easy tell. She'd noticed the pen in the right inside pocket of his open jacket and that the muscles in his left hand were more developed than his right.

What else? She needed something more significant. She dug deeper.

The back of his dinner jacket was slightly wrinkled. A longer meeting with the boys than he'd expected. An emergency meeting? Tupelo, Mississippi, had a horrific tornado. Perhaps a possible meeting to decide how much aid to give the city and state? No. Mussolini announcing the annexation of Ethiopia and proclaiming himself emperor? That was the one.

"You were in an emergency meeting with the secretary of war and a few others, but it didn't go as well as you'd hoped."

His eyes widened.

No surprise there. Those meetings never went like anyone wanted.

He studied her like a bug through a magnifying glass, then suddenly huffed. "Come see me, nine sharp, Monday morning."

As he walked away, Steven J. Williamson approached her. "Quite impressive. Now tell me what you really saw."

And that had been the beginning.

Now, four years later, Williamson walked around his desk and greeted her. "Polly."

"Sir."

"Good to see you again. How's everyone at home?"

She was sure he didn't want to know her father still wasn't speaking to her. And he especially didn't need to know her parents were "horrified and disappointed" that she wasn't married yet and seemed to have no interest in changing her marital status. They insisted she was too selective and needed to "come to her senses soon." She didn't intend to try to change. They and the rest of the world saw homosexuality as a sickness, a flaw in a person's character or moral fiber. She saw it differently. But that wasn't part of this conversation either.

"Mother and Dad are well, sir."

"Fine, fine." He motioned her to a seat across from him on the leather sofa. "We have a job for you."

"I thought you might."

He smiled. "Not just any job. This one is a priority."

"Where this time, sir? West Coast or East Coast?"

His brow furrowed. He listed toward her and lowered his voice. "Barberton, Ohio. A critical aircraft design and production plant."

Polly's heart skipped a beat. This was it, the chance she'd been waiting for to take the lead on an assignment.

"They suspect someone is trying to steal top-secret information. They've verified nothing is missing, but secure documents have been tampered with, confidential aircraft designs and plans have been out of place, and files have been rearranged. I've talked in depth with the head of the plant. They've tightened their security but have asked us to send an agent to investigate. The theft of any details from this specific factory would be detrimental to national security because of the prototype plane they're producing. You're to pose as an employee, confirm there is a spy, and if there is, find him or *her*."

Polly's attention heightened. The thought of a female spy was intriguing. It made sense. Every factory in the United States was now hiring women, and some were beginning to have more female employees than male.

"You are to eliminate the threat at any cost, Polly." His jaw tightened, and the lines at the corners of his eyes deepened. "The information at this plant cannot reach the hands of our enemies. Do you understand what I'm telling you?"

"Yes, sir. I do."

He rose and walked to his desk. "You'll leave immediately, but we're going to route you through Philadelphia to Cleveland, since that's your cover." He picked up a dossier and brought it back to her. "All your travel arrangements are in here. Your identity papers are on top. You're to stay at a private home owned by one Kalena Luisa Mikloska in Barberton. We haven't had time to investigate her and clear her of suspicion. That makes it more difficult for you, but we were barely able to get you a place to stay because of the demand for housing. It's all been arranged. All the information we have is in this folder, but the company executives will give you the specific details you need once you get there." He tapped it, as if to emphasize its importance. "Turn this over to your contact when you reach Cleveland. He'll ride the train with you to Akron, then drive you to the residence. You're on your own after that. He'll give you instructions on how to contact him." He reached into the folder and brought out two keys. "These are to your emergency safe house. One unlocks the main entrance, the other the apartment." He told her the address. "Memorize it and never write it down. Only you and your local contact know it. Your code name is Enigma. Your backup contact agent here in Washington is Agent Henson."

The mere mention of his name brought an aura of disappointment and concern. She'd have to depend on Henson for information and support. Would he do his job? The more she thought about it, the more apprehension engulfed her. But she couldn't talk to anyone about him, especially not to the assistant director. If she said anything, it'd make her look weak and petty. Now more than ever, she had to project a strong, confident front, no matter what she felt. Hopefully, if things went well, she'd have minimal contact with Henson. The critical person was her local contact, not Henson. She stood and took the file and keys.

He reached for her hand and shook it. "Godspeed in finding the enemy, Polly. Be safe. Our prayers and hopes go with you."

As she left the office, the magnitude of the moment fully struck her. The weight of it pressed down, slowing each step as the White House came into view. *At any cost!* This was the opportunity she'd worked for. Was she ready? Could she do it?

CHAPTER TWO

Kalena Mikloska folded her mother's checkered apron and placed it on the countertop beside the wooden flour bin her papa had made her momma as a Christmas gift in 1915. The once-red-painted feathers of the carved rooster on the front of the bin were now a faded rust color, but his etched initials and the year he'd made it were still visible at the bottom.

She kissed her fingertips and touched the apron, then traced the outline of the rooster. The image of her father's tired, careworn face and the steel-blue of his eyes as he bent to pick her up flashed in her mind. He'd kiss her cheek and they'd twirl. She could still feel the prickle of his rough stubble as she'd press her palms to his face. He'd reach down with callused hands and gather her in a hug, always gentle in the way he held her.

Displaying the items during the holidays usually helped ease the pain of the loss of her parents when she was four, but this year, as hard as she tried, Kalena couldn't get excited about Thanksgiving, let alone Christmas. The tragedies of the past and the turmoil of the present were overwhelming. The flu pandemic had taken both her parents and her older brother. The stock-market crash and Great Depression had wiped out Aunt Berna and Uncle Frederick's finances, and then Uncle Frederick had died suddenly of a heart attack a year ago.

Kalena was twenty-six, and she and Aunt Berna were the only ones left of their family. It didn't seem fair, but they weren't the only people who'd lost loved ones. Neighbors and friends had also suffered. Some families were annihilated, gone in a month, a week, or even a day. Their losses had somehow bonded their community, at least in the small city of Barberton, Ohio. They watched out for each other and were concerned about their neighborhood.

Kalena took a deep breath, then exhaled slowly, forcing out the memories.

Now, more devastation lurked on the horizon. The war in Europe grew closer each day. Paperboys shouted the headlines on almost every corner of the downtown streets. Radio programs blasted the updates every evening. No conversation took place without talk of war or America's responsibility. Why should we get in it? What will happen? When? These seemed to be the questions seeded in everyone's mind.

War production was gaining momentum. City officials had asked all who could to open their homes and provide housing for the increased number of workers at the Akron factories and the aircraft plant south of Barberton. Just two years ago, Portage Aircraft Inc. had forty workers. Now they employed over two thousand. Trolley cars and busses ran from sunup to long past sundown to accommodate the influx and the need for transportation. Everyone felt the sense of urgency to meet the demand.

Aunt Berna stirred beside Kalena, reminding her she wasn't alone.

She set her cup of coffee on the counter and patted Kalena's arm. "And now your momma and papa are with us once again." She smiled, her soft blue eyes twinkling, a hint of pink in her round cheeks. "If your momma was here this year, she'd especially enjoy the holidays. The house will be full of people because you opened your home. Needs will be met, and hearts will be lifted." She slipped her cotton apron over her head and drew the ties behind her, a gesture she'd made at least a million times, probably more. "I remember when she made *that*," Aunt Berna said, pointing to the apron on the flour bin. "I think it was July 1917. You were…" She gazed off, looking out the kitchen window.

"I was two," Kalena said, looking into the backyard at the bare maple trees, stripped of their glory. Only a few determined remnants of summer clung to a branch here and there, refusing to meet their inevitable fate. The trees seemed to reach out, pleading for their lost children, who now lay scattered on the ground, edges laced white from last night's frost. They were no longer the bright orange and yellow of late October, but withered and weary, speckled with varying shades of gray and brown. Snow would be here soon.

"My sunshine," Aunt Berna said in Polish. She smiled and brushed

Kalena's cheek with the back of a careworn hand. "How the years have passed by so quickly."

Kalena touched her fingers to Aunt Berna's lips. "You are *my* sunshine. I don't know where I'd be without you."

"Shh. This fine house was your momma and papa's, and now it's yours. I'm glad you didn't stay away too long."

"I don't know if I'll be able to keep it," Kalena said. "Even with the boarders, and my job at the plant, I'm barely able to make the monthly mortgage. Heating oil is up, and food prices have risen so quickly I can't keep track. You and Uncle Frederick took good care of the house all these years, but I don't know if I can do it alone."

"You don't need to do it alone. Your Uncle Frederick saw into your future, and now we're twice blessed. The house is in fine shape to take in boarders, and we have a rich supply of our home-canned goods in the cellar. We're ready to help our country."

Kalena sighed. Aunt Berna didn't understand how fast things were changing. Who knew what tomorrow would be like? Would they go to war in Europe? If so, how soon? How much time did they have to prepare? What would it be like? The questions burned in Kalena's heart. "The new boarder will make three. That's a lot of work for you to do by yourself."

"Nonsense," Aunt Berna said. "I can handle it just fine. All of you are gone during the day, and I need to fix only breakfast and supper. I'll hold back meals for those who work the second shift. You can help with Sunday dinners, and the boarders can help with evening dishes and cleanup. We can manage. Others have a much harder row to hoe."

Kalena thought of Gerald Coleman, their second boarder, twenty-two, from Warren, Ohio. He was thin but muscular and had a deep scar on his right forearm and another above his brow. Neither Kalena nor Aunt Berna had been able to find the proper moment to ask him about his injuries. He was shy and withdrawn. He ate every bite of food on his plate, and at the end of each meal, he'd take a piece of bread and wipe the dish clean, then eat the sop. He always thanked Aunt Berna for his meal and complimented how good it tasted. "Gerald walks the three miles to the aircraft plant and only takes the return bus," Kalena said.

"I worry about him in the cold weather," Aunt Berna said.

"I think he doesn't spend the money for the bus so he can send every penny back to his family," Kalena said.

"Maybe, but sooner or later he's going to have to ride the bus. It'll get too cold for him to walk in the drifting snow in January," Aunt Berna said.

"Some of the farmers are using horse-drawn wagons along the route and charging only a few pennies to ride. Perhaps he can afford one of them."

"Anything would be better than walking that far in the bitter cold." Aunt Berna shook her head. "Such times again."

Now they were getting a female boarder. Kalena didn't know much about her, except that she was from out of state and would be arriving sometime this weekend. What would she look like? How old was she? Was she married? Did she have a family? Where did she grow up? Why was she coming to work at the plant?

She was excited to have another woman in the house. Perhaps she was her age. Thinking about her brought the deep loneliness to the surface. Sometimes it engulfed her, slithering through her, seeping down into her soul so she couldn't think. She'd had several opportunities to marry, but they'd never worked out. After a few years of dating, she lost interest. She'd suspected in her late teens that something was different about her. She found women's company more appealing than men's and sometimes wondered what it would be like to be with a woman. She watched the couples in the park and daydreamed about being with someone, feeling the touch of her caress, soft but firm, her body close. She'd left Barberton and gone to Cleveland for a time, trying to discover herself, but when Uncle Frederick died, she came back to be with Aunt Berna.

She wanted to talk with her aunt about her feelings, but she could never bring herself to do it. Mostly because she feared Aunt Berna would be disappointed or ashamed of her or tell her what she felt wasn't normal. Sometimes groups of women at the plant talked in hushed tones during their breaks about *those kinds of women.* Lesbians. Bulldykers. They'd point at the women who were less feminine looking. Once an argument broke out between a husky woman named Sheryl Walker and a not-so-nice woman everyone called Tinker Bell. As Tinker Bell walked past Sheryl, she leaned in and said something. Sheryl immediately jumped up and moved toward her, fists clenched, an angry expression on her face. Tinker Bell backed away, and nothing more was said. When Kalena asked her friend Juniper Bailey what had happened, Juniper simply said, "It's nothing. Let it go."

The talk made Kalena uncomfortable. How could those feelings not be normal when it was how *she* felt? She'd met a few women she suspected felt like her when she lived in Cleveland, but she didn't feel close enough to any of them to discuss her confusion or her concerns. Surely, there had to be others at the plant. Perhaps they were also too afraid to talk about the subject. She shuddered as the memory she tried to keep buried deep surfaced.

Once, as she passed a downtown alleyway, she saw two men attacking a woman. They shouted ugly words as they held her against the wall. "Bulldyke…Queer. You're one of those lesbians, aren't you? You just haven't had a real man." The taller man moved against her, forcing her arms behind her. The other man beside him laughed.

"Let go of me, you drunken pig," the woman cried.

"Leave her alone," Kalena yelled.

"Mind your own business," the man closest to her yelled back.

"I'm getting the police," Kalena shouted, and ran down the sidewalk. She'd stopped the police officer at the corner and told him what had been going on in the alleyway, then quickly left, almost running. She couldn't bring herself to stay to see if the woman was all right. A bitter taste filled her mouth as she remembered. She'd tried to purge the memory from her mind, but occasionally it seeped in, the vile words echoing, haunting the space at the edge of sleep. Was that what men did to women who felt as she did? Did the police help? Or had they looked the other way?

At first, she thought her feelings were a phase she was going through, something triggered by the tragedy of the loss of her parents and her brother. But the thoughts didn't leave, only grew stronger as she got older. She tried to be interested in the men she dated, but something was missing. She didn't look at them the way they looked at her. She didn't feel the closeness, longing, or need they seemed to. She sighed. She wanted things to be clear, but they weren't. She wanted her future to be certain, but it wasn't. At times the loneliness and uncertainty overwhelmed her. Would she ever be able to find the fulfillment she so desperately wanted?

She'd been dating Lionel Wilcox, one of the engineers at the plant, but it wasn't what it appeared to be. They had a *special* arrangement. He was the only one she could confide in, the only one who understood. Her secret was safe with him, and his with her.

The following morning, she ripped the page off the large black-and-white calendar hanging on the back of her bedroom door. Saturday, November 22. Another week. She crumpled the paper and tossed it into the trash basket, then closed the slightly raised window. The crisp chill of impending winter hung in the air. She set the hairbrush down on her mother's dark-cherrywood vanity and looked in the mirror.

"Momma, what am I going to do? Will I ever find someone to love and who will love me?"

The answer seemed to project back from her image in the mirror. *You'll figure it out.* She squeezed her eyes shut, trying to block the overpowering loneliness. She ran the intricately carved ivory comb through her newly cut and permed hair, then touched the mid-length curls. Her hairdresser called her hair honey blond.

"Not blond, but honey blond. You're a natural beauty," she'd told her.

It was an odd feeling not to grasp long strands of straight hair, but she'd been ready for a change. She applied a small amount of black color to her eyelashes, brown pencil to her brows, and pink-rose lipstick to her lips. It didn't take much makeup to highlight her green eyes. She finished dressing, grabbed the brightly colored yellow-and-red square cotton scarf hanging from the mirror, and bounded down the steps. She was late. Again.

She stuffed the scarf into the pocket of her winter coat that hung on the wooden rack in the entryway. Every time she looked at the scratched, dark-stained oak door, she remembered her excitement as a child when Aunt Berna would swing it open, revealing a stranger or a familiar face. The mailman. Mrs. Preston, from down the street, who always brought warm cookies. Their next-door neighbor Mrs. Worten. All gone, like so many. A fleeting ache passed through her, like a pin prick in her finger.

The scent of freshly brewed coffee and baked biscuits drew her to the kitchen.

She pulled out a chair at the table and plopped into the seat. "Morning, Richard. Did Gerald leave already?"

Richard Jamison, twenty-four, from Kentucky, was the first

boarder to arrive three months ago. He worked as a welder on first shift in the engine-assembly section and liked to laugh and tease. He wolfed down the remaining egg from his plate and gulped his coffee. "Nope. He started second shift. Doesn't have to be there until four today. I just need to go upstairs for a few minutes, and then we can walk to the bus stop together." He rose. A tuft of his dark, saddle-brown hair hung almost into his eyes. He limped slightly to the stairs.

He'd told them he injured his leg in a farm accident but didn't elaborate. Kalena would have normally pushed for details, but she sensed he was embarrassed so she didn't. She had a talent for sensing people's emotions. She didn't know how she did it. All she knew was that whatever they felt would be clear to her. Maybe it was in their facial expressions, their voice, or somewhere in a subtle body movement. She didn't dwell on how she did it. It was just there, like the temperature or changes in the weather.

She nodded. "I'll be ready." She poured a splash of cream into her coffee, then buttered a warm biscuit from the batch Aunt Berna had just taken from the oven. She dipped the knife into the mason jar and slathered the golden orb with grape jelly, then took a bite and moaned. "Soooo good." She set it on the small plate Aunt Berna had placed on the table for her and picked up the cup of coffee, blowing over the top before she sipped. "Do you think she'll be here today?" She took another healthy bite and washed it down.

"If you don't slow down, you'll choke to death, and it won't matter when she gets here."

Kalena laughed. "Got to go. I'm running late. Want to try to catch the first bus."

She pushed off from the chair and stuffed the last morsel of goodness into her mouth, then darted out of the kitchen and headed for her bedroom, taking the steps two at a time.

"Come on. Hurry up," Richard yelled.

She came down the steps faster than she'd gone up and kissed Aunt Berna on the cheek.

Aunt Berna smiled and handed her the silver metal lunch pail. "Perhaps she'll be here today. Off you go, and mind your safety, sunshine."

Kalena slipped on her heavy wool coat, patting the side pocket to make sure the scarf was still in its place. "See you tonight."

Richard opened the door, waving her to go. “Maybe the new arrival will be a good dancer. That’d be swell. And a change.” He looked sideways at her with a half-smile.

“You dance?” Kalena asked.

“Hey. I’m a great shin cracker. Don’t let this bum leg fool you. I’m a killer-diller on the dance floor. Just wait till Glenn Miller’s band gets into town. I’ll show you a thing or two.”

She flicked his hat with her finger. “I can hardly wait. Come on, let’s go, bossy.”

Perhaps the new boarder would arrive today. Maybe even by the time she got back from work. What would she be like? How old was she? Would they be friends?

CHAPTER THREE

Polly placed the dossier back into the black leather portfolio, snapped the cover closed, and slid it beside her, wedging it tight between her thigh and the train window. She pinched the bridge of her nose, then scrubbed her face gently with one hand. She'd studied the dossier since she'd boarded the train, and now, as it chugged its way through the outskirts of Philadelphia, dusk was encroaching quickly. The poor lighting in the passenger car strained her eyes. The more she read about the aircraft plant, the more anxious she became.

The dossier contained just enough information to give her a clear overview of how important the plant was to war production in the United States. Where was the sensitive information stored? Who had access to it? None of that specific information was included. The first step, the easiest one, would be to verify there was a spy by confirming that someone had truly tampered with the documents. Once she established that fact, then the difficult and dangerous part of her job would start. If there was a spy, how long had they been at the factory? If they were attempting to get information, what? And how were they getting it? The questions flooded her mind, but it wasn't the questions that bothered her—it was not knowing the answers.

Eight months ago, Portage Aircraft Inc., PAI, a subsidiary of Diamond Oak Aircraft, had acquired a contract to produce a new kind of wing and engine that would make the P-51 Anaconda fighter plane faster and more maneuverable. The plant had many concerns, but keeping their wing design and engine modifications top secret and out of the hands of their competitors and the enemy was the most critical. Any data leaked or stolen from the plant would give whoever had it a wealth of information about production numbers, engineer designs, shipment schedules, and destinations.

She wiped the splotch of condensation from the train window with the heel of her hand and peered out, seeing the fields of cut corn stalks rushing by like wooden soldiers on parade, interrupted occasionally by a splash of orange from abandoned pumpkins. The gentle sway of the train lulled her into a sleepy haze. It made sense the spy could be a woman. Since the draft was established last year, thousands of men were leaving every week, which created a giant hole in the work force. Women stepped in to fill the need. A female spy would blend in perfectly. Most men considered women a non-threat, and few of them would be watching a woman closely—at least as a spy.

If it was a female, how long would it take to find her? Was the spy working alone or with someone else? What if it wasn't just one person?

The revolver in the leather holster at the middle of her back dug into her spine. She pulled at the edges of her tailored jacket and shifted to get more comfortable. She lifted her hips slightly and tugged her skirt down over her knees from where it had slid up. She hated wearing a suit when she traveled, but regulations required it. She'd much rather be in dress slacks. Women on the streets in pants in the early 1930s had caused such a stir the newspapers wrote about it. When Marlene Dietrich wore a tuxedo, Congress practically blew a gasket because of the law forbidding women to "masquerade as men." Ten years later they were still debating the fashion styles. The whole thing was ridiculous. The more Polly thought about it, the angrier she got. Her feet were aching from being in high heels for over nine hours. She half smiled, knowing she'd change into whatever she wanted when she reached her destination.

The middle-aged man sitting beside her with broad shoulders and a protruding belly pulled his fedora down over his forehead and frowned, spreading his elbows like a rooster flapping its wings. She scooted closer to the window, rested her head on the back of the seat, and tried to relax. She gazed out just as the train passed a huge billboard with a smiling, rosy-faced Santa dressed in his red suit, sitting in a rocker surrounded by his bag of presents and holding a Coca-Cola with the quote *Thirst asks nothing more*. She swallowed and wanted one. The advertisement had done its job. An almost endless stream of billboards passed by her view. She smiled, reminding herself the train was the one passing by, not the billboards. Now, one with a giant picture of Judy Garland and Micky Rooney smiling and waving encouraged the public to contribute to the March of Dimes.

The billboards mostly advertised new cars, alcohol, and cigarettes. The use of steel, instead of other metals that were demanded in war production now, made the newer cars bigger and heavier than in previous years. Polly's favorite was the Buick Roadmaster convertible, but all the rest, like the Cadillac Series 62 and the Chrysler Newport Dual Cowl Phaeton, were a waste of money as far as she was concerned. How much longer would new-car manufacturing be permitted? War-material production was increasing and would soon take precedence. This year would probably be the last for new cars for a while. Another shortage to deal with in the coming months.

The alcohol advertisements were mostly for Seagram's Five Crown, Grant's Scotch Whisky, and Blatz Beer. No shortage there, she hoped. The cigarette advertisements were for Chesterfield and Lucky Strike. She'd tried cigarettes once or twice, but smoking never appealed to her, especially the smell.

She recalled her last night in DC and the group of women she'd been with at her cousin Elizabeth's house, Edmond's sister. The living room had been so thick with cigarette smoke Polly could barely breathe. Like Polly, Elizabeth was a lesbian. She held occasional *get-togethers*. They were safe havens to discuss concerns and talk openly, relax, get to know each other, and explore interests and feelings. Elizabeth was older than Polly and had lived in Washington for more than nine years. She knew just as many people as her brother but had the confidence of those who held more secrets. She was discreet. She had to be. Lesbianism was tolerated only if it wasn't publicly discussed or observed. If Elizabeth wanted to, she could expose a third of the legislators' wives in Washington.

Polly had been fighting a headache that night and was just about to leave when Margo Harrison arrived. Margo's husband, a congressman from the Midwest, was out of town, and Margo was hot for attention. Polly ended the night at her house, as she'd done several times before.

It'd been months since she'd been with a woman, and evidently, it'd been at least that long for Margo.

After their passion was sated and the beauty beside her had breathed the rhythm of sleep, a flicker of unfulfilled intimacy intruded into Polly's thoughts. She lay awake in the dark, trying to rationalize it away. A romantic attachment would complicate her life and be too much of a risk. She had too many secrets to keep. Too many deceptions to weave. She told herself she needed sexual satisfaction, nothing more. But was that all there would ever be, a procession of beautiful women and fleeting moments?

Her life was a leviathan of secrets. She lied about her job to strangers, friends, lovers, and she lied about her sexual preference. But most of all she lied to herself about what she needed. She was lonely, but she wanted her career, and she knew what would happen if any of her fellow agents or those in charge found out she was a lesbian. She would not only lose her job, but probably go to jail. So, she lied. And the lies merged and intermingled with her needs and longing, making a powerful, austere concoction she forced herself to consume. It left a bitter, burning aftertaste, and at times she choked on it.

She wanted to be strong, but the ache of loneliness seeped into her heart and overwhelmed her.

Her parents were strong physically and mentally. Her father, Everett William Silvester, whose family had settled in Maine from England, didn't want to be a shipbuilder like his father, so he went to Cornell University when he was twenty-three, eventually graduated from business school, and then got his JD.

Polly's mother, Geraldine Ruth Wainwright, whose people came from Ithaca in upstate New York, was related to William Henry Anderton of the Newton Gun Company. Counted among the company's patrons were John Philip Sousa, Annie Oakley, and Alfred Lee Loomis.

When Polly was a toddler, her father and mother moved to Philadelphia for her father's work in a prestigious law firm. Polly grew up there. Like her father, she wasn't happy where she lived, but she wasn't ready to decide to leave home. And being like her mother, headstrong and independent, once she made up her mind, nothing could stop her.

She wiped the condensation from the window again. More houses and traffic, more roads, more billboards.

The conductor moved through the car, one hand in his dark-blue wool pant pocket, the other gliding across the backs of the seats as he passed. He took out his pocket watch, opened the worn gold cover, and slipped his glasses down slightly on his nose, peering at the watch.

"Eight minutes, folks. Eight minutes to Cleveland Union Station. Please don't get up until the train comes to a complete stop. The main concourse and cab stand are through the vestibule and at the south end of the terminal. Mind your footing."

She stretched her neck and flexed her fingers, hearing him repeat the announcement as he moved through the car. When the train stopped, she retrieved her luggage and went through the vestibule as instructed. The spacious main concourse had Botticino marble walls with high, fluted columns and marble floors. A large skylight pierced the ornamental plaster ceiling, which during daylight must have lit the concourse from overhead. The waiting room adjoined the main concourse on the west end. It looked to be almost 170 feet long, with similar flooring, encased columns, and ornately carved dark-stained wooden benches.

Her attention was drawn to a man by the newsstand, coat over his left arm, holding a newspaper in his right hand. He tipped his hat and nodded to his right. Her contact.

She started toward the exit, but a woman at the north end of the concourse, near the ticket lobby, screeched and pointed to a man running toward Polly, darting in between other passengers.

"He stole my purse," the woman yelled. "He stole my purse."

The alleged thief was almost in front of Polly, still at a dead run, a grimace on his youthful, sweaty face, a cloth purse clutched in his fist.

Polly edged her suitcase in his path as casually as she could and tripped him, sending him sprawling, sliding into the policeman who loomed a few feet in front of him, slapping his nightstick in his hand.

The officer grabbed the fifteen- or sixteen-year-old by the scruff of his collar and lifted him to his feet. "I'll take that," he said.

The boy quickly surrendered the bag.

The woman ran up to the officer, seized her purse, and slapped the perpetrator on the back of his head. "Shame on you." She turned and walked to Polly, dipping her knees slightly when she stood in front of her. "I thank you for what you done. I don't know what I'd have done if he'd got away with it. I'm on my way to my auntie's, and all my expense money is in here." She clutched the purse against her chest.

Polly smiled. "Safe travels," she said and walked to the exit.

Her contact was waiting by a parked, dark-colored Buick sedan. When she saw him, he opened the passenger door and waited for her to reach the car. He was average height, thin, dark-haired, a thick mustache and sharp jawline.

"No train to Akron?" she asked.

He had an indistinctive face. Nothing stood out. Even his eyes were a plain brown. "Change of plan," he said, surveying the surrounding cars and the people moving in and out of the station.

She reached inside her overcoat pocket and palmed the revolver she'd moved to her coat when she'd gone to the bathroom. "Inclement weather forecast for tomorrow."

"No," he said, shaking his head. "Clear skies with sunshine until late afternoon."

"Oliver?"

He nodded.

Polly relaxed and withdrew her hand from her overcoat pocket, gave him her luggage, and slid into the front seat.

He slipped her luggage into the back, then got into the driver's side and started the car. The engine jumped to life. He pulled away from the curb and into the stream of traffic.

"How long to the house?" she asked.

"About an hour and fifteen minutes. I'm sorry we changed plans, but I was able to get this car at the last minute, and it's easier to drive you directly there rather than taking the train to Akron and then driving you to Barberton."

Something didn't feel right. It wasn't anything specific. Maybe an instinct? A fleeting hesitation? Whatever it was, she decided not to give Oliver the dossier. She slid it under her overcoat on her lap, and though she knew he'd seen it, he didn't mention it.

"What do you think?" he asked.

"I feel like I'm already behind, and I'm not even there yet."

At that moment Polly realized if she didn't get whoever it was quickly, this entire thing could cost hundreds of lives and millions of dollars. Not only could the spy gain access to the schedules and production numbers, but also destinations. And if they obtained the schedules and destinations, they could notify Berlin, and then the subs could be waiting for the convoys because they could calculate arrivals. She stroked her chin.

Oliver glanced over at her and smiled. "Anything you want to share?"

She shrugged. "I'll know more after I talk with the plant executives."

"The plant's main engineer flew in yesterday. He'll be there a few days. I can't decide if that's good news or bad news for you. There'll be lots of discussions and meetings."

"Oliver?" she asked.

"Yeah, as in Oliver Twist."

Polly laughed. "Don't worry. Your secret's safe with me."

"I've heard that about you." He took a longer glance this time.

"What's that supposed to mean?"

Oliver shrugged. "Just that you do good work and are dependable and competent."

Polly nodded. "Well, I hope my reputation holds on this one."

He slowed the car and looked over at her. "You have some memorization to do." He gave her his phone number and instructed her how and when to contact him. "You'll be alone and on your own most of the time. And no cars are available, so you'll have to do the best you can with transportation."

"How strong is the probability that it's a female?" she asked.

"The executive director of the plant believes it's one, but I think he's mistaken."

"Why?"

He shrugged again and squeezed the steering wheel tighter. "Because the women at the plant don't have access to the areas where the information worth stealing is located. But they're everywhere else, so who knows?"

How did he know where the information was stored? And for that matter, how did he know what information might be stolen? Again, that unsettling feeling crossed her mind, like a shudder from a cold gust of wind. "I'm sure they're in the secretary pool and have access to the offices, and assembly-line workers could find out with a little imagination and scheming, don't you think?"

Oliver shrugged. "I suppose, but it's not my job to find out. It's yours. I've been out to the plant a couple of times but only to get a sense of the outside. I haven't been inside."

Polly noticed he'd scraped his right knuckles. "Did you get into a fight?"

He quickly inspected his hand. "Nothing much. Some jerk had

too much liquor and didn't know when to shut his mouth." He cleared his throat and changed the subject. "At this point it could be almost anyone at the plant, but Helmsworth is clean. Stanley Whitmire, head of finance, and Cecilia Morrison, Helmsworth's executive secretary, are all suspect. You have a big job ahead of you. It could be anyone, or it could just be an overreaction and it's no one at all."

Polly was surprised he'd say that, given the concern and priority Assistant Director Williamson had conveyed to her and the fact that leadership at the plant had such strong suspicions that documents had been tampered with. She kept the thoughts to herself.

"You'll be posing as Morrison's assistant. That way you can move freely around the plant. The department managers have been there for more than three years, some longer." Oliver turned right, drove two blocks, then turned again. "It could be anyone."

An hour later and halfway down a treelined street, he pulled into a driveway. The huge two-story home had a porch that stretched the entire length of the front of the house. It was quaint, homey. A wooden swing, hung on chain links, swayed gently in the crisp night breeze. Across the street was a large lake.

Oliver turned to her. "Mind your manners, stay safe, and try not to work too hard. Run along now and find the big bad wolf…if there is one."

He'd said it again. Why? Polly exited, opened the back car door, and dragged her luggage out.

Oliver ducked his head to peer at her. "Seriously, you watch yourself."

She gave him a half salute as he backed out of the driveway and drove off, leaving her standing there, watching his car disappear into the darkness, her confidence chasing it like a dog running down the street.

She could do this. She had to do this. Too many lives were at risk if she didn't get this right. *At any cost, Polly. At any cost.* The words surrounded her and echoed deep into the night.

CHAPTER FOUR

Kalena inched back the white-lace curtain on the living-room window, straining to see the new boarder. She was tall and slender and had an expression like she knew she'd have an impact on anyone near her. Her hair hung loose to her shoulders underneath a darker wide-brimmed hat and glistened in the moonlight. She appeared close to Kalena's age. Anyone could see her beauty from a distance, even in the dark. Kalena leaned closer to get a better look as the woman moved gracefully up the porch steps. She jerked when Aunt Berna touched her shoulder.

"Don't stare, sunshine."

Kalena swallowed. "I'm not staring. I'm looking." Actually, she was ogling, but she didn't want to reveal that fact to Aunt Berna.

Aunt Berna opened the door, and Kalena followed close behind, almost bumping into her.

"Come in from the cold, dear." Aunt Berna beckoned to the woman. "You must be exhausted."

The woman stepped through the doorway with her suitcase.

In her excitement of the possibility of a new friend, Kalena took in every detail. She had hazel eyes with flecks of gold around the iris, long eyelashes, and her peaches-and-cream complexion was flawless. She wore her hair in a long bob with the sides swept up, the back drifting into soft, satiny, loose curls. A scar ran along the side of her left wrist just below her little finger. How had she gotten it? She didn't wear a wedding ring. Her dark wool suit, the skirt hanging perfectly just below the knee, looked expensive. The muscles in the calves of her long legs flexed as she stood silently.

The woman coughed softly, drawing Kalena's attention to her face.

Their eyes locked.

Kalena's breath hitched. Aunt Berna was talking, but her words weren't registering. Kalena had never seen eyes so vivid and penetrating.

The woman held out her delicate, graceful hand.

Kalena reached out and gently shook it, their touch sending a surge of heat through her.

A reserved smile appeared on full lips, accented with a luscious burgundy lipstick. "Hi. I'm Polly. Polly Hollister."

"I'm Kalena." It was all she could get out. She acted like a tongue-tied adolescent.

"What a beautiful name." Polly smiled more fully, her eyes darkening to a deeper amber.

Kalena breathed again. "Here. Let me take your luggage. Did you travel far?"

"Philadelphia," Polly said.

"We have soup and bread set aside for you," Aunt Berna said. "Kalena will help you to your room. Freshen up, and when you're ready, come join us in the kitchen."

"This way," Kalena said. She began to climb the stairs, Polly following close behind.

She led her to the bedroom next to hers. There, she switched on the lamp, set Polly's luggage beside the double bed, then pulled down both window blinds. "Your room faces the main street, so just be aware people often walk in the early morning and evening."

Polly smiled. "Good to know."

Kalena crossed the room. "This is an adjoining bathroom you'll share with me." She reached inside and turned on the light. "Sorry, no shower. Just a tub but all the other conveniences."

"This is lovely. I'll be quite comfortable here, I'm sure. Thank you so much."

An awkwardness filled the room, and Kalena didn't know why. Maybe she did. It was probably from the mental picture she'd formed of Polly naked in the bathtub. It was only a momentary fantasy, but nonetheless a vivid one. "Well, I'll leave you to get settled. See you in a few minutes." She couldn't get out of there fast enough, embarrassed by her imaginings. She hurried down the stairs and into the kitchen, heat radiating from her cheeks. She ran her fingers through her hair, then rubbed the back of her neck.

Aunt Berna stood at the stove, stirring the soup. "Do you think she'll be comfortable?" She tapped the top of the pot with the long wooden spoon, then placed it on the leaf-shaped ceramic holder on the counter.

Kalena nodded, poured herself a cup of coffee, and sat at the table. "I'm sure she will be."

"She's quite lovely," Aunt Berna said.

Kalena added a splash of cream, restraining from commenting. Beautiful. Gorgeous. Breathtaking. She touched her hair again. "Yes." She didn't mean to say it so softly, but it came out as a whisper.

Aunt Berna turned and looked at her. "You're just as beautiful, you know."

Kalena stirred her coffee slowly, watching the cream swirl. "No. I think not." She heard Polly's footfalls on the stairs and straightened her posture.

Polly came into the kitchen wearing a comfortable-looking butterscotch-colored sweater that fit snugly around her waist, loose slacks, and slippers.

"Settled in?" Aunt Berna asked, ladling soup into a bowl. She carried it and a spoon to the table and set them down in front of the seat beside Kalena. "This will be your spot."

Kalena pulled Polly's chair out slightly.

"You have a beautiful home." Polly sat, placing the linen napkin in her lap, then leaned forward, sniffing the soup. "It smells delicious."

"It's called krupnik, a barley soup," Kalena said.

Polly lifted a spoonful of it into her mouth and moaned. "It's wonderful. Rich and bursting with flavor. I love the mushrooms."

Kalena passed the small basket of homemade wheat bread to her. "It's even better with this."

Polly took a slice and dipped it, then ate. She nodded. "You're right."

Kalena couldn't wait to ask questions. Where was she from? Why was she here? How long would she be staying? The questions flew out of her mouth so fast she had to stop and take a sip of her coffee to slow herself down.

Polly laughed and, in between answering, finished the soup.

She was from Philadelphia. She was hired as one of the new executive secretaries at the plant.

Aunt Berna served her a generous slice of apple pie.

Polly's eyes widened, and a brief smile crossed her soft, full lips. "So wonderful. Thank you. I haven't eaten since early this morning."

They spent an hour in the kitchen. Sometimes Polly used her hands when she talked, and when she looked at Kalena, she seemed to peer into her soul.

They stacked the dishes in the sink, straightened the kitchen, and settled in the living room, Kalena on the love seat, Polly on the full sofa. Aunt Berna excused herself and went to her room at the back of the house.

Kalena sat with her feet curled under her, watching Polly. "If you're tired, you don't have to stay up."

"No. I'm fine. Tell me about yourself. I noticed your aunt has a bit of an accent. May I assume she's not from here?"

"Our ancestors came from Poland. Through England, then New York, then to Ohio."

Polly shifted, settling deeper into the cushions. "Why Ohio?"

Kalena smiled, thinking of the way Aunt Berna told the story. "My great-grandparents didn't want to go any farther than Cleveland because of what they heard about Indians out West. They were terrified. I was born and raised here in Barberton." She saddened at what came next. "My parents and older brother died in the flu pandemic, and my Aunt Berna, my mother's sister, and Uncle Frederick raised me. This is my parents' house." She gestured around the room.

"So, does your Uncle Frederick live here too?"

"No. He died a little over a year ago. Heart attack." She'd never shared her story with the other boarders. What was different about Polly?

"I'm sorry. It sounds like it's been hard for you."

There was such sympathy in her voice, like a chorus of angels singing *Amen* to everything Kalena revealed.

"What are you, twenty-three, twenty-four?" Polly's expression grew more intense as she watched her.

"I'm twenty-six. And you?"

"Twenty-eight this past April," Polly said.

"My birthday's in April too. The eleventh. You?"

"Twenty-third."

"Did you go to college, Polly?"

"Yes. And you?"

Kalena shifted. "No. I always wanted to but didn't have the money."

"What would you have liked to study?"

Kalena looked up at the ceiling, pondering. No one had ever asked her that question. "Perhaps human behavior and history. I've always been interested in how the world reacts. The logic of it all. The things we go through and how they affect us."

"I think you would have done well."

The muscles in Polly's jaw clenched, as though she had stifled a yawn.

Kalena laughed softly. "You should probably get some rest. It's been a long day." She would have loved to sit all night and talk, but Polly was clearly tired.

Polly flushed. "I'm sorry. Traveling has gotten the best of me today. Perhaps we can talk more tomorrow?"

"Of course." Kalena's stomach fluttered. "Do come to church with us in the morning. Services start at nine. And after lunch, we can stroll downtown, and I'll show you the city. It's small but lovely."

Polly rose. "I'd like that. Thank you again for the wonderful meal. I enjoyed it very much."

Kalena rose. "You're welcome. Sleep well."

"I'll see you in the morning." Polly excused herself and went up the stairs.

Kalena flopped back down onto the sofa, as if her strength had seeped out of her body and was absorbed into the cushions. A beautiful woman was in her house, and she was going to be here for more than a day. The sight of Polly at the door played over and over in her mind. She took in the image slowly, deliberately, not wanting to release it.

How long would she stay? Why wasn't she married? Would they be close friends? She seemed easy to talk to, yet she had a mystery about her. Her eyes reflected it—deep, penetrating eyes that seemed to hold Kalena captive.

CHAPTER FIVE

Polly had been trained to tell more of the truth than a lie. That way, when she was in a situation, it wouldn't be as hard to remember the lie. But this small group of Kalena, her aunt, and the other two boarders was going to be tough. They fired questions at her so fast she barely had time to eat Sunday dinner. She leaned back in the chair and dabbed at the corner of her mouth with a beautiful white lace napkin. "I'm originally from upstate New York, but my parents moved to Philadelphia when I was small, before the influenza pandemic hit."

Everyone at the table grew silent. Gerald bowed his head and crossed himself. Richard cleared his throat, and Kalena and Aunt Berna sat quietly.

"Who'd you lose?" Richard asked, matter-of-fact. "It's best to get the question out there and have at it. It helps the pain."

"I was very blessed. I'm an only child, and both my parents survived, but I lost many of my extended family members," Polly said.

Gerald's hand shook slightly when he reached for a biscuit and began to butter it. He remained silent, the pain of his loss written on his face and in his eyes. From his reaction, it was someone close and important to him. Parents? Siblings? He was reserved and shy. She wanted to offer physical comfort, something brief, like a touch on his arm, but hesitated. She didn't know him, and from the way he sat, feet close together, arms tight against his body, he clearly didn't want the contact.

Aunt Berna changed the subject. "I hear Glenn Miller's coming to town next week. Are you all going?"

Richard's face lit up. "Who isn't? That's all everyone's talking about at the plant."

"Do you dance, Polly?" Kalena asked, pouring the hot brown gravy into the small hollow in her mashed potatoes, then placing a pat of butter into the lake she'd made. She swirled her fork through the mixture.

Polly watched, intrigued. These people were so open and gentle, not like the Washington crowd, whose goal at a dinner was to find out who could help them on their way up the ladder or to get a tidbit of gossip to use as leverage in some way. "I do dance. But I'm not sure I'll be able to make it."

Richard slapped his fork onto his almost empty plate. "Not make it? Why, that's just nuts. Of course you're going. No one will be working at the plant Saturday night. Second shift is letting out early. Everyone will be at the dance." He served himself another heaping spoonful of green beans, then potatoes, drowning them in gravy.

Kalena looked at Polly. "I guess you're going."

Polly laughed. "I guess I am."

"You'll have a great time. What about you, Gerald?" Richard asked.

"Haven't decided yet. We'll see. I think I'll stay here and write to the family. Maybe go for a walk around town."

Richard didn't protest like he had with Polly.

Gerald seemed reluctant to discuss anything personal. Whatever happened in his life had obviously been bitter and traumatic.

After they cleared the table, and the dishes were done, Kalena asked Polly if she wanted to go for a stroll. They changed into their walking shoes, slipped on their heavy coats, and started down the sidewalk.

A slight mist hovered in the crisp, chill air, reminding Polly that Thanksgiving was right around the corner.

Kalena slipped her hand from her glove and held it out, like she was checking the weather. "It's going to snow soon." She slid her slender fingers back into the glove.

Polly looked up. Darkish-gray clouds, the color of light charcoal with traces of deep purple, were gathering in the west.

"Those are snow clouds," announced Kalena with confidence, as if it was second nature to know the mind and will of the season.

"You that sure?" Polly asked.

"Oh, it's going to snow by morning."

They walked on, their footsteps the only sound on the cement. They were at the edge of town in just a few minutes. Kalena steered her one block to the right, then to the left. A little later they were at the corner of Tuscarawas Avenue and Fourth Street.

Kalena pointed to the right. "Down there are the Lake Theater, the ice cream shoppe, the butcher, and the grocery store. Up this way," she pointed left, leaning slightly toward Polly, "are Woolworth's, Mr. Hartley's shoe store, the bookstore, and old man McGregor's toy store. Nothing much in there but ancient toys. He lost his four children during the pandemic, and mostly I think he has things that remind him of his kids. I don't go in there much. It's too sad. Woolworth's has a good variety of merchandise. Plenty of choices. But if you want the new nylon stockings, which don't run as bad as the silk, you can only buy two pair, and you better get them soon because they can't keep them in stock. With all the new female workers coming to the plant, you have to get things you need quickly or go without. There are shortages of everything, but especially makeup, hose, slips, and hair products. We have at least twenty hair stylists in this town, but it takes a month to make an appointment just to get a haircut, and if you want a perm? Forget it."

Polly watched her, fascinated. Kalena barely stopped for air. She was so cute when she got going like this. She wanted to eliminate her from the list as soon as possible, and in order to do that, she had to find out about her life. Who were her friends? What did she do outside of work? She'd already learned at dinner that she worked on the assembly line at the plant.

"Engine parts," Kalena had said.

Richard welded wing parts, and Gerald worked the heavy-machinery lift. They'd all wanted to know what Polly would be doing. "Assistant secretary to Cecilia Morrison," she'd told them.

Richard let out a long, low whistle. "Nice."

Lying to these genuine, open people, especially Kalena, stung, and she was uncomfortable doing it. But she had no choice. It was part of the job, part of her cover.

Kalena slipped her hand in the crook of Polly's arm. "I'm so glad you're here."

Kalena's loneliness was blatant. It flowed from her like water over a spillway after a heavy rain. Polly didn't want to get close to her. She didn't want to make any friends because she'd be gone in a little while, and if they became close, it'd be harder to lie to her. Kalena was beautiful and open and had a natural charm. She could be dangerous, not physically but certainly emotionally. Polly had sensed it the moment she'd stepped into the house and looked at her. She was drawn to her, and when they'd touched, Kalena's warmth had radiated into her, like she'd been wrapped in a soft, woolen blanket. She'd have to be careful, but Kalena was alluring and almost irresistible.

She patted the sleeve of Kalena's coat and held on to it, trying not to say the words, but she said them anyway. "I'm glad I'm here also." She stroked the fabric of the sleeve of her coat once more, and they walked toward the ice cream shoppe.

"The ice cream shoppe and the theater are the only two businesses open on Sundays," Kalena said, releasing Polly's arm and stepping into the doorway.

The withdrawal of her comfort was immediate.

The small bell above the entranceway jingled a pleasant announcement of their arrival.

Every booth and table was mostly filled with women, an occasional man tucked in here and there. Only three seats remained open at the fountain. Kalena grabbed Polly's hand and led her to the empty stools. She sat quickly and patted the seat beside her. "Sit, before someone else does."

"Moment, please," said a stout, gray-haired man at the end of the counter, shouting over the jukebox next to the counter that was blaring out "Elmer's Tune" by Glenn Miller.

Kalena waved to the man and greeted him in what sounded like Polish.

The man smiled and said something back.

"My neighbor, Mr. Bakowski," Kalena said, glancing over at the jukebox. "Wow. That's beautiful. It's the Wurlitzer 850 Peacock. Brand-new. Mr. Bakowski has done nothing but talk about getting it for two months. He said it can play up to ten records without a reset."

A few minutes later Mr. Bakowski appeared in front of them, smiling brightly. He spoke briefly to Kalena, again probably in Polish, then motioned toward the jukebox. "Is not she beautiful?"

Kalena nodded and laughed enthusiastically. "She is."

"What can I get you?"

Kalena looked at Polly, as if sizing her up and down. "A hot-fudge sundae all right?" she asked.

Polly nodded.

When the dessert arrived, Polly dipped into the luscious treat, making sure the first bite was loaded with hot fudge, ice cream, whipped cream, nuts, and the cherry.

The music, the crowd's laughter, and the chatter made it almost impossible to talk.

Kalena put her finger up to her ear. "I can't hear myself think."

Three women maneuvered their way up to them, and one wrapped her arm around Kalena's shoulders. "Kalena. Come over and join us?" She pointed to two tables pushed together with eight women jammed shoulder to shoulder.

Kalena looked closely, then back to the woman embracing her. "No, thanks. We couldn't hear what anyone said anyway. We're just here for a few minutes." She turned on her stool and leaned toward the small group. "This is Polly Hollister from Philadelphia. She starts tomorrow at the plant and is boarding with us. Polly, I'd like you to meet Perta Howard, Juniper Bailey, and Beverly Anderson." She indicated each woman. "Perta is a welder, one of the first women to do the job at the plant. Juniper works on the assembly line by me, and Beverly is in maintenance."

Beverly raised her hand. "Trash," she said with an exaggerated frown. "Someone has to do it."

They all laughed and greeted Polly.

Perta tugged Kalena's arm. "Come on over and sit with us."

Kalena shook her head. "No. We can't stay long."

"Why? Do you have to go get ready for a date or something?" Beverly asked.

"Date?" Juniper asked. "There're no dates because there're hardly any men. Besides, Kalena is exclusive. She only dates Lionel Wilcox, the engineer on the second floor of the administration building." She elbowed Kalena.

Kalena fidgeted in her seat.

Polly noticed her discomfort.

The three women returned to their group after securing a promise from Kalena to go out with them soon.

Kalena ate her sundae, then quietly waited for Polly to finish hers. She looked around at the crowd. "Come on, Polly. Let's get out of here."

They made their way through the press of people and, when outside, turned toward the theater.

"We can walk this way and then back toward home. We'll eventually pass the bus stop we'll be going to tomorrow morning."

They strolled in silence as the chill in the air bit deeper into Polly's cheeks. These people were so different than what she was used to. Their sense of family and neighborly affection was deep and abiding. How would she be able to keep the secret of why she was here? Could the spy be one of these seemingly good people? Of course—under the right circumstances anyone could be a spy. That's what she'd been taught. That's what she believed. She couldn't let her own feelings interfere in the investigation. But how could she not be drawn to these people who were so friendly and open? Was she really that lonely and starving for friendship? Her anger rose at the thought of someone taking advantage of these people and their trusting nature. But wasn't that what she was doing? She shook her head. It wasn't the same thing.

Kalena paused to look at the brightly colored theater marquee ad announcing Cary Grant and Joan Fontaine in *Suspicion*. She moved to the next poster. "Look! A new Bud Abbott and Lou Costello film's playing next week. *Keep 'Em Flying.*" She leaned closer to the display. "I think they're funny." Her wide smile made her nose crinkle.

It was adorable. "The Hitchcock movie looks good too," Polly said.

Kalena pulled Polly's collar up around her neck. "We better get you home. Don't want you to catch a cold the first week you're here." She touched her elbow and nudged her gently.

A group of five teenagers hurried past in animated excitement, heading into the theater.

"Hey, Miss Mikloska," one called out.

Kalena smiled and waved. "Hey, Eddie. How's your mom?"

"She's much better."

"Tell her I said hello. Enjoy your movie."

The familiar exchange triggered a yearning in Polly. She'd separated herself too much from others.

"Do you think we'll get into the war soon?" Kalena asked as they sauntered down the sidewalk.

Polly recalled the conversations in the social groups she was a part of in Washington. The gossip and criticism of politicians and business leaders. The whining and chatter. The jockeying for power and position. Kalena just wanted to know Polly's opinion. She hadn't had such an easy encounter with anyone in a long, long time. It was refreshing and genuine. "I'm afraid everything points to it. No one wants to go to war. A lot of people feel we should remain isolated and neutral. But President Roosevelt's fireside chat last month made it clear we need to protect our ships. Hitler's aggression will probably force us in, whether we want it or not. We can't let him claim the open seas and get away with his submarines sinking our ships and not answering for it."

Kalena sighed and slipped her arm around Polly's once again. "I listened to that speech. I agree. It's war in Europe for us. President Roosevelt practically said it in his talk. He said 'times call for clear heads and fearless hearts.' But I'm scared, Polly."

Again, Kalena's willingness to reveal her most intimate feelings struck a chord in Polly, and she responded with equal sincerity. "So am I." She placed her hand on Kalena's arm, which rested comfortably in the crook of hers. The war was closer to Kalena than she knew—even at her door.

Kalena stopped and turned toward Polly, releasing her.

Polly felt the immediate separation again. She wasn't as comfortable, as content, as she'd been a moment ago.

"Will you be with us for a while?" Kalena asked the question with intensity, punctuated with longing.

Polly sensed its urgency. She hated the lies and deception. She didn't want to lie to Kalena, who was so exposed and bare of pretense. "I imagine I'll be here for a while, as long as there's work for me."

"Do you have a steady fella back in Philadelphia?"

Polly said what she had to say, as the acidic taste of her lie slid down her throat. "He's an officer in the Army Air Corps and is already in Europe." She glanced at Kalena, the pink blush on her soft skin, the perfectly formed mouth and full lips. A flash of sunlight through a momentary opening in the clouds caressed a few golden strands of her hair as it danced gently on the breeze.

Kalena nodded, as if in deep thought, the silence thick as they walked on.

"How about you? I bet you have to fight them off with a club. Is Lionel anyone special?"

Kalena smiled shyly and nodded. "You'll come to the dance, won't you? Please say you will. I couldn't bear it if you didn't."

Kalena had changed the subject too quickly. Something was there. But what? "Yes. I'll go to the dance if I can."

Kalena picked up her pace. "Good." She patted Polly's arm. "Let's get home before we both freeze to death. Perta, Juniper, and Beverly come over to the house often and are fun to be around, but I'm glad you're here."

Polly's analytical nature suddenly kicked in. Was it a reactive response? A way of protecting herself to prevent others from getting too close? She was here for a reason. A critical reason. Emotion had no place here. Was Kalena genuine? She appeared too open, too quick to reveal her emotions. Could it be a cover for something else? How did Lionel fit into her life? She was charming, and it would be intriguing to get to know her. But Polly didn't have the time, and the risks were too great. She couldn't let herself get distracted. Not with the work she had to do. And she hadn't cleared her yet. For all she knew Kalena could be the spy. No one was above suspicion.

CHAPTER SIX

Polly scooted over as far as she could. Every seat on the bus was taken, and anyone else who could push their way on stood in the aisles and grabbed a seat back to claim their territory.

The driver yelled at the woman standing on the first step to either get in or get out. "I'm closin' the door with or without you, lady. Move it." He gripped the operation handle to the double doors.

She skittered up the steps, pushed her way forward, and grabbed the back of the first seat she could. The forty or so people left gathered at the bus stop crowded together like they were about to stampede. The large, wet snowflakes clung to their scarves and hats, and the shoulders of their coats.

Polly shouldn't have doubted Kalena's weather prediction.

The driver waved the hopeful passengers away. "No more. Wait for the next one." He shut the doors abruptly.

The bus chugged down the street, leaving behind great puffs of black exhaust, as if it were some giant metal animal marking its territory. Its movement must have been a signal for everyone to talk louder.

Polly raised her voice, hoping Richard could hear her. "Is it always like this?"

He yelled back from the seat in front of her. "Always. You should have seen it before they started a second shift."

Perta, one of the women Polly had met at the ice cream shoppe, stood next to Richard, gripping the corner of his seat when the driver shifted gears and the bus jerked forward. Her brown hair was knotted in a tight bun. "Why don't you get up, Richard, and let a lady sit?"

"I would, but you ain't no lady."

Perta playfully slapped the shoulder of his heavy coat.

He got up slowly and pointed to his seat. "Remember I did that."

Perta quickly changed places with him. "Thanks. That's swell of you."

Polly needed a car. She couldn't waste valuable time in the investigation taking public transportation and standing around. She made a mental note to work something out as soon as possible.

The ride took about fifteen minutes to the plant's main gate, then a few more to the employee entrance. The facility stretched out over five hundred acres, with a runway at the south end by the last building. Polly followed Kalena off the bus and eased into the line with the rest of the group at the entrance.

"Personnel is in the administration building." Kalena pointed at the two-story, smaller building on the east side of the main plant. "Let's try to catch the end-of-shift first bus together if we can. If not, I'll see you when you get home." She touched Polly's shoulder. "Have a good first day. Don't worry. You'll get used to it."

Polly lingered, watching Kalena blend into the group and move forward, slowly disappearing. She didn't know why she watched her. Another lie. She knew exactly why. She just didn't want to admit it. She turned and made her way to the administration building.

A stocky woman at the reception desk was instructing a group of about ten women dressed in coveralls and holding scarves. "It's simple," she said curtly. "A square cotton scarf works better than silk because it doesn't slide off your head as easily. Fold it diagonally, position the long fold at the back of your head, and bring the tip even with the bottom of your forehead. Tie the long end twice, left over right, right over left, then tuck your hair in, and there you have it." She turned to Polly. "How can I help you?"

"Personnel?"

The woman pointed to her right. "Down that hall. First door on your left."

Polly went as instructed into the large room. Six women sat in different areas, some typing furiously, one carrying a bundle of manilla folders in her arms. Folder lady looked up and smiled at Polly. "Be right with you." She hurried over to a far desk, set her bundle down, and quickly returned to the counter. She adjusted her glasses and smiled once more. "Hi. Are you new?"

Polly nodded. "Hello. I'm Polly Hollister. I'm supposed to report to Cecilia Morrison."

The woman drew back and raised her eyebrows. "Oh. I see," she said, evidently impressed. "Please follow me."

They made their way through the corridor and up a flight of stairs, entering a hallway with several offices on each side. They stopped at the first door on the right. Four women were working at desks—one was on the phone, another clacked away at her typewriter, one shuffled through what looked like lists of supply orders, and another had three ledger books open and was running her finger over the columns, probably trying to find an error. The scowl on her face gave it away.

"Kitty, is she in there?" the woman escorting Polly asked.

The one with the ledgers stabbed her finger on the paper to mark her place and looked up. "Are you Polly?"

"Yes," Polly answered.

Kitty got up from her desk. "I'll take you to her. Thanks, Evie."

Evie wished Polly good luck and left.

"She's just down here," Kitty said, motioning for Polly to follow.

They passed the offices marked *Production*, *Assembly*, and *Engineering.* Men's voices on the other side of the entry marked *Shipping* were almost vibrating the opaque windowpane.

"I can't meet that order if the trucks don't get here on time. Section four in the assembly area is sitting with their thumbs up their butts because *you* people can't get me my engine parts. And I'm tired of waiting for rivets. We're down two crates. I have enough for another day and a half, and then we'll be at a standstill…Again."

"If your workers would stop wasting rivets, you'd have enough. Train those damned women better."

"Listen, jackass. They're *trained.* If this company would pay a little more to get better quality rivets, we wouldn't have so much waste."

"We're having some problems," Kitty said.

Polly nodded. "So I hear."

They came to an unmarked door at the end of the hall.

Kitty opened it into a spacious reception area. An older woman, about fifty, with salt-and-pepper hair, looked up from a large, finely polished dark-wood desk.

"This is Polly Hollister," Kitty said. She motioned to the woman and looked at Polly. "This is Cecilia Morrison, Mr. Helmsworth's executive secretary."

"Thanks, Kitty," Cecilia said.

Kitty nodded and left.

"It's just Celia." She rose and offered her hand.

Polly shook it.

"We're so glad you're here. Mr. Helmsworth's waiting for you. May I see your identification?"

Polly retrieved her credentials from the inside pocket of her jacket and showed them to her, revealing her true name. "Celia, I need to get into a decent pair of shoes. I can't spend the day tromping up and down stairs and doing my job in these heels." She held up a canvas bag containing her walking flats.

Celia laughed. "We all wear heels to work but bring a more comfortable pair with us. We've got an office ready for you. You can store your shoes in there. I'll take them for now."

She took Polly's bag and placed it under her own desk, then led her to the large oak door. "You're a lot younger than I thought you'd be. Mr. Helmsworth, Mr. Whitmire, the chief financial officer, and I were trying to figure out what you might look like, and believe me, we were way off." She laughed. "You're quite stunning."

"Thank you. That's very kind."

Celia rapped, then opened the door without waiting for an answer. "She's here at last, Mr. Helmsworth," she said.

Mr. Helmsworth smashed his half-smoked cigar into the cut-glass ashtray on his desk and pushed his rotund body up from his worn brown-leather chair. He lumbered toward Polly. "Thank God. If we don't get this mess straightened out, we'll lose the war before we even get in it."

The inside heel of his right shoe was slightly scuffed, and he didn't lift it as high as his left. He'd broken it at some point, probably before the age of thirty because he wasn't limping. His face was accented with worry lines, etched especially deep at the corners, near his eyes. How much of it was from the current concern was hard to tell.

He stopped in front of Polly and looked her over like he was buying a new DeSoto. "This plant makes wings and engine parts that make the P-51 Anaconda fighter plane faster and more maneuverable than any plane in the world. And I'll be damned if I'm going to let my competitors, or those German SOBs, get their mitts on one of them or any information about them." He didn't say anything else for a few seconds, just stared at her like he was inspecting an assembly line for productivity. "Why didn't Washington send me a man? They getting short-handed because of the draft?"

"No. They just thought I might do a better job."

Helmsworth smiled. "A better job, huh? We complete forty planes a week here. We fly 'em out on Friday by one o'clock in the afternoon. Give me another year, and we'll be cranking out a couple hundred a week, maybe even a thousand." He stopped talking, as if waiting for Polly to respond.

"Where do you fly them to?" She knew. She just wanted to see his reaction.

He studied her, rubbing his chin. "Joe DiMaggio batted the longest hitting streak in history from May to July. Fifty-six games. It lasted two months and two days."

A challenge? A battle to see if she could hold her own with him? He didn't trust her. He obviously needed more assurance that she was who she claimed to be, and that she could do the job she was sent here to do. She was up to it. "Whirlaway is the fifth winner of the Triple Crown. He was sired by English Derby winner Blenheim II and foaled at Calumet Farms in Kentucky. I knew Seabiscuit would beat War Admiral at Pimlico in '38. Man o' War sired War Admiral and Hard Tack, who was Seabiscuit's daddy, so Seabiscuit beat his uncle."

Helmsworth squared his shoulders. A counterattack. "General George Patton had to go to Sears and Roebuck to get nuts and bolts to repair three hundred tanks, and he hasn't been reimbursed for them yet."

Polly tried to keep a straight face but couldn't. "I wore the *Hell with Hitler* badge to President Roosevelt's inauguration."

Helmsworth belly-laughed and put his stubby fingers on her shoulders. "What's your code name?"

"I can't tell you."

"I know you have a code name. What is it?"

"I can't give it to you."

"You're a persistent little thing, aren't you?"

"Yes. It's what makes me good at my job, Mr. Helmsworth."

He let go of her shoulders. "I like it. Now let's get to work and catch that bitch."

Polly grimaced. "We're not sure yet it's a woman or that you actually have a spy."

"Oh, we have a spy. And whoever it is, you find them. And fast. Or I swear I'll shut this plant down and lock every single employee in here until we do."

"I like your enthusiasm, Mr. Helmsworth."

He nodded. "Whatever you need, you'll have it." He looked at Celia. "Anything. Where do you want to start?"

Polly clasped her hands loosely in front of her, trying to look relaxed. "I want to see the secure areas of the plant, where you store the sensitive documents, and what evidence you have regarding why you think you have a spy. I need to see what you think has been tampered with or stolen. Once I concur, then I'll need employee records. I want the ones of all executives first, then management, and then we'll look at employees who may have access to sensitive information."

"But many of us have already been cleared," Celia said.

"Well, according to your policy, all your employees have been cleared, yet you suspect someone is stealing information. So, we start at the top and work our way down."

Celia nodded. "Right away. The offices you'll want to see are just down the hall."

She led Polly to the engineers' offices, then through the secure storage areas, showing her the plans and documents and reviewing their protocols. Polly meticulously eliminated any frivolous rumors or undocumented incidents.

Celia opened the cabinets and brought out a large group of papers. "This is a report of the testing phase of the new modified wingspan." She turned the pages, then pointed. "These two pages were out of sequence. They weren't like that when I personally put the report in the file cabinet."

Polly requested the report and thumbed through it. "Was the cabinet locked?"

"Absolutely." Celia grimaced. "And not only were the pages out of order, but one page was upside down."

"As far as you know, has anyone taken this report out since you put it there?"

"No, not since I took it out to get some information for an order and discovered the changes. No one would have need of it now."

Polly handed the report back to Celia, then checked the cabinet, noting the subtle scratches around the lock. She walked to the outer door, inspected it, then came back and rechecked the metal cabinet, running her fingers along the handles. "How old is this?"

"We just got it last year. Lights have been coming from this room when the outer offices were closed."

"What kind of lights?" Polly asked.

"Flickering lights."

Polly carefully inspected the floor, seeing multiple scuff marks in the immediate area. "How many people have access to these files, and how often do they come in here?"

Celia picked up a book that was marked *Log-In* on top of the nearby desk and turned the pages slowly. "This area is off-limits to almost everyone. According to the entries, only four people have been in this room since last month: Mr. Helmsworth; Mr. R. K. Smyth, the head design engineer from Dayton, Ohio; our lead engineer, Randy Warton; and me."

Once Polly considered what she'd observed, and the information Celia had given her, it was obvious Portage Aircraft Inc. had something to worry about. "While I'm investigating, I'd like a guard posted at the entrance to the document room, and anyone who enters must be escorted. No one can remain in this room alone. When the floors are cleaned, the door must always remain open and in full view of the guard."

Celia nodded, her eyes fixed on Polly. "So, it is what we suspected?"

Polly returned her gaze but didn't answer.

She and Celia once again went to Mr. Helmsworth's office.

"Based on what I saw, there is a strong probability someone is trying to steal information."

Mr. Helmsworth grunted. "Now what?"

"I'm going to initiate a full-scale investigation. I'd like to clear a few people first so I can get some assistance. The more help I have, the faster we can find who we're looking for. How many people know you requested an agent from Washington?" Polly asked.

Helmsworth turned toward Celia. "I'm not sure."

"Mr. Helmsworth, Mr. Whitmire, and me," Celia said.

"Who dictated and then typed the letter to Washington?"

"Mr. Whitmire dictated it, and I typed it," she said.

"Did you send it through regular interoffice mail, or did you personally deliver it to the post office?"

Celia glanced at the floor. "Inter-office post."

"Who made phone calls to the Office of American Defense?"

"I did," Helmsworth said.

"Did you mention it to anyone else except Mr. Whitmire and Celia? In a board meeting? Out to lunch? At the country club? Anywhere else?"

"I don't believe I did."

"That's a *yes*," Polly said.

"Damn, you're good," Helmsworth grumbled. "I'd like to invite you to supper tonight at the house with my wife and me."

"I'd love to, but I don't have the time. Perhaps later in the week?"

They sat, and Polly reviewed with Mr. Helmsworth and Celia how she would proceed through the process of finding the spy.

"The first person I'd like to interview is Mr. Whitmire. Is he available?"

"Celia will check, and she can set it up for you." Helmsworth nodded at Celia.

"No one mentions anything about me being here from now on," Polly said. "I've been hired to assist Celia. No one is to use my real name, just Polly Hollister. That's all anyone needs to know. And the less said, the better. Security rules and regulations need to be tightened immediately. There's one more thing, Mr. Helmsworth."

He stopped from sitting at his desk and turned toward her.

"Is it possible I can get a car? I have to be more mobile, and public transportation is a nightmare."

"I'll have one here for you by the time you're ready to leave today."

"Nothing that stands out or draws attention to me."

Helmsworth nodded. "Understood."

Celia and Polly left his office.

"I need three people to help me immediately. Trusted employees, able to keep strict confidences and read quickly. I'll need their employee records first. As soon as I've cleared them, I'd like to assign them tasks."

"Whatever you need," Celia said. "I'll pull the records myself."

"And I'd like Mr. Whitmire's employment record."

Celia half-smiled. "You're going to have your hands full with him."

Polly entered the office Celia had assigned her. It had two windows, good overhead lighting, and a working radiator. The view to the west overlooked the plant. She would need to go through the factory, watch the process, and see where the employees worked and didn't work.

Celia brought the files and the executive staff records, including her own, with a note listing her and Mr. Helmsworth's office phone extensions and their home phone numbers. She was very thorough. "Your meeting with Mr. Whitmire is at three."

Polly nodded, took off her suit coat, pulled out the chair, and began to sort through the documents and information. She managed to get through half the files before she looked at her wristwatch, a Rolex Prince Elegante she had bought for herself last year. She'd been sitting for more than four hours.

She stood and stretched, massaging her lower back. She walked to the office where Kitty and the others worked. The room was empty. She went around the counter to the opposite end and followed the sound of female voices. They were sitting with Celia in a side room, at a small table, eating packed lunches. Polly hadn't brought a lunch. It hadn't entered her mind. She was embarrassed at the neglect.

"Are you not eating, Polly?" Celia asked.

"I didn't remember to pack something."

Celia patted the chair next to her. "Here, share mine. I have plenty."

"I couldn't impose."

"No. Please. I really do have more than enough."

Polly sat.

Kitty held up what looked like sweet bread and broke it in half. She laid one portion on a small paper napkin and slid it toward Polly. "I'm happy to share."

"You're very kind. Thank you."

"I'm Shirley Weismann." The woman with ash-blond hair blushed slightly.

Polly said hello.

"I'm Margie Williams," said the woman with brown wavy hair down to her shoulders, probably in her mid-thirties, with a twinkle in her eyes.

Polly smiled. "Nice to meet you." She took a bite of the sweet bread. "This is delicious. Did you make it, Kitty?"

"Yes. It's my grandmother's banana-bread recipe, but I changed it a little. It has pumpkin in it."

"It's really good. Where's the other secretary?"

Celia finished her mouthful of food and swallowed. "Patty went down to the main employee lunchroom. She likes to take her breaks with family or friends when it's not raining or snowing."

They ate and talked. Polly tried to give as little information as possible. When the questions became overly probing, Celia steered the group to different topics.

"Margie raises goats," Celia said.

Margie nodded. "I do. Have you ever had goat's milk or cheese, Polly?"

"I have not."

Margie gave a ten-minute dissertation on the benefits of goats.

Their break ended, and Kitty, Shirley, and Margie shuffled out of the lunchroom to go back to work.

Polly assumed it was Patty who came running up the stairs a few minutes later, breathless, clasping a pair of high heels, and hurried toward the office.

"Sorry, Kitty."

"Another late one, Patty, and you won't be leaving the building," Kitty said.

Patty nodded.

When only Celia and Polly were in the small room, Celia lowered her voice and leaned close to Polly. "Did we pass?"

Polly laughed. "Yes. With flying colors."

Celia shoulders relaxed. "What now?"

"Now we start digging for clues and fitting the pieces of the puzzle together."

"I love a good mystery," Celia said.

How much time would they have? How dangerous was it going to be?

At fifteen minutes to three, Polly's phone rang.

"Just a reminder," Celia said.

Polly thanked her and got ready for her meeting with Mr. Whitmire.

His office was located on the left at the end of the hall. His secretary, a small petite woman, greeted Polly and buzzed his office.

"Polly Hollister is here, sir." She looked up at Polly and smiled.

The smile was genuine, but something in her eyes confirmed everything Polly had read. This man was a tyrant.

Polly steeled herself. She'd dealt with men like this before and remembered what her father had taught her years ago. "Never sail without knowing the weather."

His secretary opened the door for her and whispered, "Good luck."

Polly smiled and whispered back, "Stormy seas ahead."

"Don't I know it," the secretary said, shutting the door behind her.

Mr. Stanly F-for-Franklin Whitmire looked up from his desk. No greeting. No sentiment of any kind, except a gesture for her to sit in one of the two chairs in front of his big wooden desk.

She complied.

His thin, dark hair was slicked and combed straight back. His tie was fastened with a diamond-studded clasp, precisely positioned, and his fingernails were perfectly manicured. Her first instinct was to challenge his authority. She could make him so thoroughly unhinged he would probably urinate in his pants. But she needed information quickly, and that tactic always took time. She observed him carefully.

According to his file, he was five-eight, forty-two, and had been with the company for a little over three years. He had a degree in business from a college in Virginia and had worked at one of the big rubber companies before coming to Portage Aircraft Inc. He was married with no children.

Sweat was forming at his temples. Why was he so nervous? He knew why she was here. She suspected he had lots to hide, but was giving away confidential information a part of it?

She'd gone through his file and talked with Celia about him and found out his wife had a drinking problem that she concealed. No surprise there. Lots of secrets. The way he dressed, his physical appearance, his file history, and his aloofness all painted a clear picture. He was a mean, domineering man who craved control. But was he who she was looking for? She could find out very easily. This man was bottled up so tight it would take only one question to shake him up and watch him explode. And she knew the question.

They stared at each other like they were about to lunge for a weapon and the first one who got it would win the battle. He gripped his pen tighter. She'd already grabbed the weapon and was ready to deliver the coup de grâce.

"Mr. Whitmire, are you betraying your country by giving confidential and sensitive information to the enemy?"

She watched the red heat start at his neck, spread to his face, and then to his ears. His face turned a deeper shade of crimson. He threw the pen down on the desk and stood, pushing his hands against the top of the desk so hard his fingers blanched. "How dare you ask me that question!"

His instant indignation gave her the answer. If he'd been guilty, he would have gone on the defensive with explanations and excuses. She stood. "Thank you for your time."

He had lots of secrets, but being a spy wasn't one of them. She smiled as she turned and left his office. On to the next person.

CHAPTER SEVEN

Kalena massaged her stiff neck. Her knees ached from standing in one position too long. She slipped her head scarf off and fluffed her hair, looking more closely at herself in the mirror that ran the length of the four sinks.

Perta gazed at her own reflection, puckering her lips. "I hate that we can't reapply lipstick once we get to the building. What does it matter if we wear lipstick or not? Like that's going to make a difference welding or torquing bolts into those stupid engines. Why *torquing*? Why not screwing? I like screwing better."

Kalena laughed. "Hair. That's what bothers me. I just got a cut and a perm, and now all I do is tuck it under this scarf." She pointed toward her head. "It's a mess. I may as well have not gotten anything done to it." She slipped the scarf back on her head and retied it, frowning at herself.

Perta leaned over the counter, studying herself like she was looking for a revelation. She was cute. Not beautiful or lovely, but cute. Her nose turned slightly upward, and she had high cheekbones and a sensible expression when she smiled, like she was saying, "I agree and find that very amusing."

"Say, are you sure you're going to the dance Saturday night?" Perta asked. "You don't act like you want to."

"I want to," Kalena said. She did, but she didn't know how to dance, and Perta knew better than to bring it up. It embarrassed her to admit it. Her friends had tried to teach her, but she had two left feet and did nothing but stumble over herself and her partner. It'd been years since she'd tried to learn again.

Four more women came into the bathroom, as three came out of the stalls and up to the sinks. One looked at Kalena in the mirror. "It's going to be a swell dance. You can't go wrong with Glenn Miller. Anyone know who the singers will be?"

A woman in one of the stalls yelled back. "Paula Kelly, and of course Tex and the Modernaires."

Freda, a tall, stout woman with a green-and-purple scarf wrapped around her head, pulled at her ear as she looked in the mirror. "I hope those dead-hoofers don't come down from Cleveland and take up all the dance floor. He was just in Cleveland a couple of months ago. They need to stay in their own city."

Kalena's stomach tensed at what Freda might do at the dance.

She didn't seem to have a problem speaking her mind. A few weeks earlier, just before a lunch break, Freda had started a ruckus when she told the foreman in assembly-line two that he was nuts if he thought they were going to stand more than three hours without a break. Kalena and the other women near her had gathered around to watch.

The foreman, Sammy Lichfield, a smaller man with thinning hair, who all the women nicknamed "the bald eagle," told her she'd work until he told her to stop.

Freda took one step closer toward him and said, "We'll work as hard as we can, and do all we can, but we're taking a break."

Sammy looked around at the other women, who had nodded in agreement with Freda. "We'll see about that," he said, and left.

Freda evidently went to the employee offices, because the next week signs were posted announcing all employees would take two fifteen-minute breaks, one mid-morning and one mid-afternoon.

After that, Sammy glared at Freda every time he came down the assembly line.

The room began to fill with more women, and a line formed against the far wall.

"Did you hear there's a federal agent in the building?" Freda asked, adjusting her scarf.

The chatter around the room stopped. A toilet flushed. Everyone turned toward her.

"A federal agent?" Perta asked, as if by saying the word, they'd all be herded up and interrogated. "What for?"

Freda shrugged. "Beats me. I saw him and Mr. Whitmire talking with a group of men by the steps in the administrative offices when I went over there the other morning." She held her hand up and inspected her fingernails.

Kalena squinted. "How did you know he was a federal agent?"

Freda turned toward her. "Because Kitty, in personnel, told me they were expecting someone from Washington."

Suddenly Juniper Bailey stuck her head in the doorway. "Amscray. The bald eagle is on the prowl. Anyone late back on the line is going to be written up." She disappeared as suddenly as she'd appeared.

Everyone pushed their way out of the bathroom, scrambling to get back to work.

Kalena went to her position, picked up the torque wrench, and tightened the bolts on the flywheel that attached to the crankshaft. She looked up at the large wall clock. Two more hours. What was Polly doing? How was her day going? Would she be working late on her first day? Would they be able to ride home together?

When the shift ended, Kalena waited for Polly, but she didn't show. Finally, she reluctantly boarded the bus and held on to the back of the seat nearest the driver. She watched out the window, hoping she might see her at the last possible second. But no Polly.

Still no sign of her at supper. Kalena listened for the front door to open and glanced periodically at the empty chair beside her.

Aunt Berna buttered a slice of bread. "She must be a hard worker."

"You don't think anything's happened to her, do you?" Kalena asked.

Richard dipped his spoon into the plentiful vegetables in his bowl of beef soup. "Naw. She's fine. I'm sure she'll be here soon. Office staff don't work the same hours as shift workers."

She heard the front door open and turned toward the living room, a flutter of excitement shooting into her stomach. Polly was home.

She appeared in the kitchen with a smile but looked weary.

"Good evening, everyone." She took her seat at the table.

Aunt Berna served her.

Polly sniffed the warm mixture. "It smells delicious."

"How was your first day?" Richard asked, before Kalena could say anything.

She wanted to ask the questions. She wanted to talk with Polly. She was the one who had waited all day to visit with her, not Richard.

Polly nodded as she began to eat. "It was good, but it's really busy."

Kalena made her move before Richard took over the conversation. "Did you see the federal agent?"

Polly choked on her soup. She dabbed her napkin at the corner of her mouth. "I'm sorry. What?"

"Today in the bathroom, Freda, from assembly-line two, said she saw a federal agent in administration talking with a group of the executives."

Polly wiped the corners of her mouth with the napkin and continued to eat. "I don't know anything about it."

Richard laughed. "Yeah, and if you did, you wouldn't tell us." He dipped his bread into the soup and wolfed it down. "I'm sure you're one of those kinds of people."

"What kind of people?" Aunt Berna asked.

"The kind you have to pry the time of day out of," Richard said.

Polly smiled slightly, as if she agreed but didn't care if anyone else did.

Kalena's tension rose. Richard didn't know Polly. He had no right to say that about her. She wasn't like that. "I'm sure she'd tell us if she knew."

"Actually, I wouldn't," Polly said. "It was made very clear to me today that I'm to not say anything about what I see or hear in the administrative offices. Sorry."

"Good for you," Aunt Berna said.

Kalena watched Polly. Could she be trusted? Could she keep secrets? Would she keep Kalena's? Could she talk with her about her confusion and feelings about women, her wants and needs? Was it a want or need? Or both?

Kalena lingered in the living room after supper, stalling, hoping Polly would come down and visit, but she'd gone to her room after she finished her meal and never returned. Aunt Berna sat in her overstuffed chair, Richard on the couch, both glued to the radio, listening to Edward R. Murrow on NBC's *News Here and Abroad*. Kalena didn't want to hear the news. She didn't want to hear about Europe and its tragedy. She didn't want to hear the latest tunes or *Fibber Magee and Molly*.

She trudged up the stairs to her room, got her bed clothes, and went into the bathroom to soak in a hot bath. She lounged in the tub, occasionally pouring the steamy water over herself until it cooled to the point of discomfort. She pushed up from the tub and reached for the towel.

Polly opened the door abruptly and froze, staring at her. Her face flushed red. She backed out, almost tripping over herself. "I'm so sorry. I thought the bathroom was empty." She closed the door.

Kalena stood there stunned, trying not to admit to herself she was hoping Polly would come back. She stepped out of the bathtub and began to dry herself, feeling the heat of Polly's gaze still on her skin. The more she thought about it, the more she reacted. Those eyes. They weren't exactly hazel, but somehow a mixture of green and gold. She was wearing a nightgown, and Kalena saw the rise of her breasts and the buds of her hard, firm nipples through the aqua silk. Her breath caught as she captured the memory, not letting it go. Polly was exquisite.

Kalena dressed in her cotton nightgown and left the bathroom, closing the door loudly so Polly would know she was no longer there. She lay on the bed, motionless, quiet, remembering the sensations when Polly had looked at her. Did she like what she saw? Or was she embarrassed so badly she couldn't wait to get out of the room and discard the memory? Kalena usually didn't have problems understanding others' feelings, but Polly was different. Very different.

CHAPTER EIGHT

Polly sat on the edge of the bed staring at the bathroom door, but all she could see was Kalena reaching for a towel, her beautiful nude body in full view—voluptuous firm breasts, long legs, defined curves, a thick, rich nest of golden hue between her legs.

A door slammed. She stood and walked to the bathroom, cautiously turned the knob, and peered in. The lingering scent of Kalena's shampoo and soap filled the room. She drew her bath. Kalena had been there moments ago, naked. When the tub was full, she stepped in and sank into the warm comfort. The tensions of the day released, and her thoughts turned once again to Kalena. She'd been there only moments ago, exactly where Polly was now. She could almost feel the wet warmth of her body sliding against hers. She chastened herself, not allowing the pleasurable imaginings to continue. She was here for the job, not an affair.

She finished bathing and put on her nightgown, then realized she hadn't told Kalena or Aunt Berna about the car. She slipped on her robe and knocked on Kalena's door. What would Kalena do? It was an accident, a pleasant one, but nonetheless an accident.

Kalena peeked out.

"May I come in?"

Kalena nodded and opened the door wider.

Polly eased inside. "I'm so sorry."

Kalena's cheeks turned a light pink. "We'll have to be more careful. I might have done the same thing to you. Let's leave the door open when we aren't in there, and if it's closed, we'll make sure we knock."

Her lips were full and soft. Who had kissed them? "Good idea. I wanted to tell you I have a car."

Kalena's eyes widened. "You have a *car*?"

"Yes. It's just temporary. I'll need to spend more time at work for now, and sometimes I'll be there late at night, so they gave me one to use. I need to leave early in the morning. Will you tell your aunt, so she won't be concerned if she sees it in the driveway?"

"Yes, of course."

Polly looked deep into Kalena's eyes. Pools of liquid green gazed back, almost smoldering. Was it the reflection of the embers burning within Polly? She wanted to kiss her more than she'd ever wanted to kiss a woman, but she didn't move. She needed an excuse to stay, to linger. It wouldn't be difficult to think of something to discuss. They could talk about their day, work, the plant, Ohio, or even the weather. A smile pressed her lips, but she restrained it, thinking how ridiculous it was that she could barely keep from stepping toward Kalena. Polly's body seemed to have a will of its own. Yes. She could think of many things to talk about—and do. "Well, good night." She turned and retreated to her bedroom.

The next morning, she wasn't sure if she wanted to leave early to avoid Kalena, or she was just anxious to catch a spy. Maybe it was a little of both. She got halfway to the front door before Aunt Berna called to her.

"Polly, you must eat something, and I have a lunch for you."

Polly cringed, did an about-face, and walked to the kitchen.

Aunt Berna pointed to the food on the table. "Eat."

She couldn't protest or pretend she wasn't hungry because she was famished. "Thank you." She surrendered into her chair.

Aunt Berna immediately filled her cup with rich-smelling coffee and brought a bowl of hot oatmeal. "Would you like brown sugar in it? I couldn't get raisins at the store this week."

"Brown sugar would be wonderful." Polly poured a generous amount of cream into her coffee.

"I'm afraid we're going to have to do without more things soon. There was also very little coffee and sugar. It seems like every time I go in, I see less and less. And the prices. Last month a loaf of bread was six cents. This week it's seven. Butter went up to forty cents a pound.

And eggs? I considered getting some chickens, but I hate their stink and noise."

Aunt Berna had a lot to talk about this early in the morning.

Polly removed the paper lid from the milk bottle, then poured milk into the bowl of thick oatmeal and dipped in the spoon. "I'm sure you're right. Things are going to get more expensive and harder to find."

"I'm glad Kalena is back with me. I wouldn't want to go through this by myself."

"Where was she?" Polly asked.

"She was in Cleveland for a time. Her leaving surprised us. It was sudden. One day at the supper table she announced she was going to live in Cleveland with a friend. A week later she'd moved there."

"Why did she go? She seems to like it here."

"Oh, she loves Barberton. I'm not sure why she left. She won't say much about it, only that she had to get away."

Polly heard the floorboards squeak above her. Kalena's room.

She ate faster, drank half her coffee, then quickly stood. "Delicious breakfast, but I must be going."

"Where are you off to so early? Buses won't start running for at least another thirty minutes."

"I have a car."

"A *car*? Mercy sakes." Aunt Berna offered her the meal in a brown paper bag. "If you'll pick up a lunchbox and thermos at the five-and-dime next time you're out, it will save you money in the long run."

Polly nodded, took the sack, and headed for the front entrance to grab her coat and purse she'd left on the end table. She hurried out the door.

By two o'clock she was ready for a break. She rubbed her temples and looked at the long table piled with documents and employee files separated by job assignments. She'd interviewed the rest of the executives, scrutinized their reactions to her questions, gone over their files, looked at their backgrounds, and dismissed them as suspects. The process of elimination was much easier for the secretarial staff because they were closely watched and, for some reason, were held to a much higher criterion of security than any other group in the plant. They couldn't have gotten their hands on an extra note pad, much less a secure document without someone knowing about it. They were a tight-knit group and had full accountability wherever they went in the plant. Celia had seen to it and was very good at her job. All the executives and the secretarial staff had been screened. She was sure it wasn't any of them.

Patty and Margie shuffled through the files, continuing to sort.

"What's the next group?" Margie asked.

"Go ahead and take a break. I'll be back in a little while," Polly said.

She went directly to Celia's office.

"Besides secretaries and executives, who else has access to these offices?"

Celia stopped writing and laid the pen on her desk. "How much access do you mean?"

"Entrance during all shifts."

"No one except maintenance, custodial staff, and runners."

"What are *runners*?"

"Employees on special assignment. They deliver modified plans, instructions, anything that needs communicated to the foremen on the floor."

"Good God!" Polly scrubbed her face. "How many on a shift?"

"None on third shift but three on first and second shift. How many used depends on the production run for the day and where the plant is in the process."

"How do I get their names?"

"The plant foremen will know. There are three foremen on each shift—Walter Henry, Bill Shannon, and Sammy Lichfield—one at each assembly station on first shift." Celia shuffled through her papers, picked up a green bound notebook, and read from it. "And Harold Stanton, Emmitt Brewster, and Mac Tenbury on second shift."

"I'll need to talk with them."

On the plant floor, the constant noise was a mix of clanking, voices, and muffled echoes of the movement of parts and machinery. Polly saw Kalena on the far assembly line and waved when Kalena smiled at her.

"Listen, sweetie. I don't have time to stand here and talk all day." Walter Henry stood with his legs slightly apart, his large frame towering over Polly. He seemed to be inspecting her, trying to figure out what she was doing there and why she was asking him so many questions.

"I understand, Mr. Henry, but do you use specific runners?"

"Like I said, it depends on what I need or what's sent from the office."

Getting information out of him was like trying to pour molasses from a mason jar on a winter morning. "Sir, it's important."

He swooped his arm. "Honey, it's all important." He surveyed the assembly line. "We use Herb Stanford, Carl Enright, or Kalena Mikloska."

Kalena? "No one else?"

Mr. Henry shook his head. "Only them three."

She quickly wrote the names. "One more thing. Why them?"

"I know what's going on here, toots. I'd trust them in a storm."

"I'm sorry. I don't understand."

"I mean I know all about what this plant builds and how important it is. I don't use anybody I don't know or trust. And Bill and Sammy are the same way. And if you're trying to find out how well we all do our jobs, I'm telling you first-shift does ours. If we have any problems with production, they're not on first shift."

Polly smiled. "I'm sure you all do a fine job, Mr. Henry."

"Damn right we do. You won't find shoddy work here. And another thing, some of these women do a better job than the men. They talk too much and complain a lot, but other than that, I don't have any problems with 'em."

"That's good to know, sir." Polly thanked him and went to the other assembly lines, ferreting out the needed information from the remaining two foremen.

By six that night she'd cleared all the runners and foremen from both shifts, including Kalena. Each runner had limited access to the offices and received only information that specific executives gave them. They were never permitted to obtain information on their own. Once they were handed any documents, they signed for them, wrote the date and time they left the offices, and were escorted back to the assembly line. They then signed and wrote the time when they handed the documents to the shift supervisor. The shift supervisor had to return all documents to the offices at the end of their shifts. Polly meticulously reviewed all the records and processes connected with the runners and found no evidence of tampering or illegal activity. Whoever the spy was, they weren't getting information by being a runner.

Celia came into the room. "You all right? Long day?"

Polly nodded. She placed Kalena's file on the stack with the others, then rose, flexing her neck and yawning. "I'll be done shortly."

"Don't forget to turn the light out when you leave." Celia said good night and left.

When Polly was sure she was alone, she went to the hallway and checked all the office doors. Locked. Celia had given her a key and told her it was a master, and that all department heads had one. She stopped at the engineers' office and unlocked the door. She walked around, looking at the paperwork and items on desks and stacked in trays. She reached into the trash can and pulled out several wadded pieces of paper. She sat at the nearest desk and smoothed out the wrinkles. One was a partial draft for a new fuselage, the other a list of aircraft-production numbers for the next year. They contained sensitive information. The papers should have been shredded, not wadded and tossed into the trash can. It was a major security breach. She slipped them into her pocket, keeping them as evidence for later. She returned to her office and continued to review more employee records. The sound of the elevator's motor penetrated the silence. The pulleys creaked and moaned, and a loud thump sounded as the elevator stopped. Then came the sound of the doors opening. She walked to the hall. Two women in faded green coveralls pushed their cleaning carts down the corridor. Polly recognized the taller one from the ice cream shoppe. Beverly Anderson.

"Evening," said Beverly. Her key ring jingled as she opened the office door across from where Polly stood.

Polly smiled. "Hello."

They entered.

Polly watched as they dusted the desks and windowsills, emptied the trash, then swept and mopped the floor. Beverly relocked the door, and they continued to the next office. Polly went to her desk and returned to the hallway when the women later approached the elevator with their carts.

"What do you do with the trash in your carts?" she asked.

They exchanged a glance.

"We empty it in the first-floor dumpster," Beverly said.

"And then what happens to it?"

"It's burnt in the incinerator out back," the shorter woman said, as if anxious to get on with her work.

"By whom?"

"Beats me. We just empty it," Beverly said, watching Polly closely.

Short woman nodded. "We don't want any trouble. We do exactly what they tell us to. I need this job. I got two kids at home."

Polly was irritated with herself. She should have been more discreet with her questioning. "I'm sorry. I was just asking because I'm new and trying to understand how things work around here."

Short woman's shoulders relaxed. She settled her hand on her cart. "I think they burn the trash sometime before the end of second shift."

Polly had found two carelessly discarded secure pieces of information. It would be easy to correct an unintentional error, but had someone discarded the information on purpose? Critical information wadded and tossed openly into a trash can was clever. Anyone walking by wouldn't give it a second thought. If that was the case, more than one person was involved, and it was a much deeper problem. Whoever was trying to get information was skilled and well trained. As hard as Polly had been searching, so far, she'd found no trace of who it was. She hadn't vetted Beverly or the short woman yet. Or, for that matter, several others. She was still a long way from putting the pieces of this puzzle together.

Mr. Helmsworth had added guards, but that wasn't the security problem. It wasn't about people getting in but about information getting out by people who already worked there. That was the key to finding the spy. She needed more help.

By the time Polly left the office, it was eight thirty, pitch-dark, and the temperature had dropped drastically. She shivered and rubbed her hands together, waiting for the car to warm up. Mr. Helmsworth had made a good choice for her. It was a black 1939 two-door Austin 8, simple yet functional. It'd been a year since she'd driven a car, and she was still grinding gears and riding the clutch.

She purposely headed downtown, stopping at the phone booth at the corner of Fifth Street and Tuscarawas Avenue to call Oliver. But he didn't answer. She reinserted the nickel and called again. Still no answer. When she got back to the house, Aunt Berna, Kalena, and Richard were in the living room listening to what sounded like a radio drama.

Polly waved hello to everyone, not wanting to interrupt their story. Kalena waved back.

She quickly climbed the steps, shut the bedroom door, and took the papers out of her pocket. Where to stash them without anyone finding them? She scanned the room, weighing her options. She'd cleared Aunt Berna of being a spy, but Aunt Berna cleaned Polly's room weekly. She was sure she wouldn't invade her privacy by going through her suitcase or the dresser drawers, but she couldn't take the chance.

She'd put her backup weapon, another .38 snub nose, in the small false compartment on the inside of her suitcase, along with the dossier she'd brought with her, but she couldn't stuff another piece of paper in there. She inspected the room once more, finally deciding on a viable option. She moved the dark-wood dresser far enough from the wall, taped the papers to its wooden back, then returned the furniture to its original position, being careful not to scuff the floor.

Why didn't Oliver answer when she'd called? Was something wrong? She'd phone him tomorrow, and if she couldn't reach him, she'd check the safe house. While this wasn't an overtly dangerous mission, she didn't want to be without support. Especially if things went wrong.

CHAPTER NINE

Kalena sat with her feet up in the overstuffed chair, watching Aunt Berna crochet a row of white thread in one of her doilies. The minute she heard the water running upstairs, she couldn't focus on the radio program. She'd lost interest as quickly as Polly had swooped in and gone upstairs. Would she come back down and visit? She must be exhausted.

Kalena had thought about her off and on all day. Why had she been talking to the foreman on the assembly line? Why was she working such long hours? She waited as long as she could, but her curiosity got the best of her, and she went upstairs, stopping by Polly's room, seeing the light under the door. She had to be done with her bath by now. She hesitated and took a deep breath, then rapped on the door.

"Come in."

Polly was sitting in the cushioned armchair beside the bed. She'd been writing something in a small brown leather notebook and closed it when Kalena entered.

"Am I disturbing you?"

Polly's lips curved slightly upward, and her eyes focused directly on her. "Not at all. I'm glad for your company. I wanted to say hello this afternoon when I was on the assembly line but didn't get the chance. How was your day?" She wore loose-fitting pants and a light-cream-colored knit sweater, and her feet were covered in embroidered silk slippers.

Kalena went for a quick dip in those eyes again. This morning, when she came down for breakfast and heard Polly go out the front door, her heart sank. That's when she concluded she was now infatuated with her and couldn't do anything about it. She'd never experienced this feeling before. The more she was around her, the more she wanted to be with her.

"You all right?"

She found herself caught between Polly's gaze and her question. She nodded and brushed a piece of fuzz from the bottom of her skirt. She should leave. Run. What was she doing here?

"Are you excited about Thanksgiving and the dance on Saturday?"

Kalena realized she was still standing in the doorway. She hadn't moved an inch since she stepped in. "I'm sure Thanksgiving will be good. Aunt Berna's already started getting ready. We're having quite a few people for supper. You'll be there, won't you?"

"Of course. I can drive us to the dance on Saturday if you'd like. Please sit." Polly motioned to the bed.

Kalena walked over and sat on the edge of the mattress. "I want to go, but I'm sure all I'll do is watch everyone else."

"Why? Every man in the room will want to dance with you."

Kalena's cheeks began to burn. She hated that she blushed. "I…I, uh, I don't know how to dance."

"You don't?"

Kalena shook her head. "Not a step."

"Well, that's going to change. Do you have a record player?"

"Yes, in the den, but I'm afraid it's not in the best shape. It's a Victrola, and the turntable sometimes sticks, and I think it needs a new needle."

"Well, we should start right away. Let's go." Polly led her out of the bedroom and down the steps but stopped halfway. "What kinds of records do you have?"

"Not many. I have two Glenn Miller and one Jimmy Dorsey, "Stardust" by Tommy Dorsey and Frank Sinatra, and the rest are Aunt Berna's."

"That'll do," Polly said.

"Hey. What ya doin'?" Richard looked up from reading the evening paper when they passed by.

"None of your business," Kalena said, shutting the sliding wooden door to the den. She walked over and pulled out the two records she had bought and set them on the table by the mahogany Victrola. "I'm afraid this is it."

"We won't need music for a while," Polly said. She began to slide the chair away from the center of the room.

Kalena helped her move the sofa and roll up the heavy, deep-colored rug next to the hearth.

Polly stepped to the center of the now-bare wood floor and held out her hand. "Don't be shy. Come here."

Kalena maneuvered in front of her. "I'm afraid many have tried before you and failed. I have no sense of rhythm."

"Nonsense. Stand beside me." Polly moved her gently.

Kalena felt the strength in her touch as she guided her.

"The swing is simple. Just a few steps and some movement. Side-step, back-step, the walk, touch-step, triple-step, and the kick-ball."

Kalena frowned.

Polly laughed. "Honest. It's not hard. Watch me." She went through each step like she was floating on air.

"I can't do that."

"Yes. You can." She repeated the motion, then moved away from Kalena. "Your turn."

Kalena hesitated, assuring herself she'd be awkward and off balance.

Polly touched her waist. "Each step is deliberate but soft." She guided her through the steps, getting closer until Kalena could feel the heat of her body.

They repeated the steps for ten minutes, then collapsed onto the sofa, laughing.

"You have a natural rhythm. But you think you don't," Polly said. "Now we'll partner. Slow dancing is nothing more than sensing each other."

Kalena raised her hands in protest. "I don't know how to slow dance."

"Yes, you do. You've already learned." Polly beckoned, then positioned herself in front of her, holding her hands even with her shoulders. "Put both hands against mine." As Kalena did, Polly pushed firmly against them. "Close your eyes."

Kalena complied. Polly's image remained distinct and clear in front of her.

"I'm going to tell you where to go, but only with my hands." She guided her back and forward and side to side by just touch and pressure. "That's perfect. Open your eyes."

Kalena did, finding Polly's sparkling gaze and a soft smile on her face.

"This is called the starting position." Polly dropped her right hand and took Kalena's right in her left. "Rest your left hand on my shoulder."

Kalena did as instructed, and when she did, Polly moved closer and slid her arm to the middle of Kalena's back, pressing in, guiding her toward her.

Kalena's breath stuttered.

"Follow me," Polly whispered.

Kalena started to step back and looked down at Polly's feet.

"Don't look down. Feel your way across the dance floor. Feel me guide you where I want you to go. Dancing is intimacy and expression. Relax. You know everything you need to dance." She moved closer, their breasts almost touching.

Could Polly feel Kalena's heart beating faster, her breath catching, how she hungered to be held?

"A good dancer will be clear where he wants his partner to go."

They began to move. Kalena followed each step as surely as if Polly whispered the instructions into her ear.

Polly stopped and broke their connection. "I'm going to add the music. Let the rhythm and feeling merge."

The slow beat and silky music of "Star Dust" began to play. Polly stepped toward her, her arm sliding firmly down the middle of Kalena's back once more.

Kalena positioned her hand on Polly's right shoulder and moved with her, embracing her, drawing her closer, feeling Polly's arm wrap more tightly around her, the warmth of her body, her toned muscles, the intimate way she held her. The music drifted on the air. They glided. Polly's breath caressed her ear. The thrill radiated down Kalena's neck and into her entire body. "Polly—"

A banging on the door made them jump.

"I know what you two are doing in there. I can help teach you how to dance." Richard's declaration was loud and full of confidence.

Polly eased away.

Nothing was said, but after they fully parted, Kalena felt only an emptiness, an absence of sensation and emotion. The room became cold and large. She was alone once again. She slid the door open.

Richard stepped into the room. "What's up? Are you dancing or just horsing around?"

"We're just finishing," Kalena said.

"Aw, come on. Don't stop. I'll dance with you."

Polly walked over to the record player and put on another tune. "Go on, Kalena. Dance with him."

Kalena took a deep breath and blew it out. "All right, but go easy on me."

Richard grinned and reached for her as "Pennsylvania 6-500" by Glenn Miller began to play. "You'll do great. Just follow me."

By the time the song was over, Kalena was laughing.

Richard let go of her. "I think you've got it." He said it like he'd been the one to teach her.

Polly moved the needle to the stand, shut off the record player, and slipped the seventy-eight back into its paper jacket. She shut the lid on the wooden cabinet and turned toward Kalena. "You're a fast learner." She said it as if she had complete confidence in Kalena's ability to win a dance contest.

Kalena couldn't stop her smile. "I had a good teacher."

Richard blew on his fingers and rubbed them against his shirt.

Kalena laughed and gently shoved his shoulder.

"Hey. I helped," he said.

Kalena laughed again. "Yes. You did. Thank you."

They replaced the rug on the floor and moved the furniture back into position.

Kalena couldn't stop looking into Polly's eyes. Did she want her, too? Did she feel the heat she was feeling? "Would you like some hot spiced cider?"

Polly touched her elbow. "That sounds wonderful."

"Yeah. That sounds swell," Richard said.

Kalena tried not to give away her disappointment that Richard had also accepted the offer. She went into the living room. "Aunt Berna, would you like a hot cup of cider?"

"Thanks, but no. I'm going to bed." Aunt Berna rose and kissed Kalena's cheek. "Good night."

"Good night. Sleep well."

Kalena heard Aunt Berna briefly speak to Richard and Polly on her way to her room. She warmed the cider, then brought the steaming cups to the living room on a tray and served Polly and Richard.

Polly curled up on the end of the sofa closest to the chair Kalena sat in.

Richard took his cup and sat at the far end of the sofa.

Polly blew the steam over the rim of the cup, then sipped. "Mm, it's delicious."

The room was quiet. Kalena hoped Richard would take the hint and leave, but obviously he didn't.

"I saw you on the assembly line this afternoon, Polly," he said. "What brought you down there?"

Polly set her cup on the coffee table and leaned back. "Just trying to get some information for Celia."

"Does it have to do with the federal agent everyone's talking about?" he asked.

Kalena rested one elbow on the chair and brought her cup forward. "I don't think those rumors are true. Why would they bring in a federal agent?"

Polly turned toward Richard. "Yes, why?"

Richard took another sip of his drink. "Because of the type of work we do. Something's going on at the plant."

"What's going on?" Polly asked.

Richard set his cup down and rubbed his knee, as if soothing an ache. "I've heard talk about lights on in the plant offices after second shift lets out. I've noticed more security guards on each shift, and men are in the offices that no one ever saw before who don't give their names and ask a lot of questions."

Kalena hung on every word. Polly sat still, as if considering what Richard had just said.

"You don't think there's a spy in the plant, do you?" Kalena asked.

Richard shrugged. "Who knows. It's no secret that the P-51 Anaconda is experimental and has been modified. I'm sure someone would like to get ahold of the plans and information."

He finished his cider, then slapped his thigh and stood. "I'm going to bed. Good night." He took his cup into the kitchen, then went upstairs.

"Polly, you don't think there's a spy, do you?"

Polly shook her head. "I have no idea. I just arrived. But Richard is correct. The work done at the plant is classified, and the information would appeal to an enemy, especially now." She looked intently at her.

Kalena swallowed hard and could barely get her words out. "A spy? It could be anyone." She looked at Polly. Could it be her? She was new to the area, after all, and sometimes it felt like she was holding things back. But surely people were entitled to have lives they didn't share with others. It wasn't Kalena's nature to be suspicious, and when she considered the way Polly's arms felt around her, she decided it simply wasn't possible.

Chapter Ten

Polly had called Oliver another three times from work the next day and still couldn't get an answer. She needed to find out what was wrong. She left the factory late, turned the headlights on, slipped the car into second without grinding the gears or riding the clutch, and drove north on Wooster Road toward the address in Akron. On a secondary street she parked across from a cobbler's store filled with brown, mahogany, and black leather shoes in the window display. The safe house was above the shop, on the second floor.

She went to the back entrance of the building and slipped the larger key into the lock, then climbed the narrow steps. Number Four was about two-thirds of the way down the dimly lit hall. She took the snub-nose revolver from its leather holster at the middle of her back and held it to her side as she made her way to the apartment. She knocked, waited, then knocked louder. No answer. She inserted the key and released the lock, then slowly pushed the door open and scanned the room. She stepped inside and closed the door behind her.

The apartment appeared empty and neglected and had a faint scent of leather and shoe polish that had seeped up from the cobbler's shop directly below. The living room had little furniture: a threadbare couch, cheaply made wooden end table, lamp, and an old Philco radio in a scratched, sun-bleached wooden cabinet against the far wall near a window with the stained blind pulled halfway down. No Oliver. The kitchenette had a hot plate. A few dishes and glasses were in the cupboard. A partially filled bag of Maxwell House coffee sat on the counter. She opened it and sniffed. Its strong scent told her it wasn't more than three or four days old. She checked the drawers, finding a few more kitchen items, then moved to the bedroom.

The bed was made with sheets, a blanket, and two pillows. She flicked the bathroom light switch. A bare lightbulb cast feeble shadows on the wall. A toothbrush and a used tube of Pepsodent toothpaste lay on the side of the sink. The bristles on the brush were dry. She searched through every drawer, under the bed, between the mattress and the box springs, behind and under furniture, closets, everywhere she could think to look. Nothing. No clue as to who Oliver was or where he'd gone.

Now what? Should she call Washington or try to work this out on her own? Protocol dictated she contact Washington, but what if they wanted answers? All she had were questions. Where did he go? Was he hurt? Why hadn't he contacted her? She shouldn't have taken this assignment by herself. It could prove to be too much and ruin everything she'd worked for.

She left the apartment and found a nearby phone booth outside a bank a block away from where she'd parked. She called the OAD and listened as the operator put the call through.

A male voice suddenly came on the line. "State your code name."

"Enigma."

"Hold, please."

After several minutes another male voice answered.

"This is Agent-in-Charge Reynolds."

Thank God it wasn't Henson. She checked her watch. Eight ten. He must have worked the first twelve-hour shift.

"Oliver is missing."

"Who?" Reynolds asked.

"My contact." Polly heard the shuffle of papers.

"How long?"

She gave him the details. She sat down heavily on the small wooden seat in the booth and ran her fingers through her hair. "I need help."

"We can't send anyone to you. All available agents have been placed in other cities. You'll have to take care of this situation on your own, Enigma. Can you find the spy?"

"Yes, but I'll have to dig deeper than I originally considered.

Whoever it is has a solid cover. I think it's going to take longer than we thought."

"How long?"

"I don't know yet."

"Well, find out who it is, and quickly…I'm sorry we can't send anyone just now. I'll contact the FBI in Cleveland and see if they can help locate Oliver, but for now you'll have to manage on your own. Do what you must, but be careful. Don't worry about Oliver. Stay focused on your assignment. I want you to report in every two days by twenty-four hundred until we find your contact or assign you another one. Is that clear?"

"Yes, sir. It's clear. I'll do my best."

Polly left the phone booth, jammed her hands into the side pockets of her wool overcoat, and hurried back to the car. The cold night air calmed her. She breathed deeply and waited for the heater to defrost the windshield. She had to put thoughts of Oliver out of her mind and focus on finding the spy. But where was he? Was he tied more closely to who she was looking for? Something was off about him. The way he'd acted, constantly scanning the area, not in the confident way agents assessed their surroundings but more like he was on the defensive. He never made full eye contact with her. Was he hiding something? His explanation of how he'd scraped his knuckles sounded vague and too rehearsed. Then there was his obvious hesitation about considering there might be a female spy at the factory. None of those things separately meant anything. But combined? Red flags were waving in the chilled night air. Could finding him lead her where she needed to go? No. Reynolds was right. She couldn't let herself get distracted.

But she couldn't help herself. She had to do something. She drove back to the plant and called the Akron and Barberton police departments, area hospitals, and the city morgues. No bodies had been reported or found answering Oliver's description. She had to let it go. It was past nine when she arrived home, tired and discouraged.

The scent of pumpkin pie filled the house. Aunt Berna and Kalena were busy in the kitchen making stuffing and cranberry sauce. Five pies sat on the wooden counter. She'd forgotten tomorrow was Thanksgiving. She should help. It would take her mind off the situation for a few hours, but she needed to focus, think things through. The answers were somewhere, and she had to find them. The ticking clock, counting down each minute the spy eluded her, pushed against her like a pulse. A pressure headache pounded in her temples. She didn't have time to be peeling potatoes, or making cranberry sauce, or doing whatever they did here in the kitchen in Ohio the night before Thanksgiving. She needed to get back to the plant and sift through more paperwork and screen more employees. The pain moved to her forehead and behind her eyes.

Kalena wiped her hands on a ruffled apron. "You're finally home. I'm so glad. How was your day?"

"Not too bad. I see you both have been busy."

"Would you like some coffee or eggnog, perhaps a piece of pumpkin pie? There's no whipped cream yet. We aren't making it until tomorrow. Sorry."

How could Polly pass that up? She'd be useless when it came to looking at documents tonight. She'd go to the plant tomorrow morning, or after the Thanksgiving festivities. Her head throbbed. "Pumpkin pie and a cup of coffee sounds wonderful. I'll just be a minute." She hung her coat on the rack by the front door and went upstairs to change into something comfortable. When she returned, Kalena had the dessert and hot drink ready. Among her many lovely physical attributes, she was also thoughtful and kind.

Kalena sat in the chair beside her. "You look beat to a frazzle."

"It's been a long day." The burden she carried was growing heavy and harder to bear by the hour. It would be comforting to share it with Kalena. She quelled the thought. She hadn't completely eliminated her as a suspect. All she'd found out was that she couldn't steal information as a runner, and if she wasn't the spy, sharing information with her would put her in danger.

Why *hadn't* she cleared her yet? It'd been five days since she'd arrived. And she was living in her house. She'd gone through her files, talked to her supervisor, discussed her with Celia, gotten to know her a little better. But why hadn't she eliminated her completely? Was it because she didn't want to know?

A burning lump formed in the pit of Polly's stomach. Deep down she knew Kalena could be the spy. She'd deliberately put off looking closer. Kalena was intelligent. She'd had opportunity. She'd been away for a significant time, and no one was sure why. She could be the spy just as easily as anyone else. In fact, the indications were quickly stacking up against her. Good God! Polly was evading the idea. That's why she hadn't cleared her yet. Her heart skipped a beat, and the blood drained from her fingertips.

"You all right?" Kalena asked with a look of concern.

Polly avoided the question, trying desperately not to rip herself apart because her thoughts and feelings for Kalena were interfering in her job. "You two look like you've been busy. Anything I can do?"

Aunt Berna smiled and set the creamer on the table. "Heavens no. You've had enough of a long day. Just sit there and relax and eat your pie." She patted Polly's shoulder.

Aunt Berna's touch brought instant comfort, a place to linger and relax. Polly sighed and looked up to find Kalena gazing at her, her green eyes the color of jade in the sunlight. The top of her apron hid her full, pert breasts, which Polly had enjoyed the feel of when they'd been dancing. She was a stunning woman, but her beauty wasn't only in her femininity, her slender legs, her subtle curves, arms that could reach out to embrace. Her beauty was in the culmination of all her attributes, including her quick wit, her intelligence, and her warm heart. She was the kind of woman Polly could see herself coming home to, sharing a life with. She couldn't be a spy. Perhaps it was Kalena's eagerness to please or engage her in conversation that always ended up without restrictions, or how she seemed to get right to the heart of the matter. Thoughts like that were far too dangerous to entertain.

"Polly? Did you hear me?" Kalena asked.

The metal pot Aunt Berna was washing clanged in the sink.

"Sorry. What?"

"Would you like me to run a hot bath for you?"

Polly sat dumbfounded. She didn't know how to respond. When Kalena asked the question, it had seemed like the most natural thing in the world to do. A hot bath waiting for her, and all she had to do was go upstairs, take off her clothes, and soak. No one had ever cared enough to do that for her. Was she making too much of it? After all, it was a bath, not a trip to the ice cream shoppe to get her a sundae. A bath for her. How extraordinary! "Yes. That'd be wonderful. Thank you."

Kalena patted her arm and rose. "You finish. I'll run up and get it ready."

Polly continued to eat the creamy spiced dessert, then sipped her coffee. All she could think about was Kalena in the bathroom holding out her hand to help her into the tub as she let the towel fall. She smiled. When an appropriate amount of time had dragged by, she excused herself, placed the dirty dishes on the counter by the sink, and said good night to Aunt Berna.

She stripped, slipped on her silk robe, and carried her bedclothes into the bathroom.

Kalena shut off the water and dipped her fingers into the steaming liquid. "Perfect timing. It's just about the right temperature." She lingered on the edge of the tub, then looked up and smiled, her eyes a silken jade.

Perfect indeed. The moment expanded and intensified.

The drip from the faucet hung in the air, then fell, splashing into the bath. The music on the radio downstairs hovered momentarily above Polly, then trickled into her ears. Her heartbeat slowed, then surged, bringing with it an overpowering urge to draw Kalena to her. To embrace. To kiss. To caress.

"Have a relaxing bath. I know you've earned it." Kalena smiled again, then closed the door behind her.

Polly stood motionless, hoping she'd return. But she didn't. A large white towel and washcloth hung draped over the sink next to the tub. She laid her bedclothes on the stand and slipped off her silk robe, then slid into the welcoming hot, wet embrace. She sighed heavily, unable to stop the sound from floating out of her mouth, then moaned as every muscle relaxed.

Finished, she dried off and dressed in her night clothes, then went to Kalena's door, hoping to thank her. She rapped. No response. Perhaps she was downstairs. Disappointed, she opened the bathroom door so Kalena would know she was no longer in it, then went to her own room and turned on the lamp. She lay on the bed, her thoughts whirling without direction.

A few minutes later she heard a sound from Kalena's room.

"Kalena, thank you for the bath," she called.

"Oh, I'm sorry, dear." Aunt Berna's voice drifted in. "It's just me putting her laundry away."

"Oh. Is she downstairs?" Polly asked, trying to sound casual.

Aunt Berna appeared in the bathroom doorway. "She went for a walk. She'll be back shortly."

"She went for a walk at this hour?"

Aunt Berna laughed. "She often goes for long walks at night. She says it relaxes her. Do you want me to tell her you want to talk with her when she gets home?"

"Yes, thank you."

Aunt Berna smiled. "Good night. Sleep well."

"Good night." Polly lay back on the bed. Why would Kalena need to go for walks this late at night? Was she meeting someone? Unwanted whispers of more doubt forced their way in. Was she handing over secrets on some back street where she couldn't be seen betraying their country? The burning in Polly's stomach raged once again, and her headache, which had begun to dissipate during her bath, resurfaced like someone had snapped her head back and flashed a bright light in her eyes. She massaged her temples, trying to get relief. Surely it would be too coincidental for her to be living with the very spy she was searching for? And Kalena seemed so sweet, so kind. But then, a well-trained spy could portray just about any nature, right? Was it poetic justice that the one woman she'd been completely attracted to would be the enemy? Polly let out an audible moan.

Twenty minutes later she heard the front door open and close. She repositioned, fluffing the pillows behind her, and waited for Kalena to come upstairs.

A few minutes later the bathroom light flicked on. Kalena peeked into Polly's room. "Did you have a good bath?"

"Yes. It was wonderful. Thank you. Did you have a good walk?"

Kalena nodded. "The night sky is full of stars. I walked around Lake Anna. Have a good rest."

"Good night," Polly said, watching her gently close the door. Feelings of confusion, uncertainty, and longing washed over her. Was she disappointed because Kalena hadn't wanted to stay and visit? Polly didn't like these emotions. They were draining her energy, and she didn't have time for them. She returned to her training. *Trust no one. Get close to no one. Stay focused.* They were cold bed partners to send her to sleep.

CHAPTER ELEVEN

Kalena started the hot water in the tub and began to undress. She did it slowly. First each button, one by one, and then she slid the blouse over her shoulders, tensing from the exposure of cool air against warm skin. She tossed her top onto the floor. She didn't lay it neatly over the towel rack like she usually did. No, not tonight. Tonight, she didn't care. It was an odd feeling. She undid her bra and let it fall. Nipples hardened from the caress of air.

What was Polly doing? Thoughts of her lingered, like the scent of spices in the kitchen. Captivating eyes watching her. The softness of her hand when they touched. Arms around her when they danced. She peeled her pants and undergarment down her buttocks and thighs, the fabric tingling and titillating as it slid over skin. She lowered herself into the welcoming water. She breathed deep and slow, sensing her need to be touched.

When would it happen? Who would it be? She'd wanted to experience sex since she was sixteen. Someone to touch, caress, and love her, and someone she could love and fulfill in return. She tried to fantasize about being with a woman, but without experience, imagination could only take her so far. Now it seemed like she had to push fantasies of Polly away hourly. She wanted to imagine what it would be like to kiss her, to touch, explore her body, glide her fingers over the curves.

A knock from her bedroom side startled her out of the moment.

Aunt Berna opened the door a few inches. "Would you get up at six to put the turkey in the oven? You can go back to bed for a couple more hours once it's in."

"Yes, of course. Set my alarm clock, will you, please?" Kalena asked.

"I will, sunshine. Thank you. See you in the morning."

"Good night," Kalena said, as she soaped the washcloth.

Aunt Berna shut the door.

The water was beginning to cool, as had her thoughts, making her flush. She finished bathing and then dressed in her nightclothes. When she flipped the bathroom light off, she saw the light from Polly's room under the door. She settled her hand on her chest. Was it more than an attraction she felt? This woman was beautiful and alive and full of intrigue. She wanted to go to her. But what if she wasn't feeling the same things? Her eyes said she did. Her touch said she did. When they'd danced, she'd looked into Polly's eyes and had seen a reflection of what she felt, of the kind of woman she was. But what if she was wrong? What if it was just wishful thinking? She'd be a fool. She'd expose her feelings to someone who wasn't interested, and she'd be rejected. That could prove to be the embarrassment of her life. And Polly was a boarder. What if she became angry and left? To knock on the bathroom door was too informal. She should leave her alone. She must be exhausted.

In spite of all the reasons she'd just rehearsed, she found herself walking through her own bedroom, out into the hallway, to Polly's door.

All she had to do was knock, see the expression on her face, and she'd know if she was intruding. But she stood there, unable to do anything. Her arms seemed made of lead. She couldn't lift them. The silence was so deafening she could hear and feel the pulsing of blood flowing through her neck and into her temples as her heart pounded. The grain on Polly's door seemed etched into the wood by a carpenter's tool. The worn metal knob was an almost luminous mixture of gray, bronze, and silver. She shifted, and when she did, the movement freed the weight in her arms. She knocked softly but firmly. Her heart beat faster. She trembled. Surges of determination, then dread swept over her. She wouldn't knock again. If Polly didn't answer, she'd leave. Was she asleep?

Polly's inviting voice floated out into the hall. "Come in."

Kalena's heartbeat slowed, but her hands continued to tremble. She opened the door and stepped in, closing it behind her to stop herself from turning and running. It was ridiculous, but it was what she had to do. She pressed her back against the door, its safety and security giving her something solid to lean on. She felt like she'd just climbed a rugged mountain peak, then congratulated herself. Now what?

Polly was sitting on the bed. The distance between them seemed like miles. Kalena wanted to go to her, but she couldn't move. She had no strength left. If she stepped away from the door, she'd surely collapse. She watched Polly's eyes as she slid from the bed and walked toward her—the flow of her turquoise silk gown, the sway of her hips, the graceful movement of her arms.

Kalena's breath caught.

Polly's eyes were dark with intensity, her expression hard to read but utterly focused on Kalena as she moved closer.

Kalena let go of the doorknob she'd clutched behind her and reached for Polly.

Polly wrapped her arms around her, engulfing her in an embrace.

Kalena couldn't get close enough. She whispered, trying to catch her breath, trying to control herself. "I'm so sorry. I tried to stay away."

Polly stroked her face and hair. "No. I don't want you to be sorry. There's nothing to be sorry about. I'm glad you're here. I felt it too."

Polly held her tighter, then eased away, resting her hand on Kalena's waist. She looked at her.

What was she thinking? What was she feeling? Kalena took a hitched breath. She looked into her eyes, those eyes full of mystery and life and…

Polly pressed her lips to hers. Soft. Warm. Sensual.

Kalena wrapped her arms around Polly's neck, aware of their breasts touching, filling her with yearning, hunger, and need.

Polly's mouth opened, and she slid her tongue into her. Wet. Hot.

Kalena returned the gesture, probing. Her entire body wanted to be a part of the kiss. The sweet taste of Polly's mouth, the scent of her skin and hair, the feel of her firm, exquisite body against her. Kalena slid her hand down Polly's arm. Polly pressed closer. The wetness of Polly's mouth and tongue and lips was all-consuming. She couldn't get enough. More, she wanted more.

Polly withdrew. "Kalena," she whispered. "We have to stop."

Kalena opened her eyes. Her breath caught. She licked her lips, tilted her head back, and swallowed. The taste of Polly's kiss lingered. Why did she stop? What had Kalena done? Did she offend her? Had she wanted too much?

Polly's cheeks were flushed. "Don't think you did anything wrong." She led her to the bed, sitting her down next to her. She stroked Kalena's arm. "We have to talk." She held Kalena's hand, softly rubbing her thumb over her knuckles. The slightest tremor in her touch betrayed her feelings.

At that moment Kalena realized this woman beside her, who was strong, and beautiful, and full of confidence, was just as nervous as she was. Kalena couldn't help but smile. She leaned near and kissed her. This time Kalena was confident. This time she intended to show Polly how much she wanted her. She held her face as she kissed her, deep and full of desire. Passion seeped out of her lips and tongue, spilling from her mouth.

Polly withdrew again, swallowing, touching her lips. "Oh, God. We can't do this." She rose and started pacing.

Kalena looked at her. Why was Polly so upset? Was it because she'd come into her bedroom? Intruded? Had she violated some sort of code Polly had? Embarrassed, she rose to leave.

Polly grabbed her hand. "Don't go. Please, don't go. We have to talk."

They froze when they heard footsteps in the hall, someone humming a soft tune. Polly shifted, tilted her head, listening. Quietly, she moved to the door and placed her hand on the worn, warm wood. With a sigh of relief that almost made her dizzy, she turned back to Kalena.

"I'm sure no one heard anything," Kalena said, her eyes wide, her expression searching as though to understand.

Polly had never kissed or been kissed like that. She could still feel Kalena's lips, her body all around her. Her skin was tingling, every nerve exposed. Kalena was inside her somehow. She guided her to the chair and eased her into it. "I don't want you to go, but we can't do this."

Tears welled in Kalena's eyes. She reached for a tissue on the nightstand. "I'm so sorry."

Polly knelt in front of her and took her hands. "You have nothing to be sorry about. I've wanted to kiss you since the moment we met."

Something inside Polly opened, and Kalena was there. Had she let her in? Could she control whatever this was? Was it real? Or was it only emotion and stress? Were the look in Kalena's eyes and her expression a reflection of her own feelings? And how could she be sure that Kalena could be trusted? In her world, trusting the wrong person could be deadly.

Polly found herself trembling. She stood and retreated from Kalena, trying to push the emotion away. But it was overpowering and consuming, exhilarating and painful all at the same time. It was as if she'd fallen into Kalena and didn't want to find her way out, yet she knew she had to. She studied her.

"What is it?" Kalena's expression changed. The smile left her lips. She leaned forward and repeated the question.

Polly slowly shook her head. What had happened? It was only a kiss. It wasn't possible to have this happen from a kiss. But she'd shifted off her axis. Time and space and distance were distorted. She ran her fingers through her hair and then scrubbed her face, trying to sift through her emotions.

"You're scaring me, Polly. What's wrong?"

"I have to get some air." Polly immediately left. She went downstairs and out onto the porch. She took in a deep, steadying breath. This could not be happening. Not now. Not when she needed to be totally focused on her assignment. People's lives were in jeopardy. She couldn't mess this up. She stared out into the darkness. A deep chill swept through her. Lights from the houses across the lake flickered in the distance. Suddenly the night was dark and lonely and cold.

The front door opened. Kalena stepped out and slipped a heavy coat over Polly's shoulders. "It's freezing out here. You're going to catch your death."

Polly turned toward her. "Kalena. We can't do this. Not now."

"I'm so sorry, Polly. I never meant to offend you in any way. I apologize from the bottom of my heart. How can I make this right? I don't want you to leave."

Polly brushed Kalena's lips with her fingertips. "Don't apologize. I wanted it. I needed it."

Kalena clasped her hand, surrounding it in warmth. "Then what is it?"

How could she reveal who she was? And how could she get

involved with Kalena when she could be the very spy she was looking for? Her emotions raged within her. She had to stop this. It'd gone too far already. She'd let herself get in too deep. "I can't do this." She'd have to lie her way out. "I'm already in a committed relationship, and we could lose our jobs or be arrested." There, she'd said it. The taste of it was metallic and bitter. She walked away and into the house.

What if Kalena wasn't the spy? What would happen then? Another lie? Another deception? She slipped the coat off and hung it on the rack. Her stomach was in knots as she trudged up the stairs. She'd focus all her efforts on clearing Kalena of any suspicion or facing that she was the spy and do what she had to do. And she had to do it quickly. She closed her door, turned out the bedroom light, and sat in the dark, waiting to hear Kalena pass by her room as the words burned in her mind—*find the spy at any cost!*

CHAPTER TWELVE

Polly rose early Thanksgiving morning and helped in the kitchen, trying to avoid Kalena's gaze. When she was sure Aunt Berna and Kalena were busy for an extended time, she excused herself and went upstairs. Richard and Gerald were still in their rooms. She stopped and listened at their doors.

No sound, no movement.

She continued into Kalena's room through the bathroom entrance and quietly went through her dresser and nightstand, then checked under the bed and mattress. She found a small bundle of letters in one of her drawers and sifted through them. Some looked like they were written in what might be Polish, but others were in German. Postmarks were from Cleveland and Germany as recently as last year. Her pulse began to race. More suspicion. Why would Kalena have anything to do with Germany?

She looked through the closet. On the top shelf, in the back, hidden among boxes and sweaters, was a very expensive Kodak Extra camera with three lenses ranging from 35mm to 153 mm, and an envelope. She took them all and went to her room, locked the door, and sat on the bed. She laid the camera and lenses on the mattress, opened the envelope, and pulled out the contents. She had to do it. She took a deep breath and went over to the window and held the negatives up against the windowpane.

"Sonofabitch." There, against the glass, she could clearly see images showing the airstrip, buildings, various parts of the assembly line, and, most importantly, what looked like three images of the structure of the modified P-51 Anaconda. Her stomach churned. She returned the negatives to the envelope and slipped it into a sock, hiding it in the top dresser drawer, under her clothes, then placed the camera and lenses in her suitcase. She could hear everyone as they began to gather. She reentered Kalena's room and dug through the closet more thoroughly, searching for a weapon, but didn't find any. She went back to her room and changed for dinner. She armed herself, shoving the gun into the holster and fastening it behind her back. "Sonofabitch," she mumbled again as she went downstairs. She wiped her lips, thinking of their kiss. It didn't seem so full of heat now, and Kalena's beauty wasn't as overwhelming as it had been the night before. She needed more information. She had to be positive, although the evidence was overwhelming. Did Kalena play her? Did she know she was from Washington? How could it be Kalena? And how could Polly be so stupid and careless?

The day dragged on. Perta, Beverly, and Juniper brought their dates. After everyone ate, Gerald went to his room. Richard informed the group it was time to dance, and they all went into the den, rolled up the rug, moved the furniture as before, and started the player. Perta had brought several records so they had no shortage of dance music. Polly excused herself and helped Aunt Berna with the remaining dishes. The last thing she wanted to do was watch Kalena sway, her beautiful body a betrayal of Polly's trust. By the time the dishes were washed, dried, and put away, the dance party was in full bloom. Polly turned to leave the kitchen and found Kalena watching her.

"Won't you join us, Polly," Kalena asked.

"I need to write a letter home," she said, and went upstairs and paced her room. She'd probably found the spy, and her job was almost complete. Wasn't she proud? She stared out the window, watching the branches of the bare trees dip back and forth as the wind blew.

After everyone left, she heard Kalena go to her bedroom. Polly prepared to follow her on her nightly walk. When Kalena left the house, Polly slipped out without being seen. It was a clear night, and she gave her as much distance as she could, staying in the shadows. Kalena turned the corner and stopped at the telephone booth by the theater. She sat down on the bench and made a call. She talked for fifteen minutes, then hung up. She retraced her steps the way she'd come but deviated when she got near the house. She started around the lake. Polly was heartsick. The closer she looked, the more evidence she found. She didn't want to follow her, but what if she was meeting someone? She had no choice. Kalena walked all the way around the lake and then back to the house with no contact from anyone. Once Kalena was in the house, Polly slipped back into her room.

Who did Kalena call? She could get the records for the phone booth, but it would take weeks. She couldn't wait that long.

The next day at work, she watched her and everything she did. Kalena took her morning break with Perta, Juniper, and three other women. Twice she was instructed by the line supervisor and left the plant floor, once to Engineering and once to Shipping. Both times she returned with paperwork and gave them to the supervisor. She spent her lunch break with her engineer-boyfriend in his office, and Polly wondered briefly why he never came by the house, and they never seemed to go on dates. A momentary flare of uneasiness was unwelcome. Was it jealousy? She pushed the thought aside. No. It was just her reasoning, her focus on the facts. Kalena spent her break in the afternoon with the women from the morning. She took the four-thirty bus and went directly home. Polly followed in the car, then parked down the street. At 6:27, Kalena walked uptown, again made a call from the booth, this time for twelve minutes, then walked back around the lake and home.

Polly needed to bring this to a close. The evidence was quickly stacking up against Kalena, but something seemed off. Was it because of how she felt about her? She admitted to herself she didn't want it to be Kalena. Her stomach churned. She pounded the steering wheel. "This is why you never get involved."

She had to be alone with Kalena so she could question her without anyone knowing or interrupting. She was confident she could get the information she needed, but how trained was Kalena? She wasn't concerned if it came to a physical altercation. Polly could overpower her. How much information had she already passed on, and to whom? How did she pass the information? Who was her contact?

Where to take her? She would have to subdue her, make sure she had control. Not the house, and certainly not the plant. Not the police station. She didn't want to involve them, because if Kalena wasn't the spy, Polly's cover would be blown. The safe house? Yes. It was an enclosed environment, she could be restrained, and Polly could do what she had to do if necessary. She drove to the house, put the items she would use in a black leather shoulder bag, then asked Kalena to go for a ride with her. Kalena hesitated at first but agreed. She was quiet in the car and finally asked where they were going.

"I need to talk with you, and I think it's best if we're alone," Polly said.

"I'm sorry about the other night."

Polly didn't respond. How could Kalena still sound so innocent?

They arrived at the apartment building, and she led Kalena up the stairs. She opened the door, turned on the lights, and motioned for Kalena to go in, then locked the door behind her.

"Whose apartment is this?"

"A friend."

"Your friend lives pretty basic." Kalena wrinkled her nose.

"Let's sit at the table," Polly said.

Kalena sat in one of the two wooden chairs, Polly in the other across from her.

Polly knew once they started down this road there was no going back. If Kalena wasn't the spy, Polly's chances to make amends were probably one in a million. Their budding romance would be over before it started. But it didn't matter. She had no time for romance. And if Kalena was the spy, she'd have to arrest her. Her mouth went dry, and her palms started to sweat. Was Kalena the spy? Did she betray her country? Her family? Was she capable of it?

Anyone was capable of anything under the right circumstances. Polly's instructors had drilled that fact into her head. Once, at the beginning of her training, she had interrogated a man who'd killed his own son because he'd discovered his father was selling corporate secrets.

The memory and sensations of their kiss washed over her. She wanted to linger in it, hold on to it for one last moment, but she had to push the thoughts away, strip herself of any feeling. It was time to question Kalena, but she hesitated. Not because she didn't know how to do her job. Not out of fear she couldn't handle any situation that arose in the interrogation. She didn't want to know if Kalena was the spy. The longer she waited, the harder it was to start. She took a deep breath and rubbed her face.

Kalena reached across the table and held her hand. "I can see this is difficult for you."

Polly withdrew from her touch. It was going to get a lot more difficult. Not for Polly, but for her. Kalena had no idea. Not yet at least.

"Where were you for over a year?"

Kalena sat back in the chair and studied her. "How did you know about that?"

"Your Aunt Berna told me."

Kalena touched her chin and looked away. "I was in Cleveland with friends."

Evasion. "Doing what?"

"Why do you want to know?"

This was going to get ugly. Polly had to subdue her immediately. She went to her and bent slightly, leaning on the tabletop as a distraction. She reached into her jacket pocket for the cuffs. "I need to know." She said it softly, like a whisper, knowing Kalena would bend toward her.

She did exactly as expected, resting her hand on Polly's. "I don't think I can talk about it."

Polly grasped her arm, slapped the metal restraint around her wrist, and cuffed the other end to the table leg.

Kalena jumped up and pulled. "Polly, what are you doing? Stop this immediately."

Polly reached into the leather bag on the table, pulled out her badge, and shoved it in front of Kalena. "Sit down."

Kalena swallowed hard and didn't move, her eyes wide, her face tense. "Who are you? What is going on? Why are you doing this? I don't understand."

"I'm with the Office of American Defense. I'm the investigator Washington sent. I'm the agent. And you're the spy. Sit down."

Kalena collapsed into the chair.

The air in the room became heavy, and it was difficult for Polly to breathe. Darkness descended like Dante's shroud. Seconds passed. Polly watched her.

Kalena jerked at the handcuffs as she glared at her.

Neither one of them spoke. Out in the hall, doors opened and closed. *Good-byes* could be heard.

Polly checked her watch. It was 7:21.

"Are you a spy? Did you betray your country?"

Kalena rubbed her cuffed wrist. "Are you crazy? Polly, why are you doing this? How dare you?"

"Answer the question."

Kalena stiffened and looked genuinely confused. If she was acting, she was an expert.

"How long?" Polly asked.

Kalena's eyes filled with tears. She stared blankly at her, probably playing dumb, formulating answers to anticipated questions. She was good.

Polly got closer, bending down in front of her. "How long?"

"How long what?"

"Cut the act." Polly reached into her bag, pulled out the camera and film, and shoved them toward her. "I know."

"You know what? What is that?"

Polly was tired of the evasion. She wanted to force her to confess, but it wasn't the correct approach. "All right. You want to play this game. Fine. You were gone for a significant amount of time and wouldn't tell your aunt or anyone else why you left or what you were doing. That's because you were training to be a spy."

Kalena's mouth dropped open, and she shook her head.

"You take long walks by yourself and make phone calls because you don't want to do it at the house. Why? Because you might be overheard?"

Kalena nodded, her eyes wide as she obviously realized Polly had been following her.

"You're dating one of the main engineers at the plant and have been since you returned from Cleveland. You're a runner on the assembly line. You play the game very well." Polly shoved the photo negatives in her face. "But not well enough." She reached into her pocket and pulled out one of the letters written in German. "How long? How long have you been spying?"

Kalena's eyes widened, and she paled.

Polly slammed her fist on the table. "Believe me, none of this is looking good for you."

Kalena raised her hand. "I'm...I'm...not a spy. I...I'm not. I swear I'm not."

Polly's heart begged for relief. She wanted so badly for Kalena's denial to be the truth, but she wasn't about to be fooled.

She was determined to remain in control and get the information she needed, all of it. It was time to slow things down, let the situation develop. She got up and made a pot of coffee. While it percolated, she sat at the table across from Kalena. She didn't ask any questions, just bided her time, waiting.

Kalena glared back in silence. Other than saying she wasn't a spy, she hadn't said anything.

When the coffee was ready, Polly turned the pot off and poured herself a cup, not offering Kalena any. She sat and sipped her hot drink, elbows on the table, holding the cup with both hands. Each time she attempted to make eye contact with Kalena, she looked away. She was scared, emotional, and angry. All good things.

Polly had to push her more. "You're awfully quiet. Don't you have anything to tell me?" She took another drink and set the cup on the table.

"You don't want to listen to anything I have to say, so why should I talk to you?"

Polly detected a slight tremor in her voice and took advantage of it. "Where were you all that time? Why did you have that camera and the pictures of the modified Anaconda? Who writes to you in German? Who do you talk to at the phone booth on Tuscarawas Avenue by the theater?"

"You tell me. You obviously know everything." Her lower lip quivered. She crossed her arm over her cuffed hand. Protecting herself?

"We aren't leaving here until you start talking and I get some answers."

"Aunt Berna will miss me when I don't come home, and she'll call the police."

"I am the police. And I've arranged it so no one will miss you." She'd left a note for Aunt Berna on the kitchen table telling her that she and Kalena had gone to Cleveland and would be back Saturday afternoon. She'd call Celia in the morning and tell her Kalena was helping her, and they would be gone until Monday morning. No one would question Kalena's absence. "Why did you stay in Cleveland?"

"I'm not a spy."

"Then answer my questions."

"Damn it. It's my own business."

"Not anymore. Not when it's a matter of national security."

"My going to Cleveland is a matter of national security?"

Polly nodded.

Kalena slammed her free hand down onto the table. "I'm not a spy."

"I'll decide that." Polly lowered her shoulders and eased against the back of the chair, then took a drink of coffee. During an interview, if the interrogator relaxed, the suspect relaxed. She spoke in a softer voice. "Why did you go to Cleveland?"

Kalena positioned her elbow on the table and rubbed her forehead. "All right. All right." She looked directly into Polly's eyes, tears running down her cheeks. "I went to Cleveland to try to find out why I was so attracted to women and not men. I stayed with a friend, who was a lesbian. I tried to meet women who were like me. I worked in a rubber factory there in Cleveland. I didn't tell Aunt Berna or anyone else because I didn't want them to know. Damn you."

She seemed either genuine or could tell one hell of a story. "Did you?"

Kalena made a fist. "Did I what?"

"Did you meet any lesbians?"

"Yes, but not anyone I felt comfortable around. Are you happy now?"

Polly ignored the remark. "What about the letters in German?"

"I resent that you went through my personal things. What right did you have?"

"I'm looking for a spy. I snoop. That's part of my job. Why letters in German?"

Kalena looked up at the ceiling, then at Polly. She inhaled deeply. "My friend in Cleveland has German ancestry. I wanted to learn to read and write German because of what's going on in Europe. I wrote to her and her cousin in Hamburg, who also wrote to me. I haven't gotten any letters from her or her cousin in almost a year."

The postmarks on the letters confirmed what Kalena had told her. "Who do you call at the phone booth? Why don't you use the phone at your house?"

"I won't tell you. It's none of your business."

"Yes. You'll tell me. You'll tell me everything, or I'll arrest you for being a spy, and you'll go to prison for the rest of your life, or maybe be put to death."

Kalena gasped and recoiled, palming her chest. "You can't do that. I'm not a spy."

"Then answer my questions. You're going to have to prove it."

Kalena touched her chin and pursed her lips. "Please don't make me do this." She started crying.

She was either the best actress Polly had ever come in contact with, or she was as innocent as she claimed. She still didn't know which it was, and given her training and talent for analyzing people, that was incredibly bothersome. She knew it was because she was emotionally involved with her. She had to dig harder to find out. "Who and why?"

Kalena's breath stuttered. She shook her head slowly, tears continuing to slide down her cheeks. She wiped them away. "You have no right. No right!"

Polly knew she was on the brink of finding her answers. She waited. Now she'd soften her questions. "I wouldn't ask if I didn't need to know. Just tell me why."

Kalena refused to make eye contact. She looked at the table and balled her fists. "I call Lionel. Lionel Wilcox, an engineer at PAI. The man I'm dating."

"You aren't dating him."

"Yes. I am."

"Why do you call him?"

Kalena glowered at her, pursing her lips tighter, rubbing her handcuffed wrist, shaking her head. "No."

This was going to take a little manipulation. "I can get the phone records. I can find out who you called, and even what you said." The latter wasn't true, but Kalena wouldn't know that unless she was the spy. "I can find out how often you spoke, how long you spoke, but it'd be better for you if you tell me."

"Then get the records. I have nothing to say."

"I'll just have to go interrogate Lionel." Why wouldn't she tell her? It could clear her. Kalena's hands were trembling. "What are you hiding? Are you a spy?"

Kalena vehemently shook her head. "I am *not*."

"Is Lionel involved in this also? Is he your partner in this?"

Kalena kept her eyes on the table, never looking up.

"You're not dating. You're using each other as a cover, a front."

"We're not."

"Do you pass secrets on to each other to betray the United States?"

Kalena made eye contact. Her shoulders relaxed. She'd conceded. "I'm not a spy. Lionel is not a spy. He's like us."

Polly tried not to react, but relief washed over her. Kalena would tell her what she needed to know. Polly now saw why Kalena was so adamant about not giving her the answer. It all made sense. She and Lionel had a secret. He was gay. But was he also a spy? He could have gotten the plans and information, then given them to her, and she passed them on.

"Why do you call him from a phone booth?"

"I don't want Aunt Berna or anyone in the house to hear our conversations. He's not doing well. He's emotional, and I'm worried about him, so I call him whenever I go for a walk, and we talk for a few minutes." She looked more intently into Polly's eyes "There's nothing wrong with it. We aren't hurting anyone."

Polly nodded. "No. There's nothing wrong with it. I understand." But there was still the camera and the negatives. Polly slid the camera over.

Kalena touched it, inspecting it closely. "It's not mine. I've never seen it before. I know nothing about it." She shoved it toward Polly.

"It was in *your* bedroom closet. It has photos of the kind of information that would be valuable to the enemy."

Kalena's facial muscles tensed, but she was pale. "I don't care what you say. That's not possible. I've never seen it before. It's not mine."

"It has pictures of the modified P-51 and the layout of the plant." Polly needed to push again. She slammed her fist on the table, making the coffee spill from the cup. "Stop lying."

Kalena repositioned herself and tried to push up, looking Polly straight in the eyes. "I'm not lying. I've never seen that camera before. It's not mine. I don't know how it got in my room, but I did not put it there. It's *not* mine."

Polly watched her closely. Kalena's eyes were wide, focused.

Her face was flushed, muscles tight, and her breathing was erratic. Her hand was pressed against the table. Her body language suggested she was telling the truth, but there was still room for suspicion. A well-trained spy could fake most of those things, knowing full well what the physical tells were. She would uncuff her and see what she'd do. If she made a run for it, Polly would know. If she didn't...She wasn't sure what she'd do next.

Chapter Thirteen

Kalena rubbed her sore, red wrist after Polly uncuffed her. She didn't move from the table. How could Polly do this? Why? Was she really an agent, or was she the spy? Everything was confusing. She felt sick to her stomach.

"I need water."

Polly motioned to the sink. Kalena got up and took a glass from the cupboard, rinsed it, and filled it with tap water. She brought it back to the table, drank half, and sat down, placing the glass in front of her. How could Polly think she was a spy? Mentally, she reviewed the points Polly had made. And when she finished, she could see why she might be a suspect.

"I want to see your identification again."

Polly handed her the leather wallet.

Kalena opened it and studied the contents. She touched the silver badge, then read the information on the opposite side. "Your last name is Sylvester, not Hollister?"

Polly nodded.

Kalena returned the wallet. "Someone must have planted the camera in my closet. Someone who knows me and has access to my room." The implication hit her full force. She rose quickly and started to go for the door. "We have to go home. Aunt Berna could be in danger."

Polly jumped up and grabbed her arm.

She fought to get away from her grip. "We have to go."

"She's fine. Whoever planted the camera doesn't know we're here, and they don't know I found it."

Kalena relaxed. That made sense, but the thought of someone leaving such things in her room made her want to retch.

Polly let go.

She had handcuffed her and treated her like a criminal. She'd lied to her. She looked into her eyes. Those eyes. Kalena couldn't decide if she wanted to slap her or kiss her. She was the one Washington had sent. She was the one everyone was talking about at work. She was the agent.

Polly led her back to the table and got her a cup of coffee. "I'm sorry there isn't any cream."

"It's okay," Kalena said.

"It's someone who had access to your bedroom. When was the last time you cleaned your closet and knew exactly what was in it?"

"Aunt Berna and I did heavy cleaning in late August. I put away my summer clothes. I restacked the shelves, re-boxed some items I wouldn't use, and got rid of a few things."

"Are you sure the camera wasn't on the upper right corner of your top shelf when you cleaned?"

"Positive. I took everything off that shelf and restacked it. The camera was not there."

"Who's been to the house since you did that?" Polly reached into the bag and offered Kalena a notebook and pencil. "Write the names."

Kalena closed her eyes and lowered her head. "Richard and Gerald, of course. Perta, Beverly, and Juniper." She wrote the names, then looked at Polly, trying to concentrate. She tapped the pencil rhythmically on the pad as more names came to her. Patty and Ilene, neighbors from down the street, had come over. "They don't work at the plant," she mumbled. She laid the pencil on the table. "That's it… wait. Carl, Raymond, and Tom, the men who came with Perta, Juniper, and Beverly on Thanksgiving. They were at the house all afternoon."

"They couldn't have put the camera there on Thanksgiving Day. I found it that morning while you and Aunt Berna were in the kitchen. Someone had to have placed it there some time before Thanksgiving Day. Are you sure no one else came to the house, especially someone who worked at the plant?"

Kalena looked up. "Lionel. He's been there several times since I cleaned out the closet."

"Lionel is a target for blackmail because he's hiding. He could be forced to do something he doesn't want to in order to keep from being outed."

"Because he's a homosexual?" Kalena covered her mouth momentarily. Tears welled in her eyes.

"It's been an exhausting few hours for you. I'll take you home." Polly rose from the chair. "I'm sorry I put you through this, but I had to know. I hope you'll forgive me. And I hope you understand now why we can have nothing between us. It isn't because you're not lovely or that I don't want to be with you, but I have a job to do."

Polly's tenderness caught her off guard. Kalena rose. She knew who Polly was now. And Polly knew her. They didn't need to hide because they had no more secrets. Polly had to do her job, and she was very good at it. "I understand." She did understand, though that couldn't stop the raging feelings inside her.

The urge to slap Polly had passed, but the need to kiss her was overpowering. She wanted to be near her, to feel her arms around her as before. She wanted the safety and comfort and thrill of her touch. It was her turn now to demand. She closed the distance between them, relieved when Polly didn't back away, despite what she'd just said about there not being anything between them. "I forgive you." She whispered the words like they were in a crowded room and didn't want anyone to hear.

She'd stifled her desire to be with a woman for so long, she felt like a caged animal. But she didn't have to be confined now. She didn't have to control herself. She could have what she wanted. And she wanted this beautiful woman standing before her, warm and soft and vibrant. The thought of Polly's kiss and touch titillated her, sent surges of desire and anticipation radiating through her. She slid her hand to the back of Polly's neck, entangling her fingers in her hair. She drew her close, and their lips touched. A moan escaped as the tip of Polly's tongue entered her mouth.

Polly wrapped her arms around her. "We shouldn't...But I can't stop this."

The heat rose, starting where Polly pressed against her, then pulsed through her. Kalena throbbed and tensed. She didn't want to stop, and knowing she wasn't going to intensified every thought, every sensation.

They kissed deeper.

The sexual pulse surged through her. She glided her hand over Polly's waist and then down her thigh, exploring, feeling the heat between Polly's legs.

Polly broke their kiss and led her to the bedroom.

Kalena found Polly's lips again, the anticipation and ache for her touch building.

Polly began to unbutton Kalena's blouse.

Kalena's fingers trembled as she lifted the bottom of Polly's top from inside her slacks. Now her entire body trembled. She fumbled with the buttons. She tried to slow her breathing, but her heart pounded, and with each beat she throbbed and yearned for Polly's touch. Was it supposed to be like this? If she couldn't calm herself, her heart was going to explode.

Polly stopped. She gazed into her eyes. She stroked her face, then brushed Kalena's lips with her fingertips. "There's no hurry." She kissed her slowly, deliberately.

Everything calmed. Kalena's heartbeat slowed. She took in a long, deep breath.

Polly slid her mouth down her neck, showering her with kisses.

Kalena's breasts swelled, nipples hardened, and the yearning and desire for Polly's touch intensified. Her fingers stopped trembling, and she unbuttoned Polly's blouse, slipping it over her shoulders. She removed her cream-colored camisole, then reached behind her and unhooked her bra. She was vaguely aware Polly was doing the same thing to her, until her bra slipped off and Polly leaned down and took one of her hard, sensitive nipples into her mouth. Kalena gasped. She laid her head back and sucked in a breath. A moan slipped out before she could stop it. She encircled Polly and breathed out her name.

They caressed, and kissed, and thrust. They merged with pleasure and ardor, erupting into a fury of wanton fulfillment. Touching with anticipation and elation, they consumed each other and moaned with arousal and satisfaction. They climaxed, and then again, and again.

They lay together, breathless.

Polly slid her leg over Kalena's thigh. "What have we done?"

Kalena kissed her neck, hoping to pull her away from the thought that this wasn't wonderful. "I never imagined it could be like this."

They began to kiss again, the heat rising once more, demanding fulfillment. Whenever Polly looked like she could become lost in thought, Kalena did her best to distract her once again.

They loved each other into the night.

Kalena woke in the early dawn when she heard something metal fall against the side of the building and a cat screeched. She eased away from Polly's arm resting on her waist. She couldn't resist the urge to touch her. She pushed strands of Polly's hair out of the way and ran her fingertips along her cheek and chin, caressing. Beauty, strength, and femininity lay at her fingertips. The light from the streetlamp outside the bedroom window illuminated just enough of Polly's form to cause her skin to glow.

Polly took Kalena's hand and kissed it. "Good morning," Her voice was husky and seductive.

Kalena kissed her. "Do you do this to all the women you suspect of being a spy?"

Polly smiled. "I don't think I was the one who initiated this."

Kalena laughed. "Maybe, but you were very good about not objecting."

They began to kiss again. Kalena's body seemed to have a will of its own. No hesitation or doubt, only pleasure and satisfaction, longing and need. Fulfilling and being fulfilled were all that mattered. It was as if they were transported to a world of their own, where no one or nothing else existed. No time, no obligations, no responsibilities. Polly taught her, and Kalena learned, as they explored and pleased one another. They lay in bed, wrapped in each other.

"Tell me about you, Polly. Where did you go to school? What did you do before you chased spies?"

Polly laughed and glanced over at her, propping herself up on her elbow. "Normally I don't talk about myself, but I can't seem to do anything but tell you everything you want to know."

"Does that scare you?"

"A little."

"Why?" Kalena reached up and brushed Polly's hair away from her face.

"You have a way of getting into my heart, and I hardly know you. If feels…unsettling."

"Ah. I think you're too private and shut off. Tell me something you haven't told anyone else."

Polly looked into her eyes.

"You can trust me."

Polly nodded. "Okay. At seventeen I went to Oberlin College in northeastern Ohio. I decided on Oberlin because I thought the leadership held women in higher regard than men. But, when I discovered I was a lesbian at the age of twenty, I soon found out that Oberlin College wasn't as liberal as I'd hoped."

Kalena laughed.

"I graduated with a degree in political science and a fascination and gift for analysis. I returned to Philadelphia and taught school for a while, not because I wanted to, but because I couldn't find anything else. Teaching wasn't where I wanted to spend my life. Obviously, I didn't prefer marriage, and rather than explain to my parents about my sexual preference, I moved to Washington DC and lived with my cousin on my mother's side of the family, Elizabeth." Polly breathed deeply.

Kalena touched her face. "Were your parents upset?"

Polly looked at the ceiling. "I love my parents, but we are…" She hesitated, a sad expression crossing her face. "We're not as close as I'd like."

Kalena kissed her. "I understand. I want to tell Aunt Berna how I feel, but I'm terrified when I think about it."

They began to touch again.

When the full morning sun shone through the window, Polly started to get up from the bed.

"I have to go. I'll be back in an hour." Already, she looked far away, her thoughts somewhere else entirely.

"Where are you going?"

"I have to make some phone calls." Polly slowly rose, dressed, kissed her, and left.

Kalena lay in bed, too tired and too hungry to move, swooning in the memories of Polly's touch and caress. Whatever happened today, she knew she wasn't alone. Polly was with her. She turned over, slowly sliding through the memories of how they'd gotten here. She ran her finger lightly over her lips, wishing Polly was next to her, kissing her once more.

A sense of foreboding slithered into her. A spy had been in her home. Someone dangerous was close to her, someone she'd trusted, and she had no idea who it was. How could something as wonderful as Polly be happening during something so awful?

❖

Polly left the phone booth and walked toward the bakery a block from the safe house. The scent of freshly made cinnamon rolls hovered in the air, and the moment she pushed the door open, pangs of hunger gripped her. She and Kalena needed to talk about so much, but they couldn't do it on empty stomachs. By the time she got back to the apartment, Kalena had bathed, dressed, and made a pot of coffee. The strong aroma caused Polly's stomach to growl.

Kalena ate in silence as they sat at the table. Polly wasn't able to decide if it was because they were both hungry or if something was wrong. "Are you well?"

Kalena nodded. "I'm in a bit of a daze." She reached for Polly.

Polly laced her fingers in hers.

"I'm afraid we've made a mess of things, haven't we?" Kalena asked.

Polly nearly sighed out loud, but she didn't want to ruin this moment between them. "No. Not at all. It's just a little more complicated now."

They finished eating, then cleaned the kitchen and straightened the apartment. They then sat at the table with a second cup of coffee. Polly poured a generous amount of cream into hers and sipped, trying to decide what to do next. Last night Kalena had revealed that, not only was this her first sexual experience with a woman, but it was also her first full sexual experience in general.

Polly wanted to be sensitive and attentive, but she had to focus on her job. Whoever the spy was had made a mistake, and she intended to take advantage of it. She encased Kalena's hand in hers. "I don't want you to think for one second that it's easy for me to keep you out of my mind, but I have to. The next few hours and days are critical. I'm going to need your help. Are you up to it?"

"It's about finding the spy, isn't it?"

"Yes."

"Can I ask about you being an agent?"

Polly shook her head slightly. "It's best if you don't. And I know it goes without saying, but you can't tell a soul, Kalena. This is a life-and-death situation, and I'm taking a huge risk in trusting you."

Kalena tensed. A sheen of tears shimmered in her eyes. "I'm so sorry. I never should have kissed you last night once I found out the importance of what you're doing here. It was selfish of me."

Polly slipped off her chair and knelt in front of her. "Did you enjoy last night?"

Kalena startled, as if not knowing how to respond. "What?"

"I said, did you enjoy our time together last night?"

Kalena pursed her lips softly, then wiped the tears. "Yes. It was wonderful, everything I wanted and needed."

"Then tell me what's wrong."

More tears. Kalena gripped Polly's shoulder. "I feel so fulfilled, but I just keep thinking of the horrible names people call…I mean, I've seen and heard things that scare me."

"What things?" Polly held her breath. Had something happened to her in Cleveland or when she was younger?

Kalena averted her gaze. She began to tremble.

Polly took her in her arms and coaxed her to her feet. She led her to the couch.

As they settled onto the cushions, Kalena began to weep.

"Shh." Polly tightened her hold on her. "It's okay. Everything's okay."

Kalena took a stuttered breath and sighed, wiping her cheek. "I'm sorry. I know you have more important—"

Polly gently settled her arm on Kalena's shoulder. "Nothing's more important than this right now. Tell me what happened to you?"

Kalena glanced at her, then quickly looked away. "I saw a woman," she bit her lip, "being attacked by two men." She inhaled, shuttering. "They called her ugly names because she was a lesbian. And," she choked out, "they were going to rape her."

"Oh, God," Polly whispered, holding her close. "Did they?" She braced herself for the answer.

"I don't know," Kalena said, shaking her head. "I went and told a policeman, but then I ran away."

Polly stroked her hair. "And you think you were wrong to leave?"

Kalena nodded.

"What more could you have done?"

Kalena wrung her hands but didn't answer.

"You couldn't have done anything without putting yourself in danger."

Kalena turned to Polly and buried her face in her neck. "I was a coward. I should have gone back and waited for the woman and made sure she got home safely."

"That was the policeman's job," Polly said, rubbing Kalena's back.

"I was so scared," Kalena whispered. "And so many times since then, I've thought that could have been me."

Polly wished so much she could assure her that that would never happen to her. But it wasn't true. Her anger swelled. As horrible as it was, it did happen, and it could happen to any of them. But they couldn't let fear rule their lives. They could only be as careful as possible. She was fortunate that the gatherings at Elizabeth's had provided such a close circle of lesbian friends in Washington. "I wish you hadn't witnessed something like that."

Kalena eased away and settled against the back of the sofa, her cheeks still wet with tears, but her breathing had calmed. She stared straight ahead. "I've never told anyone about that before. I feel lighter just from being able to say it out loud."

Polly kissed her cheek. "You can always tell me anything."

Kalena turned her head, her gaze meeting Polly's. "I'm so conflicted about how I feel about you, and women, and society's expectations and judgments. What do I do with that?"

"You have to accept your own feelings. Accept that you wanted to be with me and needed it. Accept that you prefer women to men. Lots of women feel that way. Some will admit it, but others won't. There's nothing wrong with it. It's just the way it is. Those words are just labels. They don't mean anything." Polly kissed her.

Kalena wrapped her arms around her. "I'm confused and all jumbled up inside. I'm happy, but I'm worried."

"About what?" It was important Kalena talked about how she felt and that she had the support she needed, and although Polly had to get on with the business of finding the spy, this was also a priority. She ignored the part of her that told her this was a mistake, that she was getting involved and losing focus.

"How do I act? What do I do? What do I say? I've seen what happens to women and men who feel the way we do." Tears began to flow again. Kalena wiped them away quickly, as if fighting them. This was a strong, determined woman, as beautiful on the inside as she was on the outside.

Polly stroked her hand as she held it. "Yes, we have to be careful. Someday it'll be different, but for now we need to be...discreet. What others do, how others feel about this subject won't change our need to be with women." Polly looked into her eyes, hesitant. She wanted to tell her last night was a night of complete fulfillment, that when she touched her and loved her it was as if she'd finally found her soul mate. That possibility was, perhaps, illogical, given the short amount of time they'd known one another, and it was definitely inconvenient when it came to her career. But Kalena wasn't ready. This was all new to her, and she had to be overwhelmed. The memories of their lovemaking stirred Polly. She wanted to take Kalena to the bedroom and love her again. But she had a spy to catch, and although she was relieved it wasn't Kalena, she now had a much smaller circle of suspects, which meant she could find the person she was looking for.

Kalena bent slightly forward, kissed the side of Polly's face, then slid her mouth up to her ear, her warm breath causing Polly's skin to tingle. She whispered in her ear, "I want to go back to the bedroom and be with you."

Polly ached with want, but she stopped their kiss. "I'd love nothing more, but we can't. We need to leave. Tonight's the dance, and the spy will be there. I'm sure of it."

She forced herself to focus. She mentally reviewed the list of names Kalena had written down. One of them was the person she was looking for. Everything else needed to take a backseat to the mission, no matter how difficult it was to resist her.

CHAPTER FOURTEEN

Saturday night the parking lot at the Summit Lake Ballroom was so jammed with vehicles, Kalena insisted they needed a marker to remember where they'd parked. She'd never been to the facility and was awestruck by its enormity and beauty.

"There," she said, pointing to a billboard. "We can park beside it."

Richard began pushing on the back of Kalena's seat before Polly turned the car off. "Come on, Kalena. Get out."

Kalena turned toward him. "Jeez. Easy, Richard. We've got all night."

Polly laughed.

It was strange to feel so relaxed, as though nothing was bothering her. As though Polly hadn't accused her of being a spy, then made love to her, and then figured out that the spy was within the little circle of people around them. It was a little disconcerting how well Polly used her cover. Would Kalena ever really know her?

The moment Kalena opened the door, Richard shoved past her and climbed out, practically squishing her. "Could you be a little more patient?" she asked.

Richard shrugged. "Sorry. I'll see you two in there. Perta said she'd save us some seats." And off he went.

Kalena walked beside Polly, slipping her arm in hers. "I wish we could dance together tonight, but I'm not good enough."

Polly patted her arm. "Yes, you are, but I won't push you. We can be thinking of each other." Her smile wasn't full, like she was holding a part of it back, a reminder that she'd be working even though they'd be together.

They joined the throng of people pressing toward the ballroom. Just in front, before they reached the building, was a circular flower garden with a fountain in the center. Wooden benches were lined around it and both sides of the walkway. Large four-white-orbed streetlamps lit their way.

The huge complex was made of light-colored stone with twelve arched windows in the front, going from a few feet below the roof to its base. United States flags, fluttering gently in the night's breeze, adorned the scalloped edges of the roof along the entire front of the building.

Kalena stopped to admire the scene as others walked past them. She gazed at the flowers, then back to the flags. "It's beautiful."

Polly smiled. "It is. I always get sentimental and have a sense of pride when I see our flag."

They remained quiet for a few minutes, then continued to follow the crowd toward the main entrance. The movement of the stream of people slowed, and the noise intensified. A large poster announced the Glenn Miller Orchestra and that admission was one dollar and fifty cents per person.

"A dollar fifty?" said a man beside Kalena.

A woman behind Polly moved closer to them. "Last night at the Lakeshore ballroom in Dayton they charged *two dollars* and fifty cents," she said.

"That's ridiculous," said the man, reaching for his wallet.

When they paid the fee, Kalena and Polly were given a flyer with their entry ticket. "What's this?" Kalena asked as the man took her money.

"A summary of President Roosevelt's Executive Order 8875. The Office of Price Administration was created this past August. It places a ceiling on prices of most goods, and it limits consumption by rationing. We'll all be hearing more about it in the coming weeks. Hang on to it," he said.

Kalena folded the paper and jammed it into her clutch bag as they moved forward. She stopped abruptly when they entered, standing in wonder as she surveyed the ballroom. It could hold up to five thousand people, and tonight it looked like it would fill to capacity. The domed roof had a skylight covering the middle quarter of the ceiling. The rich colors of the slick wooden dance floor glistened under the hanging crystal-glass-ball lights. Ten rows deep of round, white-clothed tables with folding chairs surrounded the dance area. The portable stage, a large, ornate gazebo without railings, dominated the back of the room. Music stands, banners, and the Glenn Miller Orchestra insignias were displayed where the band would sit. The drummer's position was toward the far right, with the piano to the left on an elevated platform. Standing microphones were scattered throughout the stage and within the orchestra area. Five bright-purple-cushioned chairs were to the left on the stage.

Kalena heard her name called as she and Polly followed a portion of the crowd on the left side of the room. She scanned the mass of people. Perta was about a third of the way from the stage, waving frantically. When Kalena and Polly arrived, Perta sat by her date, Raymond, and patted the seat next to her. Kalena looked at the chair and then the center of the room. "I want to sit across from you so I can see the band." She raised her voice over the growing conversations. "And if I'm in the front, it makes it too easy for the guys to ask me to dance."

Perta wrinkled her nose. "Oh, don't be like that."

Kalena led Polly around the table and sat opposite Perta and beside Juniper and her date, Carl.

Juniper pointed to the empty seat next to Raymond. "Richard," she said.

Kalena nodded.

"He said he didn't want to bring anyone so he could dance with whomever he wanted," Perta said.

Kalena laughed. "Of course. Where's Beverly?"

"Where's Lionel?" Perta asked.

"He's on a business trip and will be back sometime tomorrow." Kalena was glad he was out of town. She could be with Polly and not have to divide her attention between him and her.

"Beverly had to work and said she'd be here as soon as she could. Isn't Gerald coming?" Juniper asked.

"Same thing. He wasn't sure he could get done in time," Kalena said.

"They were supposed to close the shift early so everyone could attend. He's so shy he probably didn't want to come anyway," Perta said.

More people filed in, and every seat filled. Perta constantly told others the empty seat across from Polly was saved.

Kalena edged her knee against Polly's. "I don't know how much longer we can keep that seat for Beverly."

Polly pressed back, rubbing gently, and shrugged. Although she kept her expression neutral, Kalena knew she was thinking about the whereabouts of the others and determining her next move. This situation was exciting, in a way, now that she wasn't the focus of Polly's interrogation.

Polly rubbed her knee against her again, sending a shiver down Kalena's spine.

Richard strolled over and sat beside Raymond. "Man, there are some gorgeous women here tonight."

Juniper scrunched her face. "Thanks, Richard."

Richard smiled and nodded.

"Look. Here comes the announcer. We're starting," Juniper said, straightening her posture. Carl rested his arm over her shoulder.

The host stepped to the microphone. "Ladies and gentlemen."

The noise level began to ebb.

"Ladies and gentlemen, I'm Don Ballentine, your host and announcer for tonight."

There was plenty of applause. Kalena sensed the tension in Polly's body, even though she appeared relaxed. She also noticed the way Polly continued to look around the room.

"Thank you. Thank you for joining us. As you know, many of our young men are now in the service. Please don't forget to support them with letters and packages from home."

The throng gave more cheers and recognition.

"Also, our sponsors tonight, Akron Tire and Rubber, Westfield Manufacturing, and Portage Aircraft..." He stopped to acknowledge the cheers, nodded, and mouthed *thank you* as he held up his hand to still them. "They wish to remind us of the importance of conservation of materials needed to help production, including nylon."

Boos from a smaller group of women near the stage drew laughter.

Don smiled and turned to the small group who had booed. "I know hose are important, ladies." He turned back to face the larger crowd. "Also, remember to turn in all scrap metal and tires. It's important, folks, to help us conserve needed materials, even the smallest amount."

Kalena's attention was drawn back to Polly, and she had a sudden urge to kiss her. The more she resisted, the stronger it grew. She didn't dare look at her. Flashes of their lovemaking burst into her thoughts. The heat rose in her neck and then to her cheeks.

Juniper nudged her. "Are you all right?"

Kalena nodded and resisted sliding her hand under the table to stroke Polly's thigh. She had a sudden fantasy of inching Polly's dress up and touching her. The image was so vivid her heart began to pound, and her fingers flexed.

Laughter at something Don had said brought her back from her fantasy.

Polly repositioned herself, pressing her knee against her.

Kalena surrendered to the urge. She slipped her hand down and caressed Polly's thigh.

Polly leaned in, covered her mouth, and whispered, "I know what you're thinking."

Kalena was certain if she looked at her, 4,999 other people would also know what she was thinking. She continued to stare at the stage and smiled, softly rubbing her chin. Was this what it felt like to have a lover? Someone who sent rivers of heat and desire surging through you?

Another loud roar of laughter filled the room. Don must have told another joke. Kalena had to focus. She breathed deeply and pressed her back against the chair.

More dialogue from Don. He looked to his left and nodded. "Ladies and gentlemen, please join the Summit Lake Ballroom in welcoming ABC radio and RCA Victor recording artist Glenn Miller and his orchestra."

People jumped to their feet in thunderous acknowledgment. Kalena and Polly stood, clapping, and Kalena realized in that moment they weren't just expressing appreciation for the band. They were applauding for the relief it brought into their lives, for the opportunity to forget for a few brief hours the war in Europe, the tension and stress, and set aside their cares and enjoy great music and laughter and have some fun. But Polly also contributed to how Kalena felt. She wanted to turn toward *her* and applaud. Did she have any idea how completely full and overflowing Kalena was because she had come into her life?

The orchestra members took their positions. Glenn Miller strode to the middle of the stage, the lights reflecting off his brass trombone and metal-rimmed glasses.

The masses clapped and cheered even more.

The man wasn't particularly striking. His brown hair was combed back without a hair out of place. His smile wasn't full, but more serious, subdued. His dark-blue suit jacket with black velvet trim complemented the band members' lighter-colored jackets. He turned to the crowd and nodded, then motioned toward the musicians.

In one graceful motion, he almost spun and lifted his right hand. "Moonlight Serenade" began. People flocked to the stage.

Another tune played, a fast-paced swing beat. Everyone at their table quickly moved to the dance floor, leaving Polly and Kalena by themselves. A tall, lean man with sandy-brown hair came toward their table, with a determined yet pleasant expression. Kalena knew he was going to ask her to dance. What should she do? She looked at Polly.

Polly smiled and brushed her fingers over her arm. "Go on now. Spread your wings and fly."

The man's voice was deep and soft. "Would you dance with me?" He reached out and motioned her to the end of the table.

Kalena accepted. He wasn't a particularly good dancer, but then she wasn't either. A slow song, "Blue Orchid," was next. The man asked her to stay with him. The music had a nice slow pace, and Kalena followed him without either of them tripping each other. He escorted her back to the table when the song was over, thanked her, and then moved on. She was glad.

Polly patted her hand. "You did good."

Kalena took a deep breath. "It's not as easy as it looks." She watched the crowd. "So many more women than men are here tonight. Did you see some of the women fast-dancing with each other?"

Polly nodded. "It's getting to be quite common. All the men are leaving for the military, and a woman has to dance." She laughed.

After a song called "Imagination," and applause, Glenn Miller stepped to the microphone. He introduced the pianist, drummer, and which states the musicians were from. There was loud appreciation for the two Ohio band members. "Ladies and gentlemen, please welcome Paula Kelly, Tex Beneke, and the Modernaires."

Huge cheers thundered through the hall, making the room vibrate.

Paula Kelly led the small group to the stage. Her flowing yellow sequin gown dazzled when the stage lights caught it. The men wore matching yellow jackets and navy-blue pants. They smiled and waved to the crowd crammed together in front of the stage.

"How beautiful. They look like something from the Macy's store window," Kalena said, unable to take her eyes off them.

Polly smiled.

Just as the band started to play "Chattanooga Choo-Choo" and the group began to sing the words, Beverly shoved her way to the table with two other women and sat across from Polly, taking the seats that were now empty.

"It's a madhouse," Beverly said, breathless and fanning herself. "We had to walk almost a quarter of a mile from our parking spot."

Kalena leaned toward the table. "Who drove you?"

Beverly pointed to the woman beside her. "This is Betsy and Loraine from second shift. Loraine drove."

Betsy and Loraine waved hello. Kalena and Polly greeted them and then looked back to the stage. It was so strange, to be watching the people around her and wondering if one of them could be the spy Polly was looking for. She knew them. How could any of them be the one who'd put the damning evidence in her closet? Yet one of them had, and she knew Polly would find out who it was.

The group finished and immediately began playing "Pennsylvania 6-5000," but you could barely hear the song over the cheering and yelling. After that song, Glenn Miller announced the band would take a break. When the singers and musicians left the stage, the noise died down enough that they could finally have a reasonable chance of having a conversation.

Perta came to the table and grasped the back of her chair. "Why are you so late?"

Beverly waved. "I didn't finish as fast as I thought I would. How's the dancing and music?"

Before anyone could answer, Juniper and Carl, Richard, and Raymond returned. Richard wiped the sweat from his forehead with a handkerchief and stuffed it into his pocket. "Man, it's hot in here."

Kalena shook her head. "No, it's not. It's just because you were out there whooping it up on the dance floor."

Everyone at the table laughed.

"I saw you, Kalena. You did good. Polly, why haven't you danced?" Juniper asked.

"I was asked a couple of times, but I haven't wanted to. I'd rather sit here and enjoy the music," Polly said.

Beverly grazed Polly's shoulder. "Would you mind dancing a fast one with me when the band comes back? I'd rather not wait to be asked by some sod with two left feet."

Polly nodded graciously. "Sure. No problem."

Kalena grew sullen, and her stomach tightened. She felt like a kid at the playground who'd been pushed off the teeter-totter. Why should she care if Polly danced with Beverly? Beverly wasn't bad looking. Although, until just now, she hadn't noticed that she sat too straight, she showed too many teeth when she smiled, her lipstick was too dark for the dress she was wearing, and she should have never worn her hair that way. By the time the night was over, it'd be straight as a poker and hanging in her face.

Everyone discussed the great music the band had been playing and the beautiful clothes the singers wore. The horde directly in front of the stage began to applaud. The band was coming back.

Another slow song began. Kalena and Beverly were asked to dance, and each accepted. When they returned to their chairs, Glenn Miller stepped to the microphone.

"Ladies and gentlemen, while the boys and I were taking a break, some friends stopped by on their way to Cleveland and have agreed to come out and say hello. Please give a great big Akron welcome to the Andrews Sisters—Maxene, Patty, and LaVerne."

People started screaming and running toward the stage. The Andrew Sisters strolled in single file, waved, and positioned themselves at the microphones. They sang "Beat Me Daddy Eight to the Bar." After that tune, they waited for the noise to die down, then one of the trumpet players kicked off the song with a solo. Everyone knew the Andrew Sisters were going to sing "Boogie Woogie Bugle Boy." Pandemonium broke out, and even Glenn Miller was laughing.

The singers waved and blew kisses to the crowd when they finished and left the stage. The pianist started playing a fast swing tune.

Beverly jumped up. "That's us, Polly." She grabbed Polly's hand and pulled her out onto the dance floor. When they got started, all Kalena saw were arms and legs flying in the air. People around them backed away so they could watch the art in motion. They made seamless transitions from one move to the other. When it was over, the people gathered around them and cheered and clapped. They came back out of breath and sweating.

"Wow!" Richard said. "Just, wow. That was swell. Dance with me, Polly?"

Polly shook her head and held her hand up in protest. "I'm sorry, Richard. I'm going to sit this one out."

"I'll dance with you," Beverly said.

Richard led her out to the floor, and they danced to "The Woodpecker Song."

Kalena couldn't take her eyes off Polly, who was still breathing heavy and wiping her neck with a paper napkin. "I knew you had to be a good dancer from the way you taught me, but good grief."

Polly smiled. "I learned from my cousins." Her breathing was even now, and her skin had a rich blush.

An intense urge to take Polly to bed swept over Kalena. She wanted to undress her and kiss her, make love. But they might not ever be together again. The realization sank into her heart like a stone. Polly was here to catch a spy. Once she caught whoever it was, she'd be gone, back to wherever she came from, and Kalena would be nothing but a memory.

CHAPTER FIFTEEN

The plant was closed on Sundays. Polly'd been here alone for six hours, poring over reams of data and information, focusing on Kalena's list and those she'd added herself, including Ilene Stadler, the short woman with Beverly that night in the offices. One thing she had to seriously consider was that it was careless to assume the spy was working alone. They could easily have a partner. Just because they weren't in Kalena's home didn't mean they weren't involved in some way.

She'd talked with Celia on the phone for two hours about specific staff and had been able to eliminate a few more people. The girls' dates who'd been in Kalena's house and at the dance were easy to take off the list. Two were too stupid to be spies, the other was a mailman, and all three of them were leaving for military service in mid-December. The list had come down to Gerald, Richard, Juniper, Perta, Beverly, Lionel, and, yes, Aunt Berna. Polly smiled. Aunt Berna might have been suspect, but she had about as much of a chance of being the spy as Mr. Helmsworth.

She'd been able to eliminate Gerald and Richard from the list because of their work assignments within the plant, limited access to sensitive information, and their behavior. It helped to watch them daily, to see their routine, mannerisms, habits, and interaction.

She sipped the lukewarm coffee, the bitter taste burning as it went down. She'd drunk too much. Her stomach growled. She closed Lionel Wilcox's file and laid it on the stack with the other paperwork. He and Beverly were the prime suspects who'd been in Kalena's house. If she cleared them, then she'd have to start the elimination process over again and find someone she'd missed. Earlier in the day she'd called OAD and given an update to the agent in charge. Agent Henson wasn't there on weekends, so she was able to avoid any unwanted confrontations. She still didn't have any information on her missing contact, Oliver, which troubled her. Where was he? She tried to put the question out of her mind.

Earlier in the morning she'd asked Kalena to invite Lionel over when he returned from out of town. A few hours later Kalena had called to tell her he'd be at the house at six.

There was more than a slight chance he could be involved. He had the means and opportunity to place the camera in her closet. He had access to sensitive information, and he was certainly at risk for blackmail. He was vulnerable. If she were a spy and wanted information at the plant, Lionel Wilcox would be a perfect target. It was true, everyone had secrets, but exploitation was an ugly business, and so was spying. Was it a woman? Was it Beverly? A woman doing menial work in the plant would be almost invisible. And if she had a partner? Whoever it was, the person was smart and savvy, but so was she. She checked her watch. Lionel was due at the house in thirty minutes. She locked the files, turned out the lights, and drove home.

She didn't want to stay any longer at the plant than she had to, but she wasn't kidding herself. She wanted to be with Kalena. She was hoping she could wrap up her investigation of Lionel, then take Kalena to the safe house so they could be alone. The longer she was away from her, the more she wanted to be with her. She knew she'd feel this way if she got involved. She'd realized it the moment she saw Kalena the first night at the house. Now it was hard to focus on her job. If Kalena and she could just spend a little more time alone, the desire to be with her might ease, and she could pay closer attention. She'd already made up her mind to take her away for a few days after the case was wrapped up. They needed time to sort through their feelings, and she needed time to regain control. She was restless, and her mind wandered constantly back to Kalena. It bothered her. She didn't want to feel this way about her—thinking about her, wanting to be with her, to touch her. All emotion did was cloud her thinking and get in the way. And what kind of future could there be for them, anyway? Her work was in DC, where her career was, and she knew what would happen if the agency found out. Besides, Kalena had her life here.

A car was in the driveway when she arrived. Lionel was early. She parked on the street in front of the house, and when she walked in, Lionel and Kalena were on the sofa talking with Aunt Berna and Gerald. Kalena smiled at her. Polly wanted to lead her directly to the bedroom, take her clothes off, and make love to her. She blocked the thoughts. What was wrong with her? Was she using Kalena as a diversion? She didn't know her well enough to be this involved. It was just sex, a need in her that Kalena somehow completely fulfilled. It wasn't, and couldn't be, anything more.

Lionel was a handsome man. He had dark hair and a well-proportioned body, but he had a weak chin, and his eyes were dull, dark like bird eyes.

Aunt Berna glanced up at Polly from the yellow and white doily she was crocheting and frowned. "You look tired, dear. I'm glad you're home. I saved leftovers from dinner for you on the counter if you're hungry."

Polly was hungry, but other matters were more important than eating. How could she get Lionel alone to ask questions without being obvious?

"Kalena tells me you work for Celia," Lionel said, holding Kalena's hand.

"Yes. I do." She wanted to shove him away from Kalena and hold her soft, warm fingers herself. He didn't need to be touching her. She took off her coat and hung it on the rack, then rubbed her cold hands together and blew on them, glad to be in the warm house. She sat at the end of the sofa near Kalena.

"Tell me about your job," she said to Lionel.

"I'm an engineer. Can't say much more than that. Confidential and all that sort of hush-hush rigmarole. I'm sure you've been briefed."

Polly nodded. She knew all about him, but she had to engage him in specific conversation to find out what she needed. And that would require privacy. "Have you always lived here in Barberton?" she asked, not wanting to sit there and ask the boring questions she already knew the answers to. Yes, he'd always lived in Barberton except when he went to New York for his education. Yes, he'd worked at the plant for over three years. His father was dead. He was an only child. On and on and on.

What had Kalena done while Polly was at the factory today? Did she miss her? Did she want to be with her in bed and caress her body as badly as she wanted to caress hers? Thoughts of Kalena were like lions in a cage going around and around and around, always returning to the same spot.

Lionel said something, but she missed it. She had to stop this incessant mental wandering.

"Polly, didn't you tell me you had some things you'd like to ask Lionel about work? Perhaps we'd be more comfortable in the den?" Kalena had just provided the perfect opportunity to get to the real questions.

They went into the den, and Kalena slid the pocket door closed behind them. Polly mouthed *thank you* as she went by, and Kalena stroked her arm. The sensation remained long after she withdrew. This had to stop.

Kalena and Lionel sat on the leather sofa. Polly settled into the overstuffed chair, thinking of Kalena's strong, muscled back, how she'd pulled her close when they danced, her breasts and curves when her clothes fell to the floor. She looked up to find Kalena's gaze fixed on her, a slight smile on her face. She made herself focus.

"Polly's a lesbian," Kalena said.

Polly raised her eyebrows. A little blunt, but it certainly opened the door for conversation.

Lionel folded his arms across his chest. "Well, that's a surprise and turns the horse to a different color, doesn't it?" He studied Polly, then Kalena. "Oh, I see. So, is it now going to be the three of us riding around in my car and going out to supper?"

"I have my own car," Polly said.

Lionel laughed, sounding both relieved and accepting. He took Kalena's hand again and kissed it. "I'm happy for you, darling. Does this mean we're breaking up?"

Kalena patted his arm. "Of course not. I'll never abandon you."

"Thank you, pet. It's not easy being a man of my tastes in a world of Neanderthals."

Polly appreciated his pleasant nature and sense of humor. "Lionel, my job is to investigate risks of security problems at the plant."

"Good God! It's about the spy, isn't it?"

"What spy?" Polly asked.

"You can't sit there and tell me you haven't heard all the rumors?

I'm not falling for that. It's all we've talked about in the engineers' office. Suddenly there's security everywhere. Memos are going around about locking up all documents, and everyone's being watched. There simply has to be a spy. We have a pool going. My money is on someone on second shift. It's too much of a risk to get information on first shift. We lock that place up tighter than ol' man Helmsworth's belt. He's done nothing but bitch to us about security for months. We heard he finally went and hired someone to beef up security protocols." He inspected her more closely, squinting. "You. You're a perfect pick. Although I'm shocked he hired a woman. I didn't even know there were women in security, but the way things are going, it's probably better that way. Bully for you. And a lesbian to boot. The world is progressing after all."

It was time to shock him again, but this time with a lot more voltage. "Lionel, are you betraying your country by giving sensitive classified information to the enemy?"

Polly loved to ask that question cold, without warning. The normal human body responded with autonomic reflexes when threatened. Muscles tensed, and there might be a gasp or a quick breath. The body needed more oxygen, so blood rushed through it to supply that demand. Also, adrenaline flooded the bloodstream to speed up a person's movements, resulting in a change in skin color, a paling or flushing. Someone who was lying didn't have those responses. They tried to fake them or deliberately attempted to calm themselves. A trained investigator would see a slight jerk, a reflex followed by a counter reaction to elicit what the suspect thought was the correct response. Or they'd hesitate to give themselves time to think through how they should respond to protect themselves.

Lionel's mouth dropped open, and he paled. He sucked in a deep breath and shook his head. He jumped up. "Good God, woman. I may be a fag, but I assure you I would never betray my country."

A genuine response. His facial expressions matched what he was saying. His body reactions accentuated his emotions. He probably wasn't the spy. But she wanted to ask a few more questions to be sure.

"Sit down, please."

Lionel sat heavily. His hands trembled, a reaction from the sudden release of adrenaline into his body.

"Has anyone ever approached you or suggested you could help them get information?"

He took another deep breath. "No. Never." Another breath as he tried to calm himself. He closed his eyes and lowered his head. "I can't believe I'm a suspect. Is it because I'm a homosexual?"

"You're a suspect because you have access to classified information, and you have something you're trying to hide. That makes you vulnerable."

"*Hide*? How could I not hide? You have no idea what it's like to be a male homosexual in our society. A lot of people out there would just as soon stab me to death as speak to me. It's not like that for lesbians."

"I'm not going to get into a debate with you, Lionel. I'm aware that the risks and danger are much greater for you than us, but the issue right now is that you're vulnerable."

"I have no choice but to hide. To admit it openly would destroy my career, my life. And I can't change who I am, so what choice do I have?" He stiffened. "I can't help it if I'd much rather have a man in my arms when I dance."

"Thanks," Kalena said with a smirk.

Lionel patted her hand, and some of the tension seemed to leave his shoulders. "No offense, sweetie, but let's face it. You can't dance for toffee."

"I'm much better since Polly taught me."

Lionel smiled. "Heaven knows you needed a lesson or two." He looked at Polly. "I tried to teach her."

Lionel was trying to distract her from the fact that he was scared. "Lionel, I want you to protect yourself. If anyone approaches you or you get any kind of correspondence threatening you or coercing you, come to me immediately, and let me help you."

"Oh, I will. I assure you I will."

"Do you live alone?"

"No. I live with my widowed mother. Well, actually she lives with me. I bought the house when my father died."

"I know you have a telephone," Polly said.

"Yes. A party line, and believe me, those old biddies know how to talk."

"Do you have any questions for me?" Polly asked.

He studied her for a moment, as though deciding what to ask. "How can I get hold of you if I need you?"

"Call here, or call Celia at work and ask for me. Anything else?"

"No. I have to go home now and change my underwear."

Kalena and Polly laughed.

Lionel stood. He bent and kissed Kalena on the cheek. "I'll see you tomorrow at work." He turned to Polly. "And hopefully I won't ever see you again except socially. No offense."

Kalena walked him to the front entrance, then returned to the den and slid the door closed. She sat on the sofa across from Polly, not saying anything.

Polly watched her for a few minutes but couldn't stand their separation any longer. She had only one more priority name on her list, and she couldn't do anything with it tonight. "Want to go for a drive?"

Kalena snapped to her feet. "I'll get my coat and tell Aunt Berna we'll be gone for a while." She smiled and blushed.

Polly drove to Akron and parked the car just down the street from the cobbler's store. The moment they entered the safe house and closed the door, Polly gathered her in her arms. Kalena's kisses were eager and full of hope and promise. They managed to almost completely undress each other before they reached the bed.

Kalena shoved Polly onto the mattress. "All I can think about is being with you."

When their passion was sated, they lay naked in each other's arms.

"Polly, what's going to happen? Will you leave once you're done with the case?" She brushed Polly's hair from her face.

Polly didn't want to spoil the few moments they had together. She didn't want to tell her she would eventually have to leave. "Do we have to talk about this now?"

"I need to know."

Polly kissed her. "I'll have to go back to Washington after I've closed this case."

"Is that where you live?"

"Yes. I get my assignments from OAD headquarters there in Washington."

"Will you go to another city?"

"Most likely. With the increase in war production and everything going on, I'm sure I'll get another assignment somewhere."

Kalena sighed and held her tighter. "I hate the war already, and we're not even in it."

"I was thinking I could take a few days off after this case. We can go somewhere and have time to be together. Do you think you can get away?"

"That sounds wonderful. Yes. I'll get away, somehow. Do you think you'll be done soon?"

"Each day I get a little closer. I hope it's soon." She appreciated that Kalena didn't ask specifics about her investigation. She'd already shared far more than she should.

The night stars and a sliver of moonlight illuminated the bedroom.

Polly sighed. "I wish we could lie here together and sleep in each other's arms, but we have to get back."

Kalena rolled over onto her and kissed her breasts and then her mouth. "A little longer, please."

Polly wrapped her arms around her, kissing her neck. "I'm in trouble, Kalena. I can't stop thinking about you, and I'm losing focus on my job. This has to be the last time we're together until my assignment here is over. I don't want to not be with you, but it has to be this way. Do you understand?"

"Is this only a passing encounter?"

Polly turned her onto her side and looked into her eyes. She stroked her cheek with the back of her hand. "Don't you know what I'm saying? My feelings for you are so strong I have to get away from you to function." It wasn't an answer, not really, but it was the only one she had to give for now.

"Promise me we'll go away together when this is over." Kalena's eyes welled with tears.

Polly kissed her. "Yes. Yes, I promise."

She'd already said they'd go away after this, but she knew full well it wasn't what Kalena was really asking. That was a promise she couldn't make.

CHAPTER SIXTEEN

Kalena had hardly slept after she and Polly returned to the house Sunday night. All she could think about was that Polly would be leaving soon. She'd finally cried herself to sleep about four a.m.

Now she couldn't concentrate. Twice she'd stopped to re-torque the fit on the cover of the second engine block of the morning. Was Polly thinking of her? Was she in the administration building, or had she gone somewhere else?

The sharp metal tool slipped. Before she could correct the angle, the edge gouged her, tearing through flesh from her knuckle almost to the base of her thumb. Searing pain shot across her palm and up her arm. Blood dripped down her hand and over the engine block. "Damn it." She pulled the scarf from her head and pressed it against the wound, trying to stop the bleeding. She lifted it after a few seconds to inspect the cut, but the moment she removed the pressure, blood oozed out and covered her again. It was gaping, and she could see bone.

Now what? She didn't want to go the hospital. She wouldn't get paid for her time away, the rest of the day would be a waste, and she wouldn't get to see Polly at lunchtime. She pressed harder on the scarf, cradling her hand close to her body.

Walter Henry, the assembly-line foreman, came to her station. "Let me see it." He pulled the fabric away and took her hand, gently turning it over. The blood pooled in the wound and ran down her thumb and wrist. He grimaced. "Oh, hell's bells. You stuck it good. Going to need stitches for sure." He waved for another worker to take her place on the line. "Let's go to the aid station. Someone over there will take you to the hospital. I'll make sure you're clocked out for the rest of the day. Tomorrow you'll work as a runner for the assembly lines. Be more careful, will ya? This isn't the beauty shop, ya know."

Kalena nodded and pressed harder on the scarf as she followed him to the aid station.

When she got home from the hospital, Aunt Berna slipped a pillow onto her lap and set a cup of hot chocolate on the end-table beside her chair.

"I'm not an invalid, Aunt Berna. It's just a few stitches."

"Twenty stitches are not a *few*. Keep your hand on that pillow. Can I get you anything else? Are you hungry?"

Kalena shook her head. "No. This is fine." She sighed. It was only 1:45. The morphine had worn off before the aide from work had driven her home. Now the stitches ached and burned. And it'd be hours before Polly came home.

Aunt Berna went on with her cleaning.

An hour later, Kalena heard a thud upstairs, and then Aunt Berna screamed and yelled something in Polish she couldn't quite understand. She raced up the steps, holding her hand to her chest, and stopped in the doorway of Polly's room. Aunt Berna was standing by the chest of drawers she'd evidently moved away from the wall to clean behind.

"Look." Aunt Berna waved wrinkled sheets of paper at Kalena. "What are we going to do?" She yelled in Polish, "My God, she's a spy," and collapsed onto the chair beside the bed. "We must call the police." She spat out a slew of more Polish so fast Kalena couldn't keep up.

Kalena ran over to her. "No. No police. It's not necessary."

"*Not necessary*? Child, have you lost your mind? She's a spy. A spy in our house."

"Calm down, Aunt Berna."

"I won't *calm down*. I'm calling the police." She got to her feet, still clutching the papers.

"Stop," Kalena said. "Let me see them."

Aunt Berna shoved them at her.

Kalena sat on the bed and spread them out, scanning the contents. They were crumpled plans, diagrams, and descriptions of aircraft at the plant. "Where'd you find these?"

"They were taped behind the dresser."

What should she do? Telephone Polly? Tell her to come home right away so she could explain to Aunt Berna? Or should she just reveal to Aunt Berna who she was? No. It'd be better if Polly told her. She had to phone her, but she didn't want Aunt Berna to hear. "I'm going to make a call."

"I'll stay up here. I might find more," Aunt Berna said as Kalena rushed down the stairs. "Tell them to hurry. You tell them we have a spy in our house," she yelled once again in Polish.

About twenty minutes later, the tires of Polly's car screeched in the driveway, and she burst through the door.

"She's upstairs in your room," Kalena said. "I can't calm her down."

Polly looked at her bandage. "What happened? Why are you home? Are you all right?"

"I'll explain later." She followed her up to the bedroom, almost running into her when she suddenly stopped.

"It's okay," Polly said slowly and softly, raising her hands.

Aunt Berna was sitting in the chair, pointing a revolver at her. "You don't come one step closer."

Kalena screamed. "My God, Aunt Berna. What are you doing?"

"You're a spy. You're an evil, wicked spy."

Kalena recognized Uncle Frederick's handgun that he'd kept in his dresser drawer. She stepped in front of Polly. "Please put the weapon down, Aunt Berna. Polly's not a spy. She's an agent from Washington sent to get the spy."

"She told you that?" Aunt Berna asked. "It's nonsense. She's the spy. Get away from her." She shook so hard the gun was quivering.

Polly seemed to move in slow motion as she guided Kalena to her side, then an arm's length away from her, eyes fixed on Aunt Berna. "Keep pointing it at me if you like, but please take your finger off the trigger," she said. "You might shoot Kalena by mistake. I know you wouldn't want to do that."

Still shaking, Aunt Berna complied, then sprang to her feet, keeping the gun aimed at Polly.

"Would you allow Kalena to reach into my jacket pocket and get my identification?" Polly asked.

Aunt Berna remained in position, not answering for a few seconds, as if considering Polly's request. "All right, but don't try anything."

"Would you please lower the gun while she's in front of me? Then you can point it toward me again when she's out of the way," Polly said.

Aunt Berna nodded. "But don't you move a hair."

"I assure you I won't," Polly said.

Aunt Berna lowered the gun.

"Reach across me very slowly, Kalena. It's in my left inside pocket."

Kalena did as Polly instructed, then took the wallet to Aunt Berna and held it open so she could see it.

Aunt Berna raised the weapon again toward Polly. Her eyes darted from the credentials to Polly, like she expected her to make a charge for the weapon. "Don't you think about coming toward me."

"No, ma'am," Polly said firmly and clearly.

Aunt Berna continued to study the information. She squinted. "This could be a forgery in case she gets caught. It's not even the same name."

Kalena stepped away from Aunt Berna. Should she grab the weapon from her? Block her so she couldn't aim it at Polly?

Polly quietly called to her. "Kalena, don't move until she puts the gun down." She spoke to Aunt Berna in a firmer voice. "My credentials are legitimate. I assure you I'm an agent of the United States government sent here to catch a spy at the Portage aircraft plant. I don't use my real name when I'm undercover. If you like, you can call the Office of American Defense in Washington DC and speak with someone who will give you a description of me and verify my identification, or you can call the plant and speak with Mr. Helmsworth, the plant director, or Cecilia Morrison, his executive secretary. They will also verify my identity. But no one else at the factory, except those two people, the CFO, and Kalena, know who I am or why I'm here. Now you know. I hope you'll keep this information confidential. My ability to catch the spy depends on it." Polly kept her arms raised. "I'd appreciate it if you'd lower that weapon."

Aunt Berna stood rigid for a few more moments, then did as Polly requested but continued to watch her.

Polly lowered her arms but stood perfectly still.

"Aunt Berna, please lay the gun on the nightstand," Kalena said.

The moment she did, Kalena advanced toward her. Her stitches throbbed. She wrapped her arm around Aunt Berna, who was trembling.

"We should all go down to the kitchen and have a cup of coffee. Don't you think?" Polly asked.

Kalena nodded and walked Aunt Berna past Polly and down the steps.

She poured a cup of coffee for all of them and then sat at the table. No one spoke. The only sound was the tinkling of Polly's teaspoon as it touched the china cup when she stirred the cream.

Polly finally broke the silence. "I'm sorry you discovered the papers. It must have been a shock. I didn't know where else to hide them. I found them in a waste can at the plant, and I need them as evidence."

After an hour of convincing and answering questions, Aunt Berna finally accepted that Polly was who she claimed to be.

The thought that Polly could have been shot swirled in Kalena's head. She wanted to tell Aunt Berna the most important part—that Polly was everything she'd ever wanted, and she was in love with her. But would she ever be able to share that confidence with her, or Polly?

Polly looked at her wristwatch. "I've got to get back to the plant." She touched Aunt Berna's shoulder. "Are you all right?"

Aunt Berna patted Polly's arm. "I'm sorry. I'm a foolish old woman."

Polly smiled. "I'm proud of you for being brave. No spy will survive in this house." She rose from the chair.

"I'll see you to the door," Kalena said. She wrapped her arm in hers, and they walked to the entryway. Polly slipped her coat on and looped her scarf around her neck, then pulled on her black leather gloves. "I'm so sorry you were injured. What happened?"

"It was a stupid accident. I lost control of the torque wrench."

"Are you in a lot of pain?"

"Not much. I'll be fine and back at work tomorrow. I'll be a runner for a few days and maybe get to see you off and on. Will you be home late?"

Polly shook her head. "I have no idea. Celia and I are going over more information." She sighed. "I'm close. I feel it. There's just a few more pieces to fit together."

They lingered in each other's gaze.

Kalena whispered, "I want to kiss you."

Polly leaned close. "Thinking about it will only make it worse.

Trust me." She smiled. "I'll see you later. Oh, by the way, I have *my* gun on in case your aunt changes her mind."

Kalena laughed and returned to the kitchen. She did what she could to help Aunt Berna start supper, which amounted to sitting at the table and trying to cut carrots with one hand.

"Here," Aunt Berna said, taking the knife and placing the newspaper in front of her. "Read to me before you chop your fingers off. I haven't read any of it today."

Kalena scanned the headlines. "*Tokyo Postpones War Move*. That's big of them. Japan, Japan, Japan. I don't want to read the news." She folded the paper and laid it on the table.

"What is it, sunshine?"

"*What is it?* You pointed a gun at Polly and accused her of being a spy."

Aunt Berna turned the stove off, wiped her hands on her apron, and sat. "Yes, that was bad, but we got that straightened out. What is it?"

Kalena made a fist. She needed to talk about what she was feeling for Polly. She needed to get it out. She needed someone to listen to her. But she couldn't talk to Aunt Berna. What if she ended up rejecting her? She couldn't endure it. Her stomach was in knots. The stitches were aching and tight, like they were being ripped out. Her chest had a hundred-pound weight lying on it.

"What is it, sunshine?" Aunt Berna asked again. She took her hand and patted it, her grayish-blue eyes penetrating. "I want to know."

Did she? Did she really want to know? Not this. She didn't want to know this. She didn't want to know her *sunshine* was a lesbian, in love with another woman. Not this.

"Whatever it is, you can't hold it inside any longer. Tell me."

The tears started. Kalena shook her head. She didn't want to be emotional, but how could she not be? She was who she was, and her feelings wouldn't be any different tomorrow than they were today. She was exhausted, drained. She settled her arm on the table, rested her head on it, and sobbed.

Aunt Berna stroked her hair. "Talking about it helps."

Kalena shook her head. "Not about this." Now her stitches were throbbing again.

Aunt Berna leaned close and kissed her hair, then offered a tissue.

"Do you think you're the only one who's ever been in love with another woman?"

Kalena's breath caught. She bolted upright, rigid, and stared at her.

Aunt Berna patted her cheek. "Breathe, sunshine."

Kalena sucked in a stuttered breath. The released tension spewed out of her like someone had opened a radiator cap on an overheated Model-T. She couldn't utter a word. So many were in her mind, and she wanted to say them, but her body couldn't make the connection between her brain and her mouth.

Aunt Berna laughed. "I guess I hit that nail full force and square on the head. We need something stronger than coffee." She got up from the table and went into the den, coming back with the liquor bottle and two small glasses. She poured two shots of the rich amber liquid and shoved one over to Kalena, then lifted hers in a toast. "Here's to facing our fears." She drank it straight down, then gasped. She poked Kalena's shoulder. "Go on. Drink it."

Kalena tried to come out of her stupor. She brought the glass to her lips and sipped.

"No. Don't sip it. Drink it."

Kalena threw her head back and gulped. As soon as the liquor hit her throat, the pleasant burn went all the way to her stomach. It was like swallowing honey with a little red pepper on a blinding-hot sunny day. She wiped her mouth with her fingertips and set the glass on the table.

Aunt Berna poured another for each of them. "Your Uncle Frederick would have loved this." She downed the second drink and looked at Kalena. "By God, he would have loved it."

Kalena swilled hers down. "Why?"

"Because he adored you and knew how you felt a long time ago. He'd be so proud of you today for facing your fears. Another ought to do it." Aunt Berna poured the shots and gave one to Kalena. "Your turn."

Finally recovering, Kalena held hers up. "To getting what you want."

"Damn right," Aunt Berna said, and they both drank the liquor down and slammed the glasses onto the kitchen table.

Between the residual morphine, the three shots of bourbon, and the turmoil of her emotions, Kalena's head was spinning. "I love her,

Aunt Berna. She's the most wonderful, beautiful person I've ever known. How long have you realized I prefer women? I just recently admitted it to myself."

"Your Uncle Frederick and I suspected for a long time. Since you were a teenager, and especially when you went away to Cleveland. And it was confirmed the moment Polly walked into the house. I saw it in your eyes and the way you acted. Do you need another drink?"

Kalena waved. "No. I'm good."

"Do you feel better?"

Kalena couldn't help but smile so wide she felt it in her ears, at least she thought she did. Her face was getting numb. She stared at Aunt Berna in wonder. She'd known all along. Kalena's heart swelled with relief and gratitude and love. She threw her arms around Aunt Berna and squeezed her. "Thank you so much." She kissed her forehead. "I do feel better. I really do. Like a heavy weight's been lifted from my heart that I've carried almost all my life. Are you okay with it? How do you feel about it?"

"Sunshine, I'm worried for you. It's dangerous business. Most people don't understand it."

"How do you understand?"

"Your Aunt Michelina was a homosexual."

"Aunt Mickie, your older sister, liked women?"

"She and I were very close, and she talked about it often to me. I know what she went through. I know how hard it was for her."

"Did she have someone? Someone to love?"

"Yes. She did finally find someone. They were traveling together when she and Aunt Mickie were killed in the train crash."

Kalena remembered the story of how Aunt Mickie was killed. She was thirty-seven when she died on her way to Baltimore. Now she knew she'd died with the woman she loved. Suddenly she wished she'd had an opportunity to talk with her, but she was only a child when she'd died. She was tall, with darker hair, a beautiful smile, and vivid green eyes. And when she'd picked Kalena up in her arms she smelled like peppermint and roses.

Aunt Berna stroked Kalena's cheek. "You're careful, aren't you, sunshine?"

Kalena leaned into her touch. "Yes. We're very careful, and

discreet. I'm safe with Polly. You don't have anything to be concerned about. She carries a gun. You do know she had a gun all along?"

Aunt Berna laughed.

"Polly suspected I might be the spy and interrogated me." It hadn't been amusing at the time, but now it made her laugh.

Aunt Berna laughed again. "I bet she did."

Kalena blushed, feeling the effects of the alcohol course through her more strongly. "I think I'll go up to my room and rest."

"That's a good idea. Do you need some help getting up the stairs?"

Kalena rose from the chair. "No. I'll be all right. I don't think I care for any supper tonight."

She went to her room and lay on the bed, pulling the covers over her and tucking her bandaged hand close to her breasts. "Aunt Berna knows and she's okay. More than okay. What will Polly think about it? I don't want her to go." The room spun as she drifted off to sleep.

Chapter Seventeen

Polly groggily woke to banging on the front door. She looked at the wind-up alarm clock on the nightstand. Three forty-five in the morning. She and Kalena had talked until late, and now after only a few hours of sleep, the house was awakened. She heard Kalena go past her bedroom and down the steps. She slipped a robe over her nightgown and followed her, Richard close behind, and Aunt Berna joining them in the entryway. Kalena opened the front door, and two uniformed policemen stepped inside.

"What is it?" Aunt Berna asked. "Why this disturbance in the middle of the night?"

"Sergeant Snyder." The larger officer touched the bill of his hat. "And this is Officer Conners. Sorry to wake your household, ma'am, but does a Gerald Coleman, twenty-six, of Warren, Ohio, reside here?"

"Yes, he does," Kalena said. "He's one of our boarders."

"Who owns this home?" Snyder asked.

"I do," Kalena replied. "What's happened?"

"Your name, miss, and relation to Mr. Coleman?" he asked.

"I'm Kalena Mikloska, and I'm no relation. He's a boarder here."

"Is one of his family here, and if not, do you know how we might get in contact with them?" The sergeant straightened.

"He has no family here. I demand to know what's going on," Kalena said.

Polly knew. Something had happened to Gerald. Police didn't show up at your doorstep at this hour unless it was something bad. His shift at the factory had been over hours ago, and he hadn't been home when she and Kalena finally went to bed.

Snyder surveyed the others. He looked at Kalena. "May we speak with you in private?"

"Certainly, but I'd like Miss Hollister and my aunt to remain with me."

"I'll go upstairs," Richard said, and climbed the steps.

Polly sat on the sofa next to Kalena.

Aunt Berna sat in her overstuffed chair. "Mercy, what's happened?" she asked again.

"Ma'am, I regret to inform you that Mr. Coleman was killed tonight."

Aunt Berna gasped. Kalena's eyes widened. Polly waited for more details. If they didn't give them, she would get them somehow.

"Please tell me what happened," Kalena asked, gently rubbing her bandage.

"It's under investigation, but he was murdered. A night watchman found him stabbed to death at the back of one of the Portage Aircraft buildings, near a dumpster. I'm not at liberty to tell you any more," Snyder said.

If Polly showed her credentials and forced the information from the sergeant, word would get out that she was the agent Washington had sent, and her cover would be blown. Now more than ever she needed to hide her identity. She'd work through Celia to get what she needed.

The sergeant questioned Kalena about her wound. When he seemed satisfied and gave them what little information he could, he and his partner left.

Aunt Berna and Kalena were in disbelief.

"How could this have happened?" Aunt Berna asked.

"I need to go to the plant and get as much information as I can," Polly said. She called Celia, then went up to her room and dressed.

Kalena came into her bedroom. "I want to go with you. I don't want you going alone."

Polly stroked her arm. "That's very sweet, but it's my job. I've already involved you enough, and you're in danger as it is. Stay here. I'll let you know what's going on as soon as I can."

Kalena clutched her arm. "Promise me you'll be careful. We've already had enough tragedy."

"It's all right. I promise I'll be back. Do me a favor, and don't go for any walks this evening when it's dark."

Kalena nodded. "You've got to be exhausted. Be extra safe. Will someone at the plant contact Gerald's family? I feel so bad for them. Will you get me an address so we can send them a letter?"

Polly stroked her hair. "I'm sure there'll be information available soon for people to contact his family. You make sure you're in the house at dark. I don't want to be worrying about your safety."

"I will."

Polly wrapped herself in her heavy coat and picked up Celia, and then they drove to the plant.

"I heard from Mr. Helmsworth about twelve fifteen tonight," Celia said. "I was going to call you, but I wasn't sure if I should. Do you think his murder has anything to do with the spy?"

Polly grazed her lower lip with her teeth. "I think it has everything to do with the spy." How could she have misjudged him? Was he a spy? Was he working with someone? Or was it just a coincidence that she'd found the camera and documents in the same house Gerald had been living in? "I'll know more as soon as I can get more information."

She, Celia, and Mr. Helmsworth sat in his office. He leaned back in his chair and chewed on an unlit cigar.

"I need to know everything," Polly said. "Everything the police investigated, everything they know or suspect, and I need to look at the crime scene before it gets trampled over."

"I'll have the night watchman who found him go over everything with you." Helmsworth was pale. He looked at Celia. "It's Dan Abernathy. Call him up here."

Within a few minutes Dan was at the office door. Mr. Helmsworth instructed him to take Polly to the crime scene and answer any of her questions.

Dan was over fifty-eight and moved somewhat slowly. According to his work record Polly had already reviewed days before, he was an ex-policeman, had been wounded in the leg, and had been with the plant as a security guard for five years. He escorted her down to where he'd found the body.

"I knew him somewhat," Dan said. "He'd been on second shift only a little while. Nice fellow. Always said good night to me when he took the bus from the gate. He was always one of the last to leave."

"He took the bus after his shift? I know he walked to work. Did you see him last night at all?" Polly asked.

Dan rubbed his chin. "Nope, and it was odd because I always saw him at the gate. Not many people wait for the last bus. Everyone wants to get out of here as early as possible. But he always took the final one."

Dan liked to talk. Polly imagined he was lonely on the graveyard shift. He and one other guard worked security through the night, and both had Sundays and Wednesdays off. Two part-time officers covered those nights and their vacations.

The crime scene was marked with barrels and wood planks. Police were still investigating. Dan got her as close as he could. "I found him there." He pointed his flashlight beam to the left of the dumpster, then traced the set of drag marks.

"Can I see your light for a minute?" Polly asked.

Dan passed it to her, and she swept the beam across the area, then again. "I don't think whoever dragged him was very strong."

"Why do you say that?" Dan asked.

"Well, he wasn't moved in a straight line. See how it's jagged, and the blood pools at different spots. Whoever dragged him had to stop and get a better grip."

Dan nodded. "That's mighty observant of you. Say, are you one of those female cops or something?"

"No. Just want to be thorough for Mr. Helmsworth and Celia. Tell me what you've heard from the police or the coroner."

"I heard the coroner say the murder probably took place about one to two hours before the body was found. There were several stab wounds to the back, just under the rib cage, and no bruising or self-defense wounds."

Polly nodded. She took what information Dan, Mr. Helmsworth, and Celia had given her and sat in her office with a hot cup of coffee, trying to process. A strong man wouldn't have struggled dragging the body to the dumpster. Had she made a mistake in eliminating the people on Kalena's list, all except Beverly? She didn't want to second-guess herself, but had she overlooked a critical piece of information? She rubbed her forehead, concentrating on the names and mentally going over why she had eliminated them as suspects. Perta and Juniper were certainly capable of lifting the body, but their files, and what she had learned about them, gave no indication of any suspicion. They'd lived in Barberton all their lives, had no sudden wealth or increased assets, worked first shift, not second, and neither one of them owned a car.

Nor was Lionel a suspect any longer. After Polly once again reviewed her process of elimination and the evidence, only one person remained who had access to Kalena's home to plant the camera and reasonable opportunity to steal information and commit the crime. Beverly Anderson.

Polly meticulously went through Beverly's employee record one final time, but she had no doubt in her mind.

She'd go back to the house, get some sleep, then try to find out what Beverly was up to.

❖

The scent of coffee and bacon drifted in and out of Polly's awareness, finally fully waking her.

She opened her eyes to find Kalena sitting on her bed, holding a tray of food.

"It's past two. You said you needed to get up. I thought you might like something right away," Kalena said.

She poured cream in the cup as Polly sat and fluffed the pillows behind her. Once she was settled, Kalena set the tray on her lap, adjusted the stand, and started to leave.

"Don't go. Stay and visit with me while I eat. This is so sweet. Thank you. What are you doing home from work?"

Kalena sat in the chair beside the bed. "Walter felt sorry for me and told me to leave. I think he was worried I'd make a bigger mess as a runner. Everyone has heard about Gerald, and they know he was my boarder. Between my hand and people wanting to talk to me, I wasn't getting anything done."

"Does it hurt?"

"No. Not much. Just a little sore."

"Well, thank you for this."

"I'm glad to do it. You look tired. Did you find what you were looking for?"

Polly smeared strawberry jam on the toast, took a bite, chewing several times, then sipped the coffee. "That's so good. Um, let's put it this way. I'm closer than I was." She didn't want to tell Kalena that a friend of hers was the final suspect on the list, although she knew it had to be someone close to her, since they'd been in the house.

Kalena's eyes narrowed, and her face became pale. "Was Gerald the spy?"

Polly shook her head slowly. "I can't tell you anything. I'm sorry."

Kalena sighed heavily. "I understand. I can't believe he would be. Not him. If anyone is, it's Beverly."

Polly glanced up, then placed her food on the plate and the cup on the tray. "Why do you say that?"

"Because there's just something different about her. I've known her the least time of all my friends. She's been in town only about a year. Anything I can do? I'm just sitting here at the house."

Polly ignored her question. "What do you find *different* about her?"

Kalena shrugged. "She's just odd sometimes. She's there with us but then not. Someone will say something funny, and we'll all laugh, but it's like it takes her a few seconds to get it." Kalena's eyes were penetrating. "You have a suspect, don't you? And I know who it is. You're going to follow her, aren't you? Can I come?"

"Definitely not. You're going to have to mind your own business and pretend you don't know who I am."

"But I do know who you are, and you're quite lovely when you wake up."

It was an instant thing. Polly had no control over it. Before she knew it, the tray was off the bed, and Kalena was on it.

"We can't do this, Kalena."

"Yes. We can. No one's here. Aunt Berna went to a card game at her friend's house and won't be back until around four, and Richard said he had something to do after work until about eight and not to worry about him. And you just said you don't have anything to do until later this evening."

"You seem to have this all figured out."

Kalena moved closer to Polly and untied the bow to her nightgown. Polly's nipples hardened at her touch. She wouldn't be able to resist her even if she tried, which she wasn't going to do. When they kissed, she slid down into the bed and pulled Kalena close. "We shouldn't. It just makes it more difficult."

"It's *more difficult* if we don't," Kalena whispered.

"I haven't brushed my teeth yet. My breath smells."

"I'm sure it doesn't."

They kissed deep and long.

"You taste like strawberries and coffee." Kalena slipped Polly's nightgown off her shoulders, exposing her breasts. She eased down, caressing her with feather-light touches, taking a nipple into her mouth.

Polly thrummed and arched, running her fingers through the soft curls of Kalena's hair.

"Umm, you taste so wonderful," Kalena moaned.

Polly was unable to stop or resist. She began to unbutton Kalena's blouse. "What have you done to me?"

They lay in each other's arms, breathless and sweaty from the sexual release. Kalena sighed deeply, then rolled over and brushed Polly's hair away from her face. "You're wonderful."

Polly stroked her face with her fingertips. She wanted to tell her how, at the moment of fulfillment, all she could see was her, that she surrounded her and consumed her. But all she could do was smile and look deep into her eyes, seeing the comfort and safety that awaited her.

"Aunt Berna knows about us."

Polly quickly sat up. "What?"

Kalena pulled her back down beside her. "It's all right. She's known about how I feel longer than I have. We talked about it."

Kalena's eyes glowed, and a smile lit her face.

"It must have been some conversation."

"It was. And it was liberating and amazing. I feel so relieved."

Polly drew her close. "I'm happy for you."

"If you told your parents, do you think they'd accept how you feel?"

Did Polly want to share that information with her? Sharing more would only draw them closer. She was already too close to her. She already felt too much.

"That is a very complex question."

CHAPTER EIGHTEEN

Tuesday's sudden temperature climb, then the evening's chill, brought a thick fog that hung in the air, making it difficult for Polly to follow Beverly when she got off the bus and walked to her apartment. Polly watched her apartment the rest of the night from her car parked down the street, then followed her Wednesday morning. Beverly grocery shopped, returned to the house, then met Loraine, her friend from the dance, at the Coffee Pot, a small diner on Second Street. An hour later, she once again returned to her apartment, then rode the bus to the factory. Polly made certain to stay out of sight, driving well behind and giving Beverly enough distance so she wouldn't suspect she was being followed. After Beverly went into the plant, Polly called in a report. Gerald's death was upsetting, but she didn't have anything solid yet. She hadn't had any news about Oliver or getting her another contact, which meant she'd need to continue to carry on without support for a while longer.

While Beverly was at work, Polly went to Celia's office and told her what she'd been doing and asked to have Beverly observed throughout her shift. She then went home to get a few hours of needed sleep. She was suddenly awakened by Kalena.

"Celia's on the phone for you."

Polly threw the covers off and rushed to the downstairs phone. She cleared her throat, trying to fight the stupor of sleep.

"Polly? This is Celia. Beverly just told her shift supervisor she wasn't feeling well and was leaving the building."

"Can you stall her until I can get there? It should be only about twenty minutes."

"Yes. We can make her fill out paperwork and wait for approval. I'll call the shift supervisor and take care of it."

It was almost seven p.m. when Polly once again followed Beverly as she rode the bus. She got off at her normal stop and went to her apartment building. At half past eight she came out, tucking some type of portfolio inside her coat, then quick-stepped to the trolley. She rode it to the end of the line, then took the Main Street bus to the Akron train station.

It was about a third of the size of Cleveland's and not nearly as ornate. It seemed busy for nine fifteen at night. Polly took a strategic position near a corner pillar by the lounge.

Arriving passengers scurried in from the terminal platform. Men of all ages in business suits, dark circles under their eyes, with expressions of indifference, walked past her. Women with crying babies attached to their hips and bags slung over their shoulders lugged suitcases. They trudged in and out, looking forlorn and exhausted.

Beverly bought a ticket at the Cleveland express window. Had she decided to leave? Why buy groceries the day before? Where was she going? Would she continue from Cleveland to another destination? Polly's mind raced with possibilities. Whatever the situation, if she had to get on the train without a ticket, she would show her badge. The conductor wouldn't think twice.

Beverly ambled to the front row of wooden benches in the center of the large waiting area, took a seat, crossed her legs, and watched the people as if she *weren't* an enemy of the United States. She looked like every other person around her. She reached into her purse and brought out a small compact mirror, checked her face, brushed her cheeks, then reapplied lipstick. She seemed particularly interested in a woman with a sleeping baby in her arms and a little girl with ringlets of golden-blond hair, clinging to her skirt. Then she suddenly looked up, smiled, and waved casually.

Polly followed Beverly's gaze to the other side of the hall, near the entrance to the northbound platform, and froze in disbelief. Every sound and movement in the station stopped. The people who were moments ago bustling to and fro were no longer in view. The lights from the hanging chandeliers seemed to glisten and direct their beam toward the man. He wore a camel-colored topcoat, matching fedora hat, and dark-brown leather gloves. His mustache was gone, but she was sure it was him. He returned a smile and tipped his hat to Beverly. Oliver!

Polly held in a gasp. She gripped the column, its smooth, cold surface shocking her back to reality. It *was* him. Beverly walked to him, and they kissed. Not a long kiss, but more like a greeting to your lover in a public place. She threw her arms around him, and they hugged, as if happy to see each other.

Polly watched, still stunned. Beverly opened her overcoat, reached in, and subtly slid the portfolio inside Oliver's topcoat. He quickly brought his arm down to his side and continued to hold on to her shoulder with the other. He smiled and said something to her. Polly imagined it was what the people surrounding them would expect to hear. *I'll be home on the next train. Give the children a kiss and hug. I hate to leave.* Most likely it was *Thanks for the top-secret information. I'll be sure to say hello to der Führer for you. We sure fooled everyone, didn't we?*

What was Polly going to do? She couldn't follow both of them, and she didn't have time to call someone to help her even if she had anyone available. This was the ultimate dilemma for an agent who worked a case alone. She didn't have a choice. She had to follow whoever had the portfolio. And right now, it was Oliver. Beverly surrendered the Cleveland Express ticket to Oliver, kissed him on the cheek, then turned and left. She wasn't getting on the train. He was.

Polly repositioned to the far side of the pillar, avoiding Beverly when she passed toward the exit. When she maneuvered back to her original position, Oliver was gone. She frantically scanned the area but saw no sign of him. The only other place he could be was on the platform. She pulled the collar of her coat high up against her neck, ducked her chin into it, and rushed through the entrance to the trains.

The conductor motioned and yelled, "Final all aboard, Cleveland Express."

A porter started to remove the temporary step to the train just as Polly saw Oliver walking through one of the passenger cars. She leapt onto the portable step and grabbed the railing. "Excuse me. Sorry I'm late," she said, breathless and wide-eyed.

The conductor tipped his hat and welcomed her aboard, helping her up and into the entranceway. He went to the right, and she hesitated, peering through the glass of the door on her left. There were three passenger cars. She'd seen Oliver in the second one. Most likely he had a gun, but so did she. She unbuttoned her overcoat, slid her hand behind her, and pulled out the revolver, placing it in her right pocket. She'd have to go straight at him and subdue him quickly, before he could get the advantage.

He was in the right aisle seats, by the window, near the front. The seats directly forward and behind him were empty. Only three passengers sat on the left aisle, about four rows back from him. She walked quickly next to him, reached inside her pocket, held the gun, and sat down.

Oliver glanced at her, nodded politely, then paled.

"Aww. You didn't expect me."

He started to get to his feet.

"Stop." She gouged the gun through her coat pocket into his side. He sat back down.

"Give it to me," she said.

"I have no idea what you're talking about."

"Oh, Oliver, or Otto, or Wilhelm, or whatever your name is, give it up."

He reached inside his coat.

"Not so fast. Slowly." She poked the gun harder.

"You don't think I'm stupid enough to try to shoot you? Besides, it's too late. We have what we need. We did it right under your nose. You had no idea what we were up to. You were too busy playing agent to actually be one." He hesitantly pulled out the portfolio and surrendered it.

She rolled it against her hip and stuffed it into her coat pocket, then retrieved her handcuffs from beneath it. "Get up. We're getting off the train." She stood and backed out into the aisle, still aiming the gun at him.

He stood, moved toward her, then shoved her. She fell to the floor, loosening her grip on the weapon so it wouldn't accidently go off. The train jerked, metal screeched, and the engine rumbled as it started out of the station. He ran forward, toward the next car. By the time she got to her feet, he was going through the door. She managed to catch him at the connection between the two cars.

She pulled the gun from her pocket but didn't have a firm grip on it, and he knocked it out of her hand before she could aim. It landed on the floor, bounced, then went under the guardrail and off the train.

He grinned. A look of confidence and dominance crossed his face as he reached to the side of his coat and pulled out a knife. "Fräulein, you're way too clever for your health." He lashed at her, cutting the sleeve of her overcoat. Blood began to soak through the sleeve. She kicked him against the railing toward the steps, then hit him in the face with the metal cuffs.

The whistle blew. The train rocked gently, and steel against steel screamed in her ears.

He lunged.

She reached out and pulled him as hard as she could, using his momentum to slam him against the metal door behind her. He countered with an elbow to her jaw, causing her to drop the cuffs.

Dazed and her ears ringing, she kicked him in the groin. He doubled over, and she kneed him in the chin. He fell backward as the knife dropped to the floor. She bent down and grabbed it. He pushed himself off from the wall and wrapped his fingers around her neck, but she repositioned the knife and stabbed him full force in his gut. He gasped, fell back against the corner by the railing, then slid to the floor.

She hesitated for a few seconds, then bent down next to him and checked to make sure he didn't have another weapon. She hurriedly rummaged through his pockets for anything else he might be carrying and found only a wallet. She took it, slipping it into her other coat pocket, and opened his coat to see how badly he was cut. Blood gushed out around the hilt of the knife. She must have hit an artery. She couldn't do anything for him but try to get as many questions answered as she could in the few seconds he had left. "Where were you going? Who's your connection? Are you two working alone or with anyone else?"

He groaned and jerked several times.

"Answer me."

His eyes went blank. She checked the pulse in his neck. He was dead.

If she summoned the conductor, it would be hours before she could get free. They might even detain her until they completed a full investigation. And there would be mountains of paperwork. Meanwhile Beverly would be able to do whatever she wanted because Polly wouldn't know where she was or what she was up to. And it was just a matter of time before Beverly found out what had happened and took off.

Her arm throbbed, but she didn't have time to even look at it.

The whistle blew again as the train picked up speed.

She had to get back to Akron.

The train was passing a field.

Polly made her decision. She grabbed her handcuffs, unlatched the guardrails, worked her way to the edge of the steps, and jumped.

CHAPTER NINETEEN

Kalena paced in her bedroom. It was long past midnight. Polly should have been home by now. She resisted the urge to call her at the plant but finally gave in and went downstairs. She made sure no one was on the line, then dialed the number Polly had given her. No answer. She hung up and dialed again. Still no answer. She slammed the receiver down and continued to pace.

A flash of light reflected against the curtains in the living room.

She ran to the window and peered out. Polly was walking toward the porch. Kalena swung open the door and waited for her.

Her coat was wet, she had a bruise near the corner of her eye, and her legs and shoes were filthy.

"What on earth happened to you?"

Kalena followed Polly as she passed her without answering and went up the steps. Polly shut her bedroom door after Kalena entered and waved her to the bathroom, turning on the light and closing them in.

Kalena gasped. "Polly, look at you."

"Help me take this off."

Kalena held her coat while Polly slipped her arms out. One sleeve of the overcoat and her jacket underneath were ripped and bloody. Once they were removed, Kalena saw a large gash about an inch long across Polly's forearm. "We've got to get you to the hospital. That wound needs stitches."

Polly shook her head. "It's too complicated to explain right now, but no hospital. I need your help." She turned on the faucet and held her arm under the running water, grimacing. The bright-red liquid splashed over the white porcelain bowl and flowed down the drain. She scrubbed around the wound, trying to remove the dried dirt mixed with blood.

"What do you want me to do?" Kalena asked.

"I need to wash my arm and dress it."

"Like I said, it needs stitches."

"No. I don't have time to file reports or answer any questions. It's a clean cut. I can put strips of tape on it. Do you have any?" Polly asked.

"Yes, in the first-aid kit under the sink, but you need more than tape. It's going to get infected if you don't put something on it." Kalena reached into the cabinet, brought out a cardboard box, and set it on the dressing table next to the sink. "Here. Let me do that. You're making a mess."

Blood continued to ooze as she washed Polly's arm with soap and water. The cut was deep but not into the muscle. "This'll hurt. Hold this hydrogen peroxide." She opened the bottle while Polly held it, then poured the contents over Polly's arm. Then she opened a small bottle of Mercurochrome and dabbed the cut.

Polly clenched her teeth. Her face contorted and she turned pale. She threw her head back and squeezed her arm.

Kalena fanned the wound with a towel. "You need to sit before you fall down." She walked Polly to the toilet and made her sit, then folded a towel and laid it on her lap, resting her arm on it. She gave her a piece of gauze. "Press this on the cut."

Polly did as instructed.

"I can't hold the tape and rip it at the same time with my bandage on."

"We're a pair, aren't we?" Polly said. "You hold the tape, and I'll cut it."

Kalena gave her the small scissors from the kit and secured the tape. Polly pulled on it, cut several strips, then stuck the ends to the bathtub.

"Now what?" Kalena asked.

"Cut the strips in half and then make one-inch sections. Pull the skin as tight as you can, then tape over the edges. I'll pinch the skin together while you tape it."

"The fine hair on your arm is going to catch on the tape. I'll have to shave the area."

Polly nodded.

After they dressed the wound, Kalena ran a bath for Polly and helped her remove her dirty clothes. Her upper body was covered in bruises, her legs pitted with scratches and small gouges.

"You're a mess. What kind of trouble did you get into?"

"Let me take a bath, and then we can talk. Can you make some coffee?"

"Of course. Will you be all right in here by yourself?"

"Yes. I can manage."

Kalena went downstairs, trying to be as quiet as possible so Aunt Berna wouldn't wake. An anxious dread swept over her. What had Polly done? Where had she been? How did she get hurt?

By the time the coffee was ready, Polly came into the kitchen, dressed in slacks and a loose-fitting blouse and carrying papers and a billfold.

Kalena poured a cup with cream for each of them and carried the drinks to the table.

They pulled out the chairs and sat.

Polly spread the documents across the surface, then gripped the cup with both hands and sipped, staring at the stove, like she was in the room by herself.

She finally looked at Kalena. "I followed Beverly tonight. She went to the Akron train station."

Kalena drew in a sharp breath. "Beverly Anderson?" Kalena had suspected it might be her, but hearing her name was still a shock. "Is Beverly the spy?"

"One of them."

Kalena was stunned. "There's more than *one*?"

"It's much more complicated than I originally suspected." Polly's voice quavered. "Beverly was reporting to Oliver, my supposed contact." Polly's voice lowered, and she rubbed her chin. Her focus drifted. "But who is Oliver reporting to?" Polly closed her eyes and leaned her head back, obviously thinking aloud. "How long were they working together? What happened to my actual contact? Did they get any other information from the plant?"

Kalena settled her hand over Polly's and caressed the back of it with her thumb, feeling her tremble. The muscles in Polly's face tightened. The trembling increased. She slipped away from Kalena's touch, distancing herself. She moved the wallet on the table, then touched the papers.

Kalena leaned back, drinking her coffee, waiting for Polly to talk about whatever had happened. She acted like she didn't want or need comfort, but Kalena knew she did. "Tell me."

Polly stiffened. "The train was moving. I didn't mean to do it. We were struggling with the knife, and it happened so fast." She lowered her gaze. "I killed him."

An icy chill swept through Kalena. Did she just say she'd *killed him*? Polly didn't say that. She'd heard her incorrectly. She wasn't capable of harming anyone. She was too caring, too tender. Her touch when they had made love flashed in her mind. She couldn't have killed anyone. "What did you say?" She set the cup down and stroked Polly's arm. "You killed someone?"

Polly drew in a deep breath. "Oliver, my supposed contact. But he turned out to be a spy."

Kalena rose from the chair and wrapped her in her arms.

Polly slid her arm around her waist and laid her head against her.

Kalena stroked her hair. "I'm sure you did what you were trained to do. I'm sure you had to do it."

Polly's trembling subsided, and Kalena could feel her begin to relax. She kissed her head, then brought the chair next to her and sat close, so they were touching. "What happened?"

"Beverly knows about me now. She must have known I was coming before I got here. They played it perfectly. I'm sure my contact is dead. They must have tortured him to get the information about me. I thought something was off about 'Oliver.' How could I have been so stupid?"

After Polly finished telling her, Kalena slipped her arm around her again. "Are you sure he was dead?"

Polly nodded. "Positive." She took a drink of her coffee, then pointed to the items on the table. "This was all he had on him." She looked at the dregs in the cup and set it aside. "I don't have much time. As soon as Beverly knows he's dead, she'll run. I have to get what I need from her before that happens."

"Which is what?"

"Information. Were there only two of them? Who's their contact?

What happened to my real one? How are they passing the documents? Did they get any other information, and if so, what? She checked her watch. “I need to call Washington and find out how they want me to proceed.” She began to review the papers in front of her, then stopped and looked up. “Beverly knew all along I was the agent. I know Oliver told her. Why didn’t she leave with him?” Polly massaged her temple, then rubbed her forehead.

Kalena drank the last of her coffee, watching as Polly worked through the questions. She was pale. “She hasn’t left because she doesn’t know her counterpart is dead, and she still has something critical to do.”

Polly nodded. “Exactly. Or she’s getting ready to do it.”

“When will you arrest her?”

“Not until after I give her a little time. I want to watch her, to see if she’ll reveal anything useful. Will she call anyone? Will she leave her apartment? Any information I can get from her will be extremely valuable and possibly stop this type of activity from happening in other areas of the country.”

“What will you do?”

“First of all I need to sneak into her apartment building and find out if she has a phone or if it’s out in the hallway. In those types of buildings it’s usually a community phone. Her apartment’s on the third floor. Then I need to watch, and if she leaves, I’ll need to follow her like before.”

Kalena couldn’t think about what Polly had done and what she planned to do. The idea of her on the train with a killer and a spy made her skin crawl. She’d actually jumped off a moving train. And then she’d walked back to the Akron station and driven home.

Kalena inspected Polly again. She’d paid the price to do her job.

Polly rubbed her brow and tapped the papers.

“What are those?” Kalena asked.

“The final plans for the modified Anaconda, a copy of the shipping-manifest destinations, and production numbers for next year.” She shuffled through the pages again. “Good God! It’s the Akron blimp’s estimated speeds and departure schedule.” She spoke it as if she were talking to the entire War Department. “That’s why she’s waiting—to confirm that the blimp takes off when it’s supposed to.”

"It used to be a big city event when the blimp left from the Akron dock. People came from miles around to see it, but now they keep it a secret. When does it depart?" Kalena asked.

Polly pursed her lips and ran her finger down the page. "At ten in the morning, the day after tomorrow. Do you realize that with this information, German U-boats can figure out when and where the blimp patrols the Pacific coastline? I have to call Washington. I have to give them an update and tell them I lost my weapon." She grazed her lip and frowned. "I'm sure that'll go over big. I'm glad I have a backup. I'll drive down to the phone booth by the theater. I can't chance anyone listening on your party line."

"I'll go with you."

"I can go by myself."

"Yes, I know you can. But I don't want you to be alone." Kalena reached into the cupboard for the bottle of aspirin, took out two, filled a glass with water, and offered them to Polly.

Polly gulped them down.

Kalena got dressed. They hid the documents under some loose boards in the floor of Kalena's closet, then drove to the phone booth.

She watched closely, not taking her eyes off Polly the entire fifteen minutes she was in the booth.

Polly came back to the car looking forlorn. She turned the heater up as high as it would go, holding her hands over the vent. "At least now they know that the man who said he was Oliver was a spy. They'll try to get word to Akron officials about the blimp and let them know what's going on. They still haven't found my real contact."

"Do you think he's dead?"

"Yes. I'm sure of it. There's nothing we can do about the blimp taking off. The schedule's set. And they can't send anyone to help me." She slowly shook her head. "It doesn't matter. They wouldn't get here in time anyway." She yawned. "I'm going to drop you off and go to Beverly's apartment."

"I want to go with you. Maybe I can help."

Polly glanced at her. "No. It's too dangerous."

"Watching an apartment is too dangerous?"

Polly laughed. "What if she runs?"

"I can help you."

Polly stifled another yawn.

"I can get you coffee and keep you company so you won't fall asleep."

"All right. I'm too tired to argue, but you're going to stay in the car."

Polly drove the six blocks to Beverly's building and parked down the street as before. She reached into the glove box and pulled out binoculars, then started scanning. "Her apartment is there, third floor."

All the lights were out.

"What if she's not home?" Kalena asked. "What if she's left already?"

Polly sighed. "That's what I'm worried about, but she has no reason to leave, not yet, not if she needs to confirm the blimp's actual departure time. And she doesn't have any way of knowing anything happened to Oliver, or whatever his name was. I need to verify she's in her apartment."

"Her apartment is a giant corner room with a Murphy bed," Kalena said. "I was in there a few months ago, when Perta, Juniper, and I stopped to get her on the way to the movie theater. She doesn't have a phone, but there's one at the end of the hallway on the east side, near the back stairs. A friend of mine used to live on the second floor before she moved to Akron."

Polly jerked the binoculars down and glared at her. "When were you going to share that information? Why didn't you tell me when I brought up the layout of the building and the phone situation earlier?"

"I wanted to, but you were in a hurry."

"Any windows on the sides?"

"Yes. Facing east. And there's a fire escape there too."

"Good. I'll have to use it to look inside." She took the binoculars and opened the car door. "It should take me only a few minutes. Keep your eyes on the front. Blow the horn if you need me."

Polly crossed the street, walked the half block to the east side of the building, then disappeared around the corner.

Kalena surveyed the street, then the apartment complex. No movement in or out. Two cars went by. A haggard-looking man in a torn, dingy overcoat staggered past on the sidewalk, occasionally misjudging his footing and slipping into the gutter.

She checked her watch. It'd been six minutes since Polly left.

Then ten.

Where was she? Why wasn't she back?

Then fourteen.

She held her stomach and rocked back and forth.

Polly finally appeared from around the side of the building and made her way to the vehicle.

Relief washed over Kalena. "It's about time," she muttered.

Polly hopped into the car and turned up the heater, holding her hands over the blast of warm air. "She's in there, sound asleep. I couldn't see the layout of the hallway and the phone from where I was. I'll have to go through the building and up the stairs to the third floor in order to find a place where I can watch. You sit tight."

Kalena gripped her coat sleeve. "No. I'll go with you."

Polly rolled her eyes. "Are you going to argue with me about everything?"

"I'll be quiet. It's after two in the morning, and she's asleep. She probably doesn't suspect anything's wrong. As far as she's concerned, her spy buddy is off delivering their stolen, ill-gotten gain to some goose-stepping bigot Nazi in Canada, who's going to take it to Germany."

Polly laughed.

Kalena pointed toward Beverly's apartment. "There's a storage closet by the front stairwell. If *we* can get into it, it's a perfect place to watch her apartment and the phone without being seen."

Polly glanced at her, like she was expecting her to say something more.

"What?"

"Anything else you want to share?"

Kalena laughed. "Beverly told us it's always locked because people try to steal the cleaning supplies stored in it. That's it."

Polly reached into the glove box again and pulled out a small leather bag.

"Are those your burglar tools? Are you going to pick the lock?" Kalena pointed.

Polly nodded. "You can go, but you have to do exactly what I say. Come on."

They climbed the stairs. Polly scouted the hallway.

Kalena whispered in her ear. "Down there's the phone, to the left of Beverly's apartment."

If Beverly did get up in the night and make a call, what would Polly do? Or what if she made a run for it? If Polly needed her help, would she be able to do it? Kalena's heart pounded. To protect Polly, she'd do whatever was necessary.

CHAPTER TWENTY

Polly massaged the back of her stiff neck, making the throbbing in her head worse. She'd been in the cramped space for more than three hours. Kalena had fallen asleep and almost slid off a box she was sitting on, so Polly had sent her to the car.

Every few minutes she maneuvered between buckets, mops, and cleaning supplies, trying to work out the spasms in her legs. The image of Oliver's lifeless eyes recurred over and over, like a needle stuck on a scratched record. When she searched the corridor, she saw him lying there. When she scanned the stairwell, he was slouched on the floor in the corner by the steps. She'd killed him.

Her empty stomach retched at the thought. Deep regret swelled in her chest, gagging and strangling her, until it was hard to breathe the bleach-scented air in the tiny space. She'd wanted a significant assignment, one where she could prove herself. How many other agents had been forced to kill in the line of duty? She wasn't the only one, of that she was certain. But saying it was just part of the job felt callous and wrong. Granted, he'd have killed her if she hadn't killed him first.

This wasn't over yet, and she knew what the expectations were. Did this mean she'd proved herself? That she had what it takes? *At any cost* was a much higher price to pay than she'd originally thought. She'd been naïve. She gently rubbed the bandage on her forearm, trying to distract herself as she peeked out through the slit in the doorway. She'd gone this far, and now she'd see it through. No matter the cost.

Beverly had planted just enough evidence in Kalena's closet to cast the right amount of suspicion on Kalena. But Polly had shattered that façade, and she'd hit the mother lode when she took the documents from Oliver. The sheer volume of information was unbelievable: forecast production numbers, plane designs, the layout of the plant, flight schedules and destinations, and the blimp schedules. Beverly must have been gathering it for months. And an extra bonus was the film negatives from all the pictures she'd taken. But Beverly could have made another set of copies to hold on to as insurance. How had she gotten the pictures developed? Did someone in town do it? Surely a local photographer would have looked at the photos and realized what they were. Did she have a safe house like Polly but with a darkroom so she could develop her own pictures? If she had another set of the information she had given Oliver, it was hidden somewhere.

If she had a safe house, she must have a key. Did she keep it on her person like Polly did, or did she hide it in her apartment? How near was the safe house? Beverly didn't have a car, and the next closest cities were Kenmore and Akron, with easy access by public transportation. If she did have a place to run to, it could be anywhere. If it existed, Polly needed to find it. It could contain more information just waiting to be handed over at some point.

It didn't matter now if Beverly made calls. Her only remaining options were to leave or have someone come to her. Polly had thought about it all night. Beverly knew Polly was an agent. She was going to play the cat-and-mouse game for only so long because she knew her time was running out. As soon as Beverly confirmed the departure time of the Akron blimp from its docking site, she would vanish.

Polly yawned. Darkness was retreating. The faint light of the opposing force stole through the window next to the phone. She risked being seen in the daylight. Whatever happened, she'd be able to observe from outside the building.

She checked the time. Eight minutes to six.

She slipped out of the closet, relocked it, and went to the car. The motor was running, and the driver's side window was partially open. Kalena was curled up in the front seat.

Polly rapped on the glass.

Kalena startled and looked out at her. She gathered her coat tightly around herself and unlocked the door. Her hair was mussed, and a tuft of soft curls lay strewn over a portion of her face. She blew on them and flipped them back.

Polly wanted to take her in her arms and hold her, but instead, she opened the door a few inches. “I’m going to the phone booth by the bank, just down the block there.” She pointed. “I need to call Washington. You stay here. I’ll be able to see if Beverly comes out.”

Kalena nodded without saying anything, adorably rubbing the sleep from her eyes.

Polly yawned, inhaling a deep breath of the chilled morning air. The muscles in her legs began to loosen as she walked. She stepped into the phone booth, closed the door, and dialed the operator, giving her the information she needed to complete the call. As soon as the connection was made, she turned toward the apartment building and was able to see the car and the entrance through the window of the booth.

Her stomach roiled when the agent-in-charge answered. It was Henson. She gave him an update.

“Sounds like you’ve made a mess of it. I see from the notes that you lost your gun. How do you plan to find it?”

She squeezed the receiver. The chill of the metal permeated her leather glove and into her palm. If she could just reach through the phone line and knock him in the head, she’d feel a whole lot better. “The gun is the least of my concerns. I’m on my own here, Henson. I’m doing the best I can. I have a backup weapon. It’s certainly not pretty, but I think it’s going to be over soon, and any information we can get from Beverly will help us. As I said, I was able to recover the documents she passed on to her contact, so those won’t fall into enemy hands. We also know what Beverly is waiting for and why. I intend to look for the gun as soon as I can, unless you’d like to call the local police and let them find it.” She hoped he’d get the hint and follow up on it.

“Well, I’m sure they have better things to do than search for a weapon you carelessly lost.”

“Maybe, but I’m sure they’d be concerned about a loaded gun lying near a railroad track in their district. Don’t you think?”

She heard him sigh, loudly.

“Where do you think it’s located?”

She gave him as much detail as she could remember.

“I’ll contact the area police or sheriff’s office and have them send it to the agency…if they can find it. You need to be more careful in the future. This is going in your report.”

She ignored his disdain and disrespect, restraining her inclination to tell him what he could do with the report. The officers would locate the weapon if they searched hard enough. Besides, responding in the negative wouldn't get her what she needed. And it wouldn't change his attitude or his treatment of her. But someday! Right now, she needed an update on what the agency had done since last night. How would he react? She knew him well enough to be certain he wouldn't take orders from her. She had to be careful how she approached the subject. "Was the agency able to keep the news of the body on the train out of the Cleveland and Akron papers this morning?"

"Don't you read the papers? If it's not in there, then we did our job. According to the notes, they took care of it right after your last call. I'll have someone follow up. What else?"

Her face tightened. "I think Beverly's waiting to confirm the departure of the Akron blimp, and if she finds out her partner is dead, she'll make a run for it. I need—"

"Do you understand the implications if she passes on the information about the blimp's schedule, how important it is?" His voice was rough, condescending.

His final comment pushed Polly over the cliff. She seethed. She'd followed Beverly to the train station, had to fight for her life, killed Beverly's partner, retrieved the stolen information, and been up all night watching Beverly's apartment. Yes. She knew how important the damned situation was. Exhausted and on the edge, she lost control. "Look, you self-right—"

She stopped, covering the receiver with her gloved palm, holding on, squeezing. She stared at the iced window in the booth, her breath now beginning to fog her view. He wasn't worth the effort. Her blowing up at him would only feed his ego and his distorted sense of self-importance. He was a bitter, small-minded man, and in the scheme of things he mattered about as much as a rat in the hold of a ship. She had to get back to the car and do her job. She slowly lifted the receiver to her ear. "I need twenty-four hours. I understand perfectly well what could happen. Beverly thinks she's already passed the information to her contact before he boarded the train, but I'm sure she's supposed to confirm the blimp takeoff with someone. And that's my advantage right now. It's bought me some time, and I intend to use it."

"You should get wiretaps on any phones."

"It's probably not needed. There's a common phone in the apartment building, but I don't think she'll use it, at least not for any significant calls. She's not that stupid or careless. And tapping the area phone booths isn't worth it now. She'll be running soon."

"Call back this evening."

"I'll do the best I can, but I can't promise anything."

Polly hung up, then dropped the money in the coin slot and dialed Celia. "I'm tracking Beverly Anderson. It's confirmed. She's our spy."

"Are you sure? I know you've been watching her and you suspected her. She hasn't varied her routine here at work one iota, except for leaving work because of illness."

"Positive. I need someone to keep an eye on her when she goes to work this afternoon, assuming she comes in at all, but I imagine she won't vary her routine or call attention to herself until she finishes what she needs to do. Make sure she doesn't make any calls. Watch her every move. She may make a last-ditch effort to get more information. She can't leave the building. If she attempts to, keep her there and call me at home immediately. It's critical that Beverly not suspect we know anything. She has something she needs to do, and it will be a while yet. I want to give her enough room so I can find out more information. I'll be there about eight this evening, and then we can talk. Also, Kalena will be helping me all day."

She stopped at the diner for doughnuts and two cups of coffee with cream, then went to the car. She sipped from the paper cup, watching the building and Beverly's front window. People using the back door had to either go through the alley or climb over the wooden fence.

"Anyone come from around the back yet?" she asked.

"Nope." Kalena squirmed and drank her coffee as she nibbled a doughnut. "I haven't seen a single person." She yawned. "Is this all we get to do? Sit here in the car all day until she goes to work? My butt's numb, and my back's getting stiff."

Polly smiled. "Yep. Unless she leaves for some reason. Then we'll follow her."

Hours went by with no sign of Beverly, other than the light that came on illuminating her front window in the dark, overcast morning. Polly checked her watch. Eleven a.m. People left the complex, but not Beverly. The building door swung open again. Two women and a man came out. Still no Beverly.

Kalena and Polly took turns going to the diner for a potty break and more food.

Thirty-five minutes later a car slowed, pulled in front of the building, and stopped. Polly recognized Loraine and turned the car on.

"Where are we going?" Kalena asked.

Polly lifted her chin toward the building. "Recognize that woman in the car?"

Kalena squinted. "Not really."

"It's Loraine, from the dance. She's waiting for Beverly."

A few minutes later Beverly came out and got into the car. They drove to the corner and turned left on Tuscarawas. Polly followed. Twenty-five minutes later they parked in the lot of Macy's department store in downtown Akron.

"They're going in. Stay here and watch their vehicle. I'll be back as soon as they're done."

Kalena grabbed the door handle. "Can't I come with you?"

"No. Two of us make a bigger target. I don't know how long I'll be gone, but if Beverly is going to work, she has to be there by four."

"That's four hours."

"That's surveillance. Remember, you wanted to do this. We'll get a break when she goes to work. *If* she goes to work."

"I really want to go with you."

"Sorry." Polly got out when Beverly and Loraine entered the store. She turned back, holding onto the car door. "Two people can be seen a lot easier than one. Stay here, be careful, and don't get out of the car."

She followed them, pulling a soft, plain scarf over her hair and making sure to stay a good distance behind them. They went to the cosmetic counter and then to the purse section, where Loraine bought a soft tan leather clutch with a zipper on the side. Nice. They went to the shoe department, only looking, and then to the fountain and got a Coke. Beverly looked relaxed and focused on Loraine. If she was concerned about anything, she didn't show it. She was too calm, even. How long had she been a spy that she could be so unaffected? They visited at the counter for about fifteen minutes, then left and went back toward the parking lot.

They walked up to Loraine's vehicle, and damned if they didn't wave to Kalena, who was outside Polly's car, leaning against the passenger door. "Shit!"

They approached Kalena, talked a few minutes, then returned to their vehicle and drove south on Main Street. Polly waited as long as she could to avoid being seen before she went to her car, but by then Loraine had blended in with all the other black automobiles, and Polly lost her in traffic.

She got into her car and glared at Kalena. "What did I tell you?"

"I'm sorry. I got a leg cramp and had to stand up. I'd been out there only a few seconds when they saw me."

"What did they say? What did you tell them?"

"They said hello, asked me what I was doing here, asked about my hand, then said good-bye."

"What did you say?"

"I told them I took the day off and was here with a friend who went into the store to get some makeup and would be right back."

"Did they ask who it was?"

"Who what was?"

"Your friend, of course."

"No, they didn't. You're mad, aren't you?"

Polly started the car and turned out of the parking lot in the same direction Loraine had gone. "I lost them in traffic." She checked her watch, disgusted with herself more than Kalena. She never should have brought her along. More evidence that she'd lost her focus. "Beverly still has almost three hours before she leaves for work, and I have no idea where they went."

"I do! They're going to Swenson's on South Hawkins for a cheeseburger and a drink before Loraine drops her off at her apartment." Kalena smiled. "You shouldn't be so grouchy. It's not good for your complexion. That beautiful face is going to get wrinkles much too soon."

Polly laughed out loud, her tension easing a fraction. "Kalena, I swear, you're going to be the death of me."

Kalena frowned. "Don't say that. Please don't ever say that again."

Polly took her hand and squeezed it. "I didn't mean it that way. I'm sorry."

"Can we go to Swenson's and get a hamburger too?"

Polly glanced at her, wondering what she thought staying out of sight actually meant. "No. We might be seen. We'll park far enough away so we can watch them eat."

"How fun."

Polly didn't reply. Kalena was correct. It really wasn't fun watching them laugh and eat while their own stomachs rumbled from a lack of any real food, and they ached for sleep.

When Beverly returned to her apartment, Polly called Washington. Henson told her the newspaper would hold the story about the body on the train.

"They weren't happy about it, but I did it. But they'll delay for only twenty-four hours." He announced the guarantee like he'd personally arranged it.

She knew perfectly well all he had to do was make one call to check if a staff member had taken care of it.

"What about the documents?" he asked.

"They're in a safe place. I'll have a courier take them to Washington as soon as possible, or I'll bring them myself."

"Proceed with caution. We still have no agents available. As for now, continue surveillance, use local resources if you have to, and prevent her escape." He said nothing more, and she was glad to end the call.

Beverly left for work on schedule.

Polly stayed well behind the bus, then watched as Beverly followed the other employees into the main gate of the plant. "She's a monster. Look at her. Last night she believed she passed critical information that could get hundreds, if not thousands of Americans killed. Now she acts like it's nothing."

"You danced with her." Kalena grinned.

"Don't remind me." When Beverly walked through the entrance and Polly couldn't see her any longer, she yawned and stretched. "I have five hours before I come back here. Celia is making sure she's being watched closely." She looked at Kalena.

Kalena smiled. "I'm starving. We could get a hamburger at Swenson's and then go to the safe house."

"My God, woman. You're going to wear me out."

Kalena stroked Polly's arm. "I promise I'll let you sleep for a couple of hours."

"I don't want to pass that up, but I have to be at your house or at the plant. Celia will call me if there's a problem." Polly turned the car around and headed for Swenson's.

After the short time it took to get from Swenson's to Kalena's, Polly could barely climb the stairs to her bedroom. When her head hit the pillow, she knew she'd sleep for a thousand years.

The room was dark and cold when she woke. She bunched the covers tighter around her neck. How long had she been asleep? Why hadn't the alarm gone off? She saw movement out of the corner of her eye and startled, reaching for the gun on the nightstand, recoiling in pain.

"Don't worry. It's just me," Kalena said as she got into bed beside her. "I was getting ready to wake you."

"What time is it?"

"Six forty-five. You have enough time to get ready and be at the plant by eight."

Polly shot up out of the bed as a realization struck her. "Oh, God, I've made a mistake."

"What?"

"If Beverly left work early, Celia couldn't have let me know. We have to get back to the house right now."

Kalena laughed. "Polly, you're home. We didn't go to the safe house. Remember?"

Polly sighed in relief and sat back on the bed, positioning the pillow behind her, her heart slowing. She ran her fingers through her hair. "Sorry. I was so tired when I went to be bed, I'm a little disoriented."

Kalena lay down beside her.

Polly looked at her. "You look good in my bed." She maneuvered beside her and kissed her.

Kalena returned her kiss, open and willing.

Wanton heat surged through Polly. "Who's in the house?"

Kalena kissed her neck, then brushed against her nipples, already hard with the anticipation of her touch. "Aunt Berna and Richard are down in the living room listening to the radio. We can be very quiet," she whispered. She slipped Polly's gown up and took a breast into her mouth, sucking, and moaning softly.

Polly arched and flexed. "We can't be quiet. You're already moaning."

"I can be quiet."

"The floorboards creak every time I walk on them. They'll hear the bed."

"Celia called," Kalena said softly. "She left a message. She said not to worry. Two guards and the shift supervisor were watching Beverly, and she said she'd see you around eight. We have time." She slid her palm against Polly's other aching nipple, rubbing softly. "Please, can we be together? I want to be with you." She sucked with more determination.

Polly's heart pounded, blood surged and pulsed between her legs, and when she kissed Kalena all she wanted was to engulf her in a thrill of orgasm. In almost one motion, she slipped her gown off and slid Kalena's dress over her head and her underwear down her legs. She pulled them the rest of the way off and tossed them. She rolled over onto Kalena and gazed into her eyes, now bright with desire. Kalena undid her bra. Polly licked her stomach, then moved up, kissing her breasts and then her lips. She spread Kalena's thighs and slid her fingers into her hot, wet center, caressing, thrusting.

Kalena gasped, then moaned loudly.

Polly maneuvered for a better position and whispered in her ear, "We have to be quiet."

Kalena pulled her closer. "I'm trying." Her hips thrust.

The bed rocked gently.

This wasn't going to work. Polly stopped.

Kalena reached for her. "What's wrong? Don't stop. Please don't stop." Her face was flushed, lips full and swollen, and her eyes glazed.

"We can't. They're going to hear us."

Kalena pulled her to her, her racing heart beating against Polly's erect nipples. "I don't care."

Polly licked her lips, lusting to be inside her, taste her. "Maybe not this second, but you will later. Come with me." She led her to the bathroom, closing both the doors and leaving the light off. She stepped into the tub and guided Kalena in next to her. Kalena grabbed towels and spread them over the cold porcelain.

They lowered themselves, writhing, caressing, opening to each other, moving to wanton need and desire. Polly reached up and covered Kalena's mouth to stifle the sounds of her moans and gasps as she climaxed. When it was over, Kalena pulled Polly up to her and held her against her, still breathless. "The other night was wonderful, but this. My, God, what I've been missing." She showered Polly with kisses.

Polly held a laugh and got up on her knees. "I want so much more, but I need to take a bath, dress, and drive to the plant. You have to leave."

Kalena shook her head. "I want to watch you." She gathered the towels from the tub and started Polly's bath.

When Polly stepped into the hot water, so did Kalena. "You can't." Polly protested in a hushed voice.

Kalena held her finger to Polly's lips. "I want to bathe you."

Polly's nipples hardened, and a jolt of heat shot through her. "I'll never get out of this tub." She sank into Kalena's caresses and climaxed again.

Polly ran more hot water and lay in the tub after Kalena left. She'd completely lost her focus. She wasn't paying enough attention to her job. She'd let herself get distracted. She shouldn't have been with Kalena. The second Kalena was on her bed, she'd lost all sense of reason. Did she do it because deep inside she knew Beverly wouldn't leave the plant? But she could have. She could have fled while Polly was making love to Kalena. And Kalena was making love to her…with her hands and her mouth…and…

Snap out of it, she told herself. She was supposed to be at the plant at eight, and it was already a quarter till. She mentally beat herself up as she dressed. This behavior was unprofessional and unacceptable, no matter how good it felt. But she couldn't find the strength to stop it, either.

Kalena came back into her room and gathered her clothes, appearing thoughtful. "I understand now what happens to you when we're together. The same thing happens to me. You fill me so full I don't have room for anything else. I promise I won't distract you anymore. I'll wait until all this is over. I'm sorry."

Polly kissed her. "Thank you. Now get out of here. I have to get ready, and I'm not sure when I'll be back. I need to know you're here, safe."

Kalena held her face for a moment, then left.

Polly slipped the heavy coat on that Kalena had loaned her and said good-bye to Richard and Aunt Berna, who sat in the living room, their eyes fixed on her.

"You're leaving this late?" Aunt Berna asked.

"I have to go back to the plant."

Aunt Berna looked at Kalena. "She's going to wear herself out."

"Don't I know it," Kalena said, locking eyes with Polly with a sly smile.

Polly drove fast. Had she jeopardized the case by being with Kalena? Her career? Lives? How could she be so irresponsible?

CHAPTER TWENTY-ONE

Polly called Washington to check in. Henson had gone off duty, so she reviewed the day with the agent-in-charge, who was far more professional and easier to discuss things with. He'd reported from his notes that Henson had ordered a wiretap on the phone near Beverly's apartment but hadn't had any information yet. Beverly wasn't home, and Polly had already told Henson it wasn't necessary. He was grabbing at straws to feed his ego and make it look like he had some hand in what she'd accomplished on her own.

She sat with Celia in the shift supervisor's office. When Polly had scanned the *Akron Beacon Journal*, she hadn't seen any information about a dead man on the express train to Cleveland.

"I can't believe it," Celia said. "As careful as we've been, and this happened. Do you think she took anything else? Nothing's missing as far as we know. Only papers moved, things not put back as they were. Little things, but enough to suspect."

"Nothing's missing because she used a camera. That was the light people saw at night. I'm not at liberty right now to reveal what is in the documents we have, but I do know she didn't pass them on, at least the ones I have. I doubt she passed others because of the volume I have. It was probably too risky, and she might have wanted to do it all at once."

"Thank God." Celia leaned back in her chair.

Polly tapped the newspaper. "And there won't be any more if I can help it. Right now, she's biding her time until she can confirm something. But she'll take off as soon as she figures out her partner is missing, or she can't get in touch with him. Either way, my time is running out."

"What do you want to do?"

"I can't let her out of my sight. I'll have to follow her to see what she does. I need some help, though. I'm sorry to ask, but Cleveland FBI can't send any of their agents," Polly said.

"Who do you want?"

"Can you spare Dan Abernathy, the night security guard?"

"Certainly. He's off tonight, but I'll call him. I'm sure he'd be willing to help," Celia said.

Dan was at the plant by ten p.m. Polly got him a cup of coffee and filled him in on the details of the situation.

"I knew there was more to you. Imagine that? A woman federal agent." He leaned back in the chair and drank his black coffee. "Do you think Beverly killed Gerald?"

"Yes. I do. I don't believe he was involved with her in any way, so I imagine he caught her doing something. And she won't hesitate to kill again, so watch yourself."

"Why don't we just arrest her right now?" Dan asked.

"We don't have any evidence for the police to book her on the murder charge, and I need to see what she does. She might lead us to other contacts, expose more of her network. She has a safe house somewhere, and I'd like to find it. More documents or other information may be stored there."

Dan cracked his neck and took a deep breath. "Well, if she's as smart as you say she is, and if she's getting ready to leave, then she's probably cleaned it out already. To be honest, you better forget the safe house. You're right. She's going to vanish the moment that blimp takes off."

Dan was right. It was disheartening that she wouldn't be able to find the safe house, but she wasn't going to get everything she wanted in this case. Was her pride getting in the way of doing her job? Were her expectations too high? She would enjoy going back to Washington and shoving this case in front of Henson all wrapped up in a neat bow. But the real job, her only job, was to stop a spy, which she'd technically already done. The only thing left was to take her into custody. She could go to the assembly line right now and arrest her. Handcuff her and march her out of the building. But she had an opportunity to find out more and perhaps save lives, and it was worth the risk. "Do you drive?" she asked.

"No," Dan said. "Never had any cause for it. Buses and the trolley run just fine. 'Course, I've always worked night shift, so I don't need to go out late at night."

"This is what will probably happen," Polly said. "She's going to work her shift, then try to call her contact. The icing on her cake is to verify to someone the blimp takes off on schedule. But if things fall apart, she won't hesitate to run. When she doesn't get an answer from her contact, she'll either make more calls or leave. The Cleveland FBI wiretapped the phones near her apartment and will listen in and record calls. But that won't help us. They're short on manpower and don't have any agents to send us. If she takes off, we're on our own. We can't lose her."

"Does she have an automobile?" Dan asked.

"No. But her friend Loraine has one, though I don't think she'll call her. She'll most likely take the trolley or bus to the Akron train station and go from there."

"Do you know where she might go?"

"I have no idea. Her contact was heading to Cleveland, but she could go anywhere."

Dan rubbed his chin. "Well, we need to be ready to split up if we have to." He scanned the train schedule in the local paper. "Plenty of trains are going out of Akron tonight and early morning. Cleveland, Pittsburg, Columbus."

"Dan, I can't tell you how important it is that she doesn't get away."

He nodded and laid the paper on the desk. He brought out his gun from the shoulder holster under his arm and checked the load. "I get it."

❖

Polly shifted gears and moved closer to the bus after it left the plant. Beverly wouldn't be able to recognize the car no matter where she was sitting. It blended in too well with the rest of the end-of-shift traffic.

"So, I take the alleyway, and you watch the front of the apartment building?" Dan asked.

"Yes. If she bolts, you'll hear the car start."

Polly parked a block from the complex.

The cold air swept in when Dan opened the passenger door. "Hell of a night for a stakeout." He slipped on his cowhide gloves.

Polly glanced at them. "Those look nice and warm."

"My sister made 'em for me. She and her husband have a dairy farm over in Springfield."

"You going to be all right out there?"

"Sure. The buildings will block the wind." He surveyed the area. "I'll position at the far side of the alley. If she comes out the back entrance, she could jump the fence. That would take her down the embankment, and she'd have good cover by the viaduct and slip away. It's only two blocks to the trolley." He checked his watch. "It's 11:22. The trolley runs all night now because of the nightshift workers at the factories. She could easily get there. We need at least two more people. Are you sure those FBI guys can't help?"

Polly shook her head. "No. They don't have any agents to send. I'm lucky they're listening in on the phones."

"You know tapping those phones inside the building is a waste of time. She's not going to use them."

"I know. But the people in charge don't always listen, do they?"

Dan sighed, then grinned. "Ain't that the truth? Well, we'll just have to do this short-handed."

"You can't stay out there all night. And you can't go into the entranceway of the building when you need to get warm because, if she comes down there, she'll recognize you. Come to the car when you can't stand it anymore, and we'll switch places."

Dan nodded and crossed the street. Polly watched him until he disappeared halfway down the alley, near the dumpster. The windshield began to fog. She slid over and wiped the window with the sleeve of her coat, trying to get rid of the condensation.

Two men walked in front of the apartment, then crossed the next block going east. A police car passed, slowing as it came even with them. They walked to it. Polly could see their breath in the cold air as they talked with the patrolman. Their stance was relaxed, casual. Nothing important. After a few minutes, the car continued down the street, then turned left.

An hour later she stretched, feeling the pull of her sore muscles. The cut on her arm ached from the pressure of her heavy coat, and her bruised jaw spasmed in the dank chill of the night air. She tried to wipe the condensation with her sleeve again but only smeared the window. She looked out to see Dan running toward her.

He grabbed the door, jerked it open, and jumped into the car, huffing and out of breath. "She made a run for it. I couldn't get over the fence." He sucked in a breath. "She went down the embankment and headed for the viaduct like I was afraid she would. Go."

Polly started the car and drove east.

"Turn right at the next street and park at the end. Keep the lights on. Hopefully we can spot her." Dan leaned forward, as though trying to spur the car to go faster.

Polly grabbed the flashlight before they jumped out of the car, and they ran toward the embankment. A train whistle sounded, one long, then a short blast. Her heart raced. She tried to control her breathing as she scanned the underpass full of dark, shadowy crevices. "Fan out," she told Dan softly. Had she made a catastrophic mistake by not arresting Beverly at the plant? What if she got away?

They separated. She took the lower side, and Dan went up the embankment. She crossed under the viaduct, the smell of sewage and grease and earth permeating the frigid air, almost gagging her. She positioned her scarf over her mouth and continued southeast. She halted when a shadow moved on the other side of a cement pylon. She inched closer, her gun aimed forward. The shadow moved again, but it was only a scrap of old canvas sheeting wedged under a rotted log, flapping in the wind. She switched the flashlight off. There were too many hiding places, and the beam only gave her position away.

They couldn't spend this much time here looking for Beverly. She wouldn't go back to the apartment. She wouldn't go toward town. She was heading for Akron. It was the only way she could get out safely.

A crack split the air and echoed around her, and then a piece of cement flew off the pillar beside her, just above her head. Another sound, like a dart hitting a cork board, and then another piece of cement splayed by her shoulder. Someone was shooting at her but must be using a suppressor. She quickly crouched and searched for Dan, spotting him on the other side of the viaduct. She got his attention and pointed in front of her. He worked his way forward, using the cement pylons for cover, and was panting by the time he reached her.

"Shots came from over there," Polly said, pointing. "We can't shoot back. I don't know what's on the other side of the viaduct."

“Three sets of tracks. There’s a couple of side cars and a lot of fencing. South, there’s open space,” Dan said. “About a quarter of the way across the bridge, you should be able to get a clear view of the other side down below.”

“She’s got us pinned down. She could take off and we’d never know it. And if she’s still there and we stick our heads out…” Polly stopped talking and listened, not hearing anything but the rumbling of a train almost at a crawl. “I’ll get to the car and drive up onto the viaduct.” She leaned against the cold concrete. “If she slipped through, she’s on her way to the train station. We can’t allow her to get on a train. You stay here. If I don’t see her, I’ll blow my horn three times and then head for the Akron train station. Once you recheck to make sure she’s not in the area, walk to the police station and hitch a ride to Akron station. I’ll meet you there.”

Dan nodded.

“Get there as soon as you can. I don’t know when the trains run, but I’m sure she does. She left when she did for a reason.”

Polly’s heart pounded. The uncertainty of what she’d done swept over her. But she didn’t have time to regret something she couldn’t change. She’d made her choice, and wherever it led now, she’d follow it through to the end. She’d given Beverly too much time, and she’d underestimated her. Whatever happened now, she couldn’t let Beverly get away, no matter what she had to do.

CHAPTER TWENTY-TWO

Polly jumped into the car and drove to the viaduct. When she got about a third of the way over, she parked and dashed to the far side. Dan was correct. She had a clear view of the surrounding area. But no Beverly. She scanned closely, trying not to miss any movement, peering at every shadow. When she was sure, she got back into the car and blew the horn three times, then crossed the viaduct, turned around, and headed for Akron. As she passed the statue of Chief Hopocan on Wooster Road, movement in the rearview mirror caught her eye. Beverly suddenly rose in the backseat with a gun pointed at Polly's head. Polly yanked the steering wheel hard.

Beverly's head struck the right-side window as she was thrown off balance.

Polly heard the *whoosh* of the suppressor as the gun went off, hitting the metal frame, about six inches from her head.

Beverly repositioned to the middle of the seat. "Are you trying to kill both of us? Get the car under control and keep driving."

Polly's first thought was to slam on the brakes, but if she did, the gun could go off again, and this time it might hit her. What if she jerked the car hard to the left? It'd cause Beverly to lose her balance, but she still could be shot. Beverly wouldn't fall for such a move again. She couldn't reach behind her to get her gun holstered at her back without Beverly seeing it. She could only bide her time and hope for an opportunity to disarm or distract her.

Beverly leaned forward and pressed the barrel against Polly's head. "Turn right at the next street."

Polly turned east on State, past the chicken restaurant. After a few miles, the homes or farms became sparse on each side of the road. She passed Manchester as she drove farther into the remote country. She could be dead in the car for days before anyone found her. She glanced in the rearview mirror. Beverly was staring back.

"I'm not a killer by nature," Beverly said. "Gerald caught me going through Lionel's desk when he came looking for me in the offices to get some cleaning supplies for a spill. He wanted an explanation. I tried to give him one, but he didn't buy it, and when he threatened to go to the security guard, I didn't have a choice. It was messy. I don't like a mess."

"How long?" Polly wanted to ask as many questions as she could. Get her distracted, give herself time.

Beverly raised one eyebrow and shrugged. "A year."

"Are you working with someone or alone?"

Beverly nodded. "Ah, that's the question, isn't it? I never in a million years thought they'd send a woman after me. I have to say it threw me. I knew something was up when all the rumors started at the plant. Those women love to talk. Then we were able to get your contact. He didn't tell us willingly. Hans had to convince him." She smiled. "But he talked."

Polly wanted to reach back and strangle her. "Where is he?"

"Probably in the morgue. They found him right away but couldn't identify the body, and you missed it when you went looking for someone who looked like Hans. When I saw you that first night working late, I knew you were going to be trouble. Thanks for the dance, by the way."

Polly was sick to her stomach.

"Turn left at the next street." Beverly's eyes darted, then narrowed. Her face grew taut. She drew the gun back slightly.

"Where are we going?" Polly asked.

"You'll know soon enough."

Polly made a left. Now they were headed north on South Main Street. To Akron after all? Polly knew the train station was on South Main. Beverly was catching a train, as Polly'd suspected. She must not know how to drive. That's why she needed her. She was probably going to kill her in the parking lot. It made sense.

She needed to keep her talking. Distract her. Put her at ease. "Do you like America?"

Beverly laughed. "I love America. I'm going to come live here someday after the war. Only it won't be in a shithole like Ohio."

When they crested the hill, Polly could see the lights of the train station off in the distance.

Beverly looked out the window, studying the surrounding landscape. She also must have known they were getting close.

The lights became brighter, then disappeared as they started down the hill.

"What part of Germany are you from?" Polly asked.

Beverly smirked. "Don't ask any more questions."

They drove in silence. Polly could see the train station now. It was busy, which might give her more time.

"Your partner Hans was killed on the train." Polly reverted to her training. She knew how to handle difficult people. She was damn good at it. *Focus*.

Beverly shifted and sat straighter, rolling her shoulders. "I don't believe it. And if he was, that's none of your business."

She'd hit a nerve. It was time to gouge into it.

"Did you know he was stabbed in the gut? It must have been a painful death." She was almost to the parking lot. It was now or never. "I'm the one who killed him." She slammed on the brakes and turned the wheel sharply. Beverly whipped to the left, smashing her head into the door glass. The gun went off. The bullet ripped a hole in the upholstered cloth on the roof. The car tipped, then landed upright, not what Polly was hoping for. She reached back as fast as she could and grabbed at Beverly's gun, now pointed toward the side window. They wrestled for it. Blood was dripping down the side of Beverly's head onto her shoulder.

Polly punched her in the face and, with her other hand, yanked on the gun, twisting Beverly's fingers.

Beverly screeched and released her grip.

Polly snatched the gun from her.

In one motion, Beverly lunged over the back of the driver's seat, slamming Polly's head into the dashboard. The gun dropped. Everything went dark, and sound was distorted for a few seconds. She vaguely saw Beverly open the driver's side door and stumble from the car.

When Polly shook off her stupor, the deep pain in her head shot into her neck. She rolled and pulled herself up with the steering wheel, shoving the seat back into position. More pain radiated down her spine. She had to get out. She had to go after her. She scooted forward and inched out of the car until she touched the cindered parking lot. Hot, deep pain gnarled its way from her shoulders to her head. She took one unbalanced step and then another. She could see Beverly running toward the terminal. She must already have a ticket. Polly began to run too, losing sight of Beverly as she entered the building.

The posted signs just inside the station informed the passengers of two trains in the terminal, one going north to Cleveland via four stops, and then on to New York Central. The other was heading to Baltimore, then to Washington DC.

Hans had been on the Cleveland train. Would Beverly be going to Cleveland and points east, or would she be going toward Washington? Polly touched her temples. Her head was pounding, and she couldn't think clearly. Which train? Maybe she didn't get on a train. Maybe she was hiding in the station, waiting for Polly to decide which one to take. Did she circle back and take Polly's car? She'd left the keys in it. But she didn't drive. Did she?

"All aboard," yelled the conductor, positioned next to the Cleveland-bound train. She looked at him, then at the southbound train, then back to the station. She had to decide. It would make sense to go to Cleveland, on to Buffalo, then cross the border into Canada. It was the quickest and easiest way to escape. *Think. Think like them.*

"Final call. All aboard."

She stepped onto the platform of the Cleveland-bound train. But Beverly was smart. She wouldn't do the obvious thing. She could take the southbound train and transfer at any of at least three major cities before Washington.

Polly cringed when a spasm of sharp pain streaked up her back. She turned and darted to the other platform. The Cleveland train rumbled slowly out of the station. She checked the schedule. The southbound departed in ten minutes. She made her way to the row of three phone booths by the ticket counter, entering the one on the right. She sat gingerly on the wooden stool, leaning back against the booth for support. She closed the door and picked up the receiver, watching the southbound train as she gave the operator her emergency code.

She gave an update to the OAD agent-in-charge, telling him what she intended to do. Polly learned that the closest agent was in Columbus and received his description and identification phrase.

She'd made her decision and couldn't turn back. Was Beverly already on the train?

She had a good view of passengers approaching the platform. She opened the door and sat straight, ready to leap forward if she saw her prey. Had she made the right decision? She tried to work her way through the fog in her head.

When she heard the last call to board, she left the phone booth, scouted the station one last time, then hurried to the train. It had six passenger cars. She gripped the metal rail of the last car and pulled herself up each step. Beverly could be anywhere. She wanted to sit, relieve her back and head, but she had to search each section. She had to find her. And when she did, what would happen? What if she wasn't on the train at all but hiding in the terminal? No. Polly had checked it. She had to be here.

Polly inched through the end car, looking at each female passenger. Beverly was not in it.

The train jerked forward and began to move out of the station. She entered the next section. It was about half full, mostly males. She walked slowly, gripping each seat back as she moved forward. She stopped and looked through the glass to the enclave. No movement. No one hiding in the shadows. She entered and made her way through to number three. She continued her search and reached the fifth car, where she peered through the glass, scanning the shadows. There was a dark area in the far corner, but she saw no movement of any kind. She opened the door slowly, then moved to the entrance of the last section.

She started to open the door, but immediately someone's arm was around her neck, pulling her backward to the right, the sharp point of a knife in her left side.

Beverly's breath was heavy, labored in Polly's ear. She must have climbed the steps on the outside of the car, then crept back in.

"Since you don't seem to know when to quit, you're getting off the train," Beverly growled.

She forced Polly backward, toward the railing. White-hot pain shot through Polly's spine.

The train was chugging faster now, passing forests and fields, now fifteen minutes out of the Akron station.

Polly gripped Beverly's hand and pushed the knife away from her side. She grasped Beverly's fingers from around her neck and bent them back.

Beverly screamed and tried to knock Polly's legs out from under her.

Polly twisted and turned, breaking free of Beverly's grasp, and shoved her full force into the railing. She reached behind her back to draw her gun.

Beverly shoved her against the metal wall. She opened the safety railing and glanced out and then back at Polly. And before Polly could get her gun out of her holster, Beverly jumped.

Polly was stunned. If she didn't go after her, she wouldn't know if Beverly lived or died in the fall. If she did jump after her, she could be killed, or injured worse than she was now, and Beverly would still get away. Whatever her decision, she had to make it now, or it'd be too late.

Chapter Twenty-three

Kalena raced out of the house with her coat half on, taking the steps two at a time, the headlights from Lionel's car momentarily blinding her. She jumped into the passenger seat. The tires screeched as he jammed the gearshift into reverse and backed out of the driveway.

"Dan will meet us outside the police station," Kalena said.

Lionel whipped through the streets.

A sharp pain radiated through her hand as she gripped the door handle, bracing herself to keep her balance.

He skidded to a stop in front of the police station, missing the curb by inches. He glanced over at Kalena. "What if we get to the train station and Polly's not there?"

"I don't know."

"What if her car is there but we can't find her?"

"I don't know."

"What if—"

"Lionel, stop. All I know is Dan said he thinks Polly's in trouble, and the police and FBI won't or can't help. We can't leave her on her own."

Lionel looked at his wristwatch. "We've barely got enough time before the Cleveland train leaves. But there are others. Which one will she take?"

"I don't know. We'll have to figure it out. We can make it if you hurry," Kalena said.

"No way are we going to make it on time."

Dan opened the back door and slid in. Lionel took off before he could shut it all the way.

"Cut through on Third, over to Lake, then to Wooster Road," Dan said. "And make sure you go Wilbeth, not Kenmore Boulevard. It's too slow. Then take a left on South Main."

Kalena started to rub her hands together to release the nervous energy, but her stitches ached. She clutched her arms. Would Polly be upset that she showed up? Would they be able to help her? Had she already found Beverly? What if she was hurt? Her stomach roiled. When Dan had called her and told her what had happened at the viaduct and said Polly went on to the station, she knew Polly needed help. As strong and independent as she was, she couldn't do this alone. No one could. "How did you know to call me?"

"Polly said she's staying at your house, and I was desperate for a ride," Dan said. "I just hoped you had one. It's a good thing she told you about her being an agent, or this would have been hard to explain."

"Why did Washington send a lone agent to do this?" Lionel asked.

"She wasn't alone," Kalena said. "She was supposed to have a contact, but he went missing. And when she asked for help from the Cleveland FBI office, Washington told her they couldn't send anyone. They left her on her own to get some local help if she needed it. Polly said she was lucky they'd at least wiretapped the building phones."

"It's because she's a woman," Lionel said. "They don't want her to succeed."

"Well, then they're going to be disappointed." Dan smirked. "I've never seen anyone more determined."

"Not giving Polly what she needs to do her job puts her and the entire country at risk," Kalena said. "I don't believe Cleveland didn't have any agents to help her. Do you think that's true, Dan? Would someone set her up like that just because she's a woman?"

"The world's changing, and it's hard for people to keep up. Some guys would rather see Polly killed than have her succeed, no matter what the cost is to America."

Kalena thought about the men in the alley and what they'd done to the woman, and then she recalled how Polly had jumped from the train to do her job. What else would she be expected to do? "Drive faster."

Time distorted, and the minutes hovered in the air. The faster Lionel drove, the slower they seemed to go. They passed farms and endless fields. Finally, they came over the rise, down the hill, and then pulled into the train-station parking lot.

Dan pointed. "There's her car."

Lionel parked beside it.

They jumped out and peered inside.

The key was still in the ignition. Kalena gasped when she saw the bullet hole and the blood-spattered side window. She clutched her arms to her chest, unable to tear her gaze away from the cracked glass. Was it Polly's blood? She pulled at Dan's coat sleeve. "Let's go."

They rushed through the entrance.

Kalena scanned the faces of the people who filled the wooden benches of the vast waiting area, irrationally hoping to find Polly there, sitting calmly, waiting for her with a smile. She searched the sparse groups moving in and out of the platforms. She couldn't remember what Polly was wearing. What color was her coat? Tan, brown, red? No. It was a muted green. She'd helped her slip it on before she walked out the door, the last time she'd seen her. Would it be *the last time?* She shook off the thought and continued her search. The large clock on the far wall caught her attention and bore witness to the reality that the Cleveland train had long gone, and the southbound had left minutes before. Now what? She continued her search, desperately hoping to see the green coat in a desert of brown and tan.

"Let's split up," Dan yelled.

Kalena rushed out to the south platform. A few men were standing near the benches. No Polly. She approached a worker who was sweeping the planks and described Polly, asking if he'd seen her.

"Yes, ma'am. She boarded the last passenger car on the *Commodore* to Washington. I remember 'cause I was worried she wouldn't get up the steps."

"Why is that?"

"Well, she was movin' slow, real slow, like she was pained."

How badly had she been hurt? Had she gotten on board to follow Beverly? Alone? Of course she was alone. She didn't have any help. "Are you absolutely sure she got on? Maybe she got off again."

"No, ma'am. She got on. I watched her, and then the *Commodore* pulled out of the station on time."

When Kalena regrouped with Lionel and Dan, she told them what she'd learned.

"Now what?" Lionel asked.

"I'm sure he's right," Dan said. "She's not outside the station, so she must have gotten on the train."

"The only reason she'd do that would be to go after Beverly," Kalena said.

Dan checked his watch and looked at the schedule posted on the wall. "It makes four stops in Ohio. Canton's first. We missed it by only a few minutes. If we hurry, we can catch up to it there. I can get on board and get her attention. But whatever we decide, we have to do it right now."

Kalena pulled on Lionel's arm. "Let's go." They couldn't get out of the station fast enough to suit her. Every second meant Polly was alone and without help. If Kalena's heart beat any faster, it would explode.

Before they got into Lionel's car, Dan took the key from the ignition in Polly's and locked the doors. "Don't want anyone stealing this."

They headed south out of town.

"I just realized boarding the train isn't a good idea. If Beverly is on it, she'll recognize me," Dan said from the backseat.

"She knows all of us," Kalena said.

"Good point. I guess we have no choice. We should board different cars. It's faster. Lionel, you stick with me. I'll tell the conductor you're my partner."

Lionel smiled and looked at Kalena, who half grinned.

"You open your wallet, flash it quickly, then put it away in your jacket pocket. Kalena, you take the first third of the train. Run up breathless when we get to the conductor and tell him you got a call from your husband's boss and that his meeting time has been changed for tomorrow. If he asks you what his name is and says he'll relay the message, you tell him it's too important, and you'll worry all night about it if you don't tell him yourself. Offer to have him hold your purse while you board. He'll respect that. Meanwhile I'll flash my badge, and Lionel and I will split up. I'll work my way back. Lionel, you head toward Kalena."

They drove into the Canton station and heard the whistle as the Akron train lumbered slowly in.

"Let's go. Remember, we only have a few minutes, so move quickly and be careful," Dan said.

"What if Beverly sees me and wants to know why I'm there?" Kalena asked.

"If that happens, there'll most likely be trouble. Look at her like she's stupid for asking the question and act confused," Dan said. "Better yet, tell her you're here to pick up Lionel from a business trip. Lionel, if you see them together, walk up and hug Kalena, greet Beverly, and thank Kalena for picking you up. Then you both get off the train as fast as possible."

"What if we can't find Polly?" Kalena asked.

Dan looked at her but didn't answer.

Her mouth went dry. Bile rose in her throat.

When Kalena approached the conductor, he responded as Dan had predicted, except she didn't have to give him her purse. She boarded and started searching as the passengers either stayed seated or disembarked. When she entered the third car, she met Lionel.

He shook his head. "I didn't see either of them. You?"

"No."

They got off and waited for Dan, but he didn't exit. Each passing second, she grew more anxious. "Maybe we should search his part of the train?" she asked.

Before Lionel could answer, Dan stepped onto the platform and hurried to them, his expression dark.

Kalena's heart sank. He hadn't found them.

"She has to be somewhere," she told Dan. "She got on the train." Her palms were sweating. Her muscles stiffened, and she couldn't catch her breath. "Where is she?"

Dan scrubbed his face. "Either that worker was mistaken, and she *didn't* get on, or she got on, then got off."

"What do you mean she *got off*? The train didn't make a stop before here." Kalena spoke louder than she'd intended.

"You mean she jumped?" Lionel asked.

Kalena gasped. "Again?"

They looked at her like they were confused.

"She's already jumped once."

Lionel's mouth dropped open, but Dan just shook his head.

"We need to retrace and follow the tracks," Dan said.

"Beverly must have been on the train, or Polly would have never gotten on it in the first place," Kalena said. "She would have waited and taken her off when they got here." She tried to think through the situation like Polly would. "The only reason Polly wouldn't be on the train was if she'd been pushed off, presumably by Beverly, or she had to jump in order to follow her. She could be anywhere from Akron to here. We need to find her. Let's go."

Dan bought a map of the Ohio train routes and traced the Akron line under a lamppost in the parking lot. "You got a flashlight?" he asked Lionel when they were in the car.

"Yes. In the glove box," Lionel said as he pulled out of the lot.

Dan riffled through the compartment as he told Lionel which roads to take. "Slow down. Look on the far side of the tracks."

Kalena squinted into the night. She couldn't see past the rails. If Polly was out there, they'd never find her. It was too dark, and there was too much natural cover. What if she was hurt? Or worse? "Stop the car."

Lionel slowed. "What did you see?"

"I want to walk the tracks. I can't see much of anything from here."

Dan grabbed her arm as she opened the door. "You can't. It'll take too long."

"What if we miss her while we're driving? She could be anywhere. She could be hurt and not able to walk. We'll never find her." Fear clawed at her heart. She had to get out of the vehicle and run along the tracks and scream Polly's name.

Dan touched her arm. "If she's out there, we'll find her. If she's hurt, she'll get to the highway and get help. If she isn't, she's on the hunt. And we may find Beverly before she does."

Kalena looked at him. She wanted to grab him by the collar and shake him. "You don't know that. She could be injured, and we won't be able to see her."

Dan squeezed her shoulder. "Listen to me. Polly's one smart cookie. If we don't find her by the time we get to Akron, we'll walk every single mile back to Canton."

Kalena shut the door with a shaky hand and nodded.

Lionel crept along the route, Dan and Kalena scanning every movement, every shadow, peering out into the darkness. Twice Dan had Lionel stop, but they found only a dead deer and a large raccoon along the tracks.

They were ten miles from the Akron station when something

caught their attention in the distance. When the headlights captured the figure, they spotted a woman, covered in mud and grime. Was it Polly? Kalena wasn't sure.

Lionel stopped the car.

The figure trudged toward them, holding up one hand. It *was* Polly.

Kalena jumped out and ran to her.

Polly fell into her arms.

"Polly. Oh, God, Polly. You're alive."

"I lost her."

Kalena pushed her wet, dirty hair away from her forehead and wiped her bloody cheek. "What?"

"I lost her. I jumped from the train, landed on the embankment, and rolled down into a muddy ravine. I was out of it for a while, but I heard her moving. I climbed out and kept going, but I lost her. She got away."

"Well, she didn't make it to Canton," Dan said.

Polly was pale and shivering.

"We've got to get you warm and clean you up," Kalena said.

Polly pulled away and straightened. "No. We have to find her. She can't get away."

"Polly, you're obsessed. You stopped her. You found the spy. You did your job."

Polly shook her head, staring off in the distance, searching. "No. My job's not done until I catch her. She wasn't that far ahead of me. If you didn't see her, that means she went deeper into the woods."

Kalena helped her to the car and into the backseat. She took Polly's soaked and filthy coat off her and slipped her own on her.

Lionel cranked up the heat.

Dan looked at the map. "We didn't see her along the tracks. There're several acres of wetlands about six miles south of here. The only way she could cross it would be to stay on the tracks, and we didn't see her, so she hasn't made it that far yet. She's probably between us and north of the wetlands."

Polly's teeth were chattering. She pulled Kalena's coat tighter around herself. "Did you bring your gun, Dan?"

He nodded.

"Feel like going snipe hunting?" She smiled, but her eyes looked blank.

He laughed. "Always wanted to catch a snipe."

"You can't possibly think you're in any shape to go back out there?" Kalena said. "Let Dan do it."

Polly looked at her, and it was like looking at someone different. She was detached, serious. "It's my job. This is who I am."

"Then I'm going with you."

"Absolutely not. And this isn't a request, Kalena. You and Lionel need to stay in the car. Lionel, move forward every few minutes. If you have any problems, blow the horn in intermittent blasts. I need your belt and your sweater."

"My belt?"

Polly nodded and shifted. "I need to use it as support. I wrenched my back."

Kalena helped her remove the coat, tied the sweater around her middle, then tightened the belt for extra support.

Polly got out of the car and gripped Kalena's arm as if to steady herself. "That's much better." She pointed toward the tracks. "Dan, you walk no more than about fifty yards on the far side. I'll go inland about one hundred yards and walk south until I reach the swamp. If I find any trails, I'll come back, and we'll go together."

Dan looked at the map. "The old Ohio Erie Canal is a natural barrier along this route. There's a railroad crossing in about three miles." He pointed south. "We'll all meet there."

Polly took Kalena's hand. "It's all right."

Kalena intertwined their fingers. "Be careful."

Polly nodded. "Lionel, I don't suppose you have a pistol in the glove box or under the seat?"

"No, but I have a billy club."

"Not to worry." Dan reached down to his ankle and brought out a small gun and handed it to Lionel. "Just pull the hammer back and fire. She'll do the job. It's a two-shot derringer. Just make sure you point it at the other guy before you pull the trigger." Dan laughed.

Polly tightened her grip on Kalena. "You be careful and watch out. Beverly may try to get into the car. Keep the doors locked and the motor running."

Kalena bit her lower lip. "You stay safe."

Polly smiled for the first time since they'd found her. She nodded and walked off into the darkness—injured, strong, and determined.

Kalena leaned against the car. Polly wasn't a daydream or some fantasy. She was a living, breathing female agent, putting her life in danger for no other reason than it was her job. Would she still be alive in the morning?

CHAPTER TWENTY-FOUR

Polly gripped the handle of the gun. Each time she took a step on the uneven terrain, her leg muscles spasmed. The rustling leaves and snapping twigs grew louder. She stopped, holding her breath, turning her attention toward the sound. It was in front of her, somewhere in the shadows near the tree line. A deer? A small creature? Beverly?

She'd covered about two miles. The air was beginning to moisten and grow heavy. They were getting closer to the swamp. Another mile and they'd be at the railroad crossing.

A gunshot echoed ahead and to the right. The car? Dan? No. He was behind her somewhere. Kalena? She ran toward where the car should be, but it was gone. She saw the faint orange of taillights in the distance. She searched the area, frantic to find Kalena.

"Polly." Dan's voice rang out from behind her.

She turned, and when she got closer, she could see he was kneeling beside something. A man? It was Lionel. Had he been shot? Where was Kalena? Was she driving the car? Had Beverly managed to get inside? She desperately continued to search the immediate area as she hurried toward Dan.

"He's unconscious but alive. He's been smashed in the head with a rock or something," Dan said. "She somehow snuck up on him. His zipper's open. He must have stepped out of the car to take a leak. The gun's not here. She probably has it." He zipped Lionel's pants.

Waves of nausea coursed through Polly. Beverly had either shot Kalena or taken her. She looked down the road, ready to bolt after the vehicle.

Headlights flashed in their direction. The car was turning around and coming back.

Polly raised her gun.

Dan stood, also pointing his gun at the vehicle.

It slid to a stop.

Kalena jumped out.

"I saw her hit Lionel in the head. I jumped over to the driver's seat. She shot the window out and tried to get into the car. I took off. I left Lionel. I left him." She stiffened. She covered her face with her hands and started sobbing. "He's dead. I left him."

Polly held her. "It's all right. He's alive. You did exactly what you needed to do. We're going to lay him in the backseat. You drive him to the hospital in Akron. You can drive, can't you?"

Kalena stopped sobbing, her breathing still ragged. "Yes. Lionel taught me. What about you? And Dan?"

"Beverly's close. We can't stop. You call the police and tell them what happened. They'll come for us. You stay with Lionel." She started to walk away.

"But—"

"No buts. Look up the number of the FBI in Cleveland and let them know what's going on. They'll send someone. Nothing like a good manhunt to bring the FBI, short-handed or not."

"I won't leave you."

Polly wrapped her arm around her, inwardly cursing her need to stop and reassure Kalena when she needed to be moving. "You have to get Lionel to the hospital as fast as possible. I need you to do this. We can't leave. Do you understand?"

Kalena eyes widened. She nodded, then took a deep breath. "Yes."

Polly helped Dan get Lionel into the backseat, then watched Kalena drive away. As soon as she was out of sight, Polly took her weapon and fired one shot into the air, then yelled as loud as she could, "You've got one bullet left, and there's two of us. We're coming after you."

She whispered to Dan, "No more than fifty feet apart at all times."

Dan nodded.

They stepped over the tracks and into the woods.

A few minutes later a limb snapped in the distance in front of her.

She stopped. Then came an increased rhythmic rustling of leaves and twigs. Something was running. She bounded toward the sound.

She could see Beverly racing toward the train tracks.

A long, low train whistle sounded once, then again. The light from the engine flashed and bounced as it emerged from the curve.

If Beverly crossed the tracks before the train reached them, Polly and Dan would have to wait until it passed before they could follow. And by that time Beverly would be gone again. Polly surged forward.

Beverly scrambled up the embankment.

The train's rumble grew louder.

Polly yelled a warning. "Halt, or I'll shoot you."

Beverly kept climbing, then suddenly turned and fired at Polly.

The burn and gnarl of the bullet ripped into Polly's left shoulder, sending sharp, white-hot pain down her arm. She staggered backward, then caught her balance and continued the chase.

The train whistle blasted again, this time vibrating throughout her, permeating every cell until it felt like she was breathing the sound. The engine light stabbed through the darkness, illuminating Beverly as she ran.

Polly hesitated, but then she remembered her oath. She aimed. If she didn't shoot, Beverly would get away. *At any cost!* She fired.

Beverly stumbled, then lurched forward, falling in front of the oncoming train.

Polly looked away as the brakes screamed and sparks flew from the tracks, steel grating against steel. Dan caught her as her knees buckled and she went down.

❖

Polly woke slowly and winced. Pain radiated through her shoulder, and every inch of her body protested the abuse it had endured over the last several days. The water pitcher on the stand beside her hospital bed was inches away, but she couldn't get to it without reaching, which was something she didn't want to do. She laid her head back and licked her lips.

A strong arm slid under her shoulders and lifted her. Kalena leaned over her, smiling, the tenderness in her green eyes comforting and reassuring.

"You're here," Polly said. Her voice was raspy, her throat so dry she could hardly speak.

Kalena picked up the cup next to the pitcher and guided the straw to Polly's lips. "Drink."

The water was cold, and fresh, soothing the harsh burn at the back of her throat. She moaned, not meaning to, but the sound had slipped out.

The bed beneath her cushioned her like a cloud. How long had she been asleep?

Kalena eased away and returned the cup to the tray.

The withdrawal of her closeness overwhelmed Polly, filling her with a deep sadness. "Don't leave."

Kalena stroked her hair. "Oh, I'm not leaving. The surgery went well. They got the bullet out of your shoulder. The doctor said it was a good thing you were shot from a distance and that it was a small caliber. You're going to be fine, in spite of the bullet wound, sprained back, lacerations, and bruises. They gave you morphine for the pain." She wiped Polly's face with a cool cloth.

Polly closed her eyes. "What day is it?"

Kalena's voice covered her like a blanket on a cold night. "Friday, December fifth, almost eleven a.m."

"Where's Lionel," Polly asked. "Is he all right?"

"He's doing well. He's upstairs in the men's ward."

Polly opened her eyes, determined to try to stay awake until she had more answers.

Kalena's eyes danced as she gazed at her. "He'll be fine. A concussion and stitches in his head. He's quite the hero. All the nurses are swooning over him."

Polly couldn't help but smile. "That's too bad."

Kalena laughed and leaned closer. "It's not a total loss. His doctor seems a little overly concerned."

Polly chuckled. "When can I get out of here?" Not that she wanted to move an inch, but she'd never been a fan of hospitals, and she had more business to take care of.

"Later today, as long as you can eat, don't throw up, or do anything to arouse suspicion."

"I have to call Washington."

"Dan talked with the FBI from Cleveland. They called your agency and spoke with a Mr. Williamson. I believe that was his name. You're to call him as soon as you can."

"I need to talk with Dan."

"He'll be in to see you in a little while. You rest now. I'll be right here."

Polly wanted to stay awake, but her eyes were heavy, and she couldn't fight the need to sleep. When she woke an hour later, Kalena was still there, dozing beside her. She helped her eat a little, then said she'd be back later. Dan arrived just after she left. He sat in the metal chair beside Polly's bed.

Polly squeezed his fingers. "Dan." Tears welled in her eyes. She swallowed and tried to force them away. "Thank you for being my backup. We made a good team."

He patted her hand. "A hell of a night." He smiled. "You did good, kid."

She wanted him to tell her what had happened, to reassure her that Beverly was dead, but she knew. And she knew she'd killed her, even though technically the train was responsible. But if she hadn't shot her, Beverly would have made it across the tracks. She'd had to do it. It was justified. Beverly was a spy. She and Oliver had stolen information that could have killed thousands and had far-reaching implications for America.

Polly had completed her mission. But she'd let her desire for more, her pride and ego to get the job done, get in her way. Beverly could have escaped. And what about Kalena? Did she have the time or the right to get involved with her? In her heart she knew they were already involved. Could it go any further? Should it?

Chapter Twenty-five

Late Friday afternoon, Celia drove Polly and Kalena home from the hospital. Polly had talked with Celia, then called Mr. Helmsworth to update him. Before Celia left the house, she told Kalena she could take off as much time as she needed. Even if Celia hadn't told her, Kalena wasn't going back to work until Polly had to leave, no matter how long it was. But it might be only a matter of hours.

In the evening, after Polly had rested, Kalena brought her a cup of coffee and set it on the stand beside the phone in the living room. Polly had told her she needed to call Washington.

Kalena's heart sank. "So soon? Can't it wait until morning?"

Polly face saddened. "I have to report and wrap up some loose ends."

Kalena waited as Polly dialed the number, then stepped away, giving her the privacy she needed. She'd probably get new orders and be leaving soon.

After Polly finished her call, she curled up on the sofa. She watched Kalena but didn't speak. What was she thinking? Was she as sad and forlorn as Kalena? When would she be leaving? A heaviness of dread hung in the air.

The front door opened, then slammed. Richard. A cold chill swept through the room, and Polly shivered.

Kalena retrieved one of Aunt Berna's quilts from the closet and covered her.

"Thank you," Polly said, pulling it up around her chin.

An uncomfortable silence filled the space between them, like a wall had been suddenly erected. Was it because she couldn't bear to say good-bye to Polly and was distancing herself from the pain? She didn't care why. The reality of having to separate from Polly hung over her like a pall of dark foreboding.

"Richard, I thought you were working a double shift. It's only six o'clock. Why are you home?" She didn't mean to sound so sharp, but she'd looked forward to being alone with Polly. Aunt Berna had gone to a card game with her friends for the evening, and now Richard was here spoiling it.

"I'm here for only a few minutes, and then I'm back to work. They gave me a break. I need to eat and get a few things."

"Oh, okay." Kalena spoke with more acceptance than she felt.

"Where were you two last night?" he asked.

"Polly and I were in Cleveland." Kalena was surprised at how easily the lie came out of her mouth.

"What happened, Polly?" he asked.

"I wasn't watching where I was going, tripped on an uneven sidewalk, and tumbled down an embankment."

What good liars they both were!

"Ouch! Will you be coming back to work soon?" he asked.

Polly grimaced. "No. I'll be taking some time off."

And there it was. She must have gotten her orders and would be leaving. For a moment Kalena had hoped she would stay just a little while, so they could talk and be together, but even if Richard didn't know the truth, the reality of Polly's words slapped her in the face.

She'd already talked with Celia, called Mr. Helmsworth, and now was saying her farewells. Kalena hated it. Polly was leaving and would soon say good-bye. Kalena would no longer be able to watch her as she moved gracefully around a room or gaze into her eyes and see her face light up when she smiled. She'd known she had to go eventually, but the thought made her heartsick. She couldn't endure it any longer. She excused herself and went to her room, where she slumped onto the bed and stared out the window. It had snowed in the afternoon, and a dusting of white covered the trees and ground.

A few minutes later she heard a knock.

Polly came in and closed the door. She eased down next to her, wrapping her arm around her. "I made an initial report and gave OAD the information they needed. They said the local sheriff's office found my gun beside the railroad tracks. They're going to mail it to the agency."

"What would have happened if they hadn't found it?" Kalena only superficially wanted the answer. It was more a question to distract her heartbreak.

"Someone could have picked it up and used it in a crime, or a child could have come across it and harmed himself or others." She paused. "It's tradition to take some time off after completing an assignment. I don't have to report back until December sixteenth."

Kalena's heart fluttered, and the heavy weight lifted. Was Polly staying until then? Even if she wasn't, she obviously wasn't in a hurry now. She moved carefully against Polly, and they kissed. "That's wonderful news."

"When I talked with Mr. Helmsworth, he said I could use a vehicle until I was ready to leave. He wasn't even upset about the mess we made of the other one. I thought we might get a cabin somewhere and spend the week together."

Elated, Kalena couldn't stop smiling. "Oh, Polly, that's wonderful. Thank you. I know a perfect place. It's about an hour from here, in Chardon. I'll call and make a reservation. Let's leave right away. I don't want to waste a minute."

Polly laughed. "We can go in the morning. It's too late to make the drive tonight."

The front door closed. Richard had left. They were finally alone.

"Polly?"

Polly pressed her cheek to hers. "There's time to talk, but not now. Let's just lie here and be together. I need to have you next to me."

Kalena positioned the pillows and lay down beside her. The evening sun broke through the clouds and shone brightly in the window just as the sun began to set. A sliver of hope wedged its way into her. Somehow everything was going to be all right. It had to be.

❖

Polly studied Kalena's lissome, naked body and the dance of firelight on her soft skin.

Kalena stoked the red-hot coals like she was conducting a symphony, each movement precise and purposeful. She added another log. A flicker of fire danced on its edges, then began to consume it in a heated embrace.

They couldn't have gotten a more perfect cabin. It was secluded and allowed full privacy in a dense forest, beside a beautiful lake. Saturday afternoon they strolled along the wood-chipped path, shared a hot, luxurious bath, and then lay entwined in front of the fire, covered by a beautiful, thick homemade quilt.

Kalena had told her it was an Ohio star pattern. "It's a traditional quilt. The pattern was started back in 1803 when Ohio became the seventeenth state in the Union. I have one in my dowry chest that my mother made."

Kalena replaced the poker in the stand on the hearth and returned to their nest, sliding in beside Polly. They merged, as if fitted and molded for each other. Polly kissed her, gliding her fingers over her curves and then down her thigh, hearing Kalena's soft sigh of desire as they caressed each other.

Polly hadn't wanted to be this close to her. She'd told herself nothing could come of what was between them. But she couldn't stop herself, not now. She needed Kalena. She ached for her comfort and support, but mostly she craved her affection, and the strength and confidence it brought.

They explored each other, their bodies like a gift between them.

In those tender moments, Polly wanted to be nothing more than Kalena's. It was the most she could ever aspire to be if she lived a thousand years. They were together, united, bonded. When had it happened? How had it happened? She didn't know. It was a force beyond her comprehension.

They made love slowly. Only now existed. No measure of time. No past. No future. Only this moment when touching, caressing, and loving each other defined their existence.

Sunday, they walked in the woods again. Then they made a delicious soup of lentils and beef and ate it with a loaf of bread from the local market.

They consumed each other until the evening. The temperature dipped. They dressed in their heavy sweaters, pants, and socks and curled up by the fire. Kalena read aloud a few chapters of a book by J.R.R. Tolkien, called *The Hobbit or There and Back Again*, from the small library in the corner of the cabin.

"When you made the reservation, how did you explain there would be two women," Polly asked.

Kalena smiled. "I lied, like you."

Polly's breath hitched. Had she lied so much in the short time they'd been together that Kalena identified her with it? She regretted every falsehood she'd ever told her. "What did you say?"

"That you're a widow and need some time away. They understood and said how nice it was that I had brought you."

"Do you feel guilty about what you told them?"

"Only that your husband had been killed overseas. I should have said it was an automobile accident or something. I think I did it to get their sympathy, so they'd be more understanding."

Polly stroked Kalena's arm. "It's okay. It's not our fault society acts like we have a disease or something. I—"

Someone pounded on the door. Polly jumped up, then looked at Kalena and hesitantly went to the door. Did the owners suspect they weren't who they said they were? Were they going to kick them out? Did they have a gun? Was it the police? She opened the door a crack.

Mr. Rhitenhower, the proprietor, stood with a stoic expression, blowing into his bare, stubby fingers. The buttons and the buttonholes on his navy-blue checkered winter coat looked like they were in a territorial dispute over his protruding belly. A red muffed cap dangled over his ears. "Sorry to bother you ladies." He looked first at Polly, then at Kalena. "You have a call. Do you mind coming to the main house? A Berna Iwan…Iwon…"

"I-wan-ow-ski?" Kalena asked, now at Polly's side.

Mr. Rhitenhower smiled. "Yes, that's it. She said she'd call back in a few minutes."

They waited at the Rhitenhowers' kitchen table for the call. When Mrs. Rhitenhower answered, she gave the receiver to Kalena, who then quickly handed it over to Polly.

"Hello, Polly," Aunt Berna said. "Some assistant director, a Mr. Williamson, called for you. He said it was urgent that you get in touch with him. Do you have something to write this number down with?"

"Hold on." Polly covered the receiver with her palm. "I'm sorry to trouble you, Mrs. Rhitenhower, but do you have a pencil and something I might write on?"

Mrs. Rhitenhower opened a small wooden drawer under the counter and handed Polly a tablet and pencil. "Here you go, dear."

"I appreciate it." Polly wrote the number on a sheet of paper. She thanked Aunt Berna, then hung up. She looked at Kalena and then at the others. "I'm afraid I must ask another favor. May I use your telephone? I'll gladly pay the cost."

"Certainly. I hope it's not more bad news," Mrs. Rhitenhower said. She looked at Polly as if she might break out in tears and hugged her, then smoothed her graying curls behind her ears and backed away.

Polly felt a tinge of guilt. They shouldn't have lied. But what else could they have done? Tell them the truth and be arrested or run off at gun point? Polly needed privacy for the phone call, but how could she ask for it discreetly?

Kalena must have sensed her need. "Is the call confidential?" she asked.

Polly nodded.

"Oh, dear," Mrs. Rhitenhower said, grabbing her husband's arm. "Come along, Carl."

Kalena followed Mr. and Mrs. Rhitenhower into the living room.

Polly dialed the operator for assistance.

Assistant Director Williamson answered on the second ring.

"This is Agent Sylvester, sir."

"Thank you for calling back so quickly, Polly. I'm sorry to tell you, but you must return to Washington immediately."

"Why, sir? I have leave until the sixteenth."

"The Japanese have bombed Pearl Harbor. It happened early this morning, Hawaii time. President Roosevelt will go before Congress tomorrow and ask for a declaration of war. You're needed here."

Polly swayed as the news hit her, entering like a bolt of lightning striking the ground in front of her, searing the earth. He gave more bits of information, but Polly's mind reeled. All she heard was *Pearl Harbor* and *war*. The silence was deafening when he stopped talking.

"Did you hear me, Polly?"

"Yes. I understand, sir. What about the loose ends here? We still haven't found the safe house Beverly might have had, and there may be other documents. I also haven't discovered yet who she was reporting to, aside from the man I knew as Oliver."

"We're turning it over to the Cleveland office of the FBI and letting them finish up. Our agency just got other priorities. You've done enough. We need you back here."

"I'll be there as soon as I can, sir." She hung up and tried to settle her emotions. America had been attacked and was going to war!

Still stunned, she walked stiffly to the living room. She thanked the Rhitenhowers and informed them she and Kalena would have to cut their vacation short and would be leaving in the morning.

Pale, Kalena stared at her questioningly.

"I'm sorry to hear that, dear," said Mrs. Rhitenhower. "We're so sorry for your loss. We'll refund five of your days."

Mr. Rhitenhower frowned.

"Thank you. That's very kind," Polly said. "I'll leave some money on the kitchen table in the cabin when we leave. For the phone call and any inconvenience this may have caused you."

Mr. Rhitenhower smiled. "Well, that's mighty nice of you. We appreciate it."

"Not at all. And thank you again. I suggest you turn on your radio to NBC."

She and Kalena stepped out into the frigid night.

"You have to go back to Washington?" Kalena asked.

Polly nodded. "Let's go to the cabin, and I'll explain."

She stoked the fire and added more logs, then went into the kitchen and poured two shots of whiskey and carried them to the living room, giving one to Kalena. "I know this is a disappointment. Drink."

They sat on the couch together and sipped the whiskey without talking, and then when their glasses were empty, Polly said, "What I'm about to say is going to be a shock. Do you understand? It's why I told the Rhitenhowers to turn on their radio."

Kalena nodded. She rubbed her palm on her thigh. "It's bad, isn't it?"

Polly slipped her arm over her shoulder. "The Japanese bombed Pearl Harbor in Hawaii earlier today. The damage to our navy ships was catastrophic."

Kalena shook her head and took in a deep breath. "I knew something like this would happen."

Polly held Kalena's hand. "President Roosevelt is going before Congress tomorrow to ask for a declaration of war." The implication of what she'd said out loud finally sank in. What would happen? Japan? Not Germany? "The United States is going to war." The words tumbled out like they were boulders she'd been forced to hold for hours and finally let go. She struggled to get a full breath. She fought back her tears that were now demanding release. She focused on Kalena.

Kalena's cheeks were wet, her unrestrained sobs piercing the stillness.

They sat close to one another, unable to speak, each second, each moment feeling like leaves floating along on the current of a stream. Polly was unable to stop them or get them back. This fracture in time had changed everything. She would leave. Would she ever return? Would she ever see Kalena again?

Chapter Twenty-six

Kalena clung to Polly, taking in the unique scent of her skin mixed with Ivory soap and flowers. And when they kissed, the taste of cinnamon toast and coffee lingered on her lips. She kissed her again and glanced at the bed. Polly's suitcase was closed and locked, her borrowed coat draped carefully over it. She was ready to leave.

All morning the waves of desperation had crashed over Kalena. She couldn't bear it. They had no time left. All the angst and anxiety of a last farewell loomed over her like a tornadic storm.

Their time together was ending, but there were things that needed to be said, things she shouldn't feel but did. Should she tell her how much she'd miss her? How her heart ached at the thought of not being with her? How she'd give anything if she could stay? Would the memories of their time together fade in the chaos of war?

She hated feeling so desperate. She needed to tell her, but she held the words in. What was she waiting for? She'd known her only a few weeks. She shouldn't feel this way about her, but she did.

Polly held her tighter. "I have such strong feelings for you. I didn't want to. I fought them so hard. I don't understand how everything happened, or why now of all times. But I can't get you out of my mind and heart. I'll call you as soon as I can. I don't know when it will be. I wish I had more time to tell you, to show you, how grateful I am you came into my life, how you've filled me, touched me in ways no one has or ever will again. A part of me is staying here with you."

Kalena kissed her once more, barely holding back another sob.

"I don't want you to go to the train station with me. Celia will have someone pick up the car," Polly whispered.

"No. I want to go."

Polly stroked her hair. "I can't bear saying good-bye to you in public."

"Then stay another day."

"I wish I could, but I should have left last night."

Polly kissed her.

It was deep, and long, and full of the bittersweet that only a last kiss could impart.

Every muscle in Kalena's body tensed. Her pulse surged. The pain and sorrow of their good-bye clung to her like thistles on a blanket. She buried her face in Polly's neck. "Don't go." She murmured the words like a prayer, desperation oozing from her.

"I have to." She carried her suitcase down the stairs and set it by the foyer.

Aunt Berna hugged Polly, wished her well, then sat in her chair once more, picking up her crochet needles and thread, to continue her task.

Polly opened the door and looked back at Kalena with obvious reluctance, mirrored longing in her eyes.

Kalena was unable to move, held in her gaze. Only Polly was in front of her, a faint smile on her lips, a hope of someday, somewhere in the future.

President Roosevelt's voice echoed through the room from the radio.

"Mr. Vice President, Mr. Speaker, Members of the Senate and House of Representatives: Yesterday, December 7, 1941, a date which will live in infamy, the United States of America was suddenly and deliberately attacked by naval and air forces of the Empire of Japan..."

In that moment Polly was ripped from her, and America was plunged into war.

She watched the car pull from the curb. She ran to the sidewalk, her hand in the air as she watched the love of her life drive away. Yes. She loved her. And now it was too late to tell her.

❖

Kalena sat next to Lionel on the sofa, clasping his hand.

"Her telegram said she'd call sometime tonight. It's been only ten days. You'll make yourself sick if you don't stop this," Lionel said.

She checked her watch and suddenly realized what the problem might be. She picked up the receiver and recognized the female voice. No wonder Polly couldn't get through. "Mrs. Evans, would you please get off the line? I'm expecting a very important call."

"Oh, dear. I'm sorry. Of course. Ester, talk to you tomorrow."

Kalena replaced the receiver and paced. She traced the scar on her hand, the skin between her finger and thumb still tender and pink.

"She'll call," Lionel said, eyeing her.

Kalena checked the time again. Another ten minutes. What was taking her so long?

Aunt Berna brought her a cup of tea. "Lionel's right. I'm sure she's very busy and doing the best she can."

They were trying to comfort her, but their efforts only made her more anxious. She sighed and continued to pace, occasionally sipping the drink.

Another hour passed.

Finally, the phone rang.

Kalena jumped to her feet and grabbed the receiver. "Hello?"

"Kalena. It's so good to hear your voice."

"Polly." The connection was bad. She could barely hear her.

"I have only a few minutes. People are lined up waiting for the phone. Can you write something down?"

Kalena grabbed the notepad and pencil from the end table beside her. "Yes. Go ahead."

Polly gave her an address and a phone number. "It's my cousin Elizabeth's home here in Washington. I gave up my apartment. I won't be there much longer. I've been…Washington…the twenty-seventh."

"Polly, you're breaking up. I didn't hear that last part."

"I said, I'll be leaving Washington on the twenty-seventh. I'm being sent overseas. I can't tell you more than that."

"No. That's only nine days from today. Will you have time to come here before you leave?"

"I can't get away. I need to pack and settle everything here. I know it's the holidays, and I'm sorry to ask, but can you come to

Washington? You can stay at my cousin's house. We won't have a lot of time together, but at least it's something. I can't bear the thought of not seeing you before I leave. Please say you'll come."

"Yes. Yes, of course I will. I'll take the next available train. I'm not sure when it will be, though."

"Call Elizabeth and give her your travel information. I'll meet you at Washington Union station. It's a madhouse here, but I'll find you. Hurry. I can't wait to see you. I have to go."

"I'll be there as soon as possible."

After she hung up, Kalena stood motionless, her heart pounding, hands shaking.

Lionel came up beside her and wrapped his arm around her. "I'll drive you to the Akron station. Some things you need to know. Take only one suitcase that you can carry easily. Stuff it in the rack above your seat, and don't let it out of your sight. Take some food. There could be delays. The trains are packed."

She'd been on the local train to Cleveland only once, and she'd never been out of the state. She should be full of anxiety and apprehension about traveling alone, going somewhere she'd never been, but she wasn't. All she could think about was being with Polly.

The next day she called the Akron depot. Nothing was available until December twenty-sixth. After she hung up, she paced the living room. "That's not possible." She stalked into the kitchen, yanked the drawer open, and pulled out her address book. Her heart raced. She couldn't catch her breath. She skimmed the list but couldn't find Lionel's work number. "Damn it," she yelled, and pounded the counter.

Aunt Berna came in. "What on earth is the matter?"

Kalena burst into tears. "There's no available seats in Akron until the twenty-sixth, and I can't find Lionel's work number."

"Calm down. I know it's in there." Aunt Berna wrestled the book from her and began searching. "Here it is." She handed it back and pointed to the entry.

Kalena wiped her eyes. "Thank you." She returned to the living room and grabbed the receiver, so upset she could barely dial.

"You better sit," Aunt Berna said.

Kalena slumped into the chair.

Lionel finally answered.

"Lionel, I can't. I tried." She began to sob. She couldn't stop herself. Not being with Polly before she left was unbearable. What was she going to do? She'd have Lionel drive her if she had to or take a bus. She was going to see her, and nothing was going to stop her.

"Kalena, I can't understand you. Take a breath," he said.

Her fingers and toes began to tingle. She became dizzy. She bent and lowered her head onto her knees, talking into the phone sideways. "I can't get a ticket."

"Oh, my. No wonder you're so upset. I'll take a long lunch break and be there in a little while."

Lionel arrived twenty minutes later, calm and collected.

Seeing him was just what Kalena needed. She told him the details of what had happened, managing to hold back her hysteria this time.

He listened quietly, sipping the tea Aunt Berna had brought him. "I think you're forgetting that Akron isn't the only station in the area. You can catch the *Capital Limited* in Elyria. I can drive you there. Let's call and see if they have any available tickets."

She was on the train and on her way to see Polly by five the next morning. She watched the other passengers as they boarded. Every available seat was taken by the time the whistle blew, announcing their departure. Her heart skipped a beat. She would miss Christmas with Aunt Berna for the first time in her life. Although Aunt Berna had friends she'd be celebrating with, *she* wouldn't be with her. Did that make her irresponsible? A bad niece? Aunt Berna had assured her she would be fine, but would she? How could she leave her to run into the arms of a woman she barely knew? She remembered what Aunt Berna had told her.

"If you don't do this, you'll regret it for the rest of your life. Go to her and find out. We'll have Christmas together when you get back."

Twinges of guilt inched their way into her heart, but she ignored them. Being with Polly overrode everything else. She wasn't being rational, but Aunt Berna was right. She had to find out.

It was hard to grasp how much her life had changed in just a few weeks. She remembered the morning before Polly had arrived, how she'd looked in the mirror and wondered if she would ever find someone to love. Now she had, but their time together had been limited and ephemeral.

It would be almost a fourteen-hour trip, but she was on her way. How much time would they have together? What would her life be like now? At this moment she knew only that she could never return to the way she'd been before she met Polly.

CHAPTER TWENTY-SEVEN

Polly couldn't sit any longer. She paced the Union Station's grand hall, hardly noticing the brightly decorated gigantic Christmas tree or the wreaths hanging in the waiting area. Christmas carols played in the background over the sounds of the bustling crowd, but they didn't distract her. She was focused on one thing only—Kalena. She glanced at her watch. The train should arrive in twelve minutes. When she'd checked with the station agent for the third time to see if it was on schedule, he'd become irritated.

"Look, lady, I told you. It left the last stop on time. That's all I know."

Polly continued to pace, weaving in and out of the press of people making their way through the depot. Her heart raced. It'd been only twelve days since she'd seen her, but it seemed like months. Was it even appropriate to ask her to come to Washington to be with her? She rebuffed the thought. Kalena was an adult who'd gone off to Cleveland to find like-minded women. What would it be like for Kalena after Polly left? Was it fair or even realistic to expect Kalena to have any kind of relationship with her under the circumstances? Her head throbbed.

She wanted to make the most of the time she and Kalena had together, but they needed to ask each other questions and discuss their concerns. She had no idea how long it would be before they could be together again. They had a few days now, which was all that mattered.

She watched as more passengers boarded another train to depart. She'd never seen Union Station this busy. The engine rumbled as it powered up. Her mind slipped back to Akron and Beverly.

Assistant Director Williamson had been pleased with how she'd conducted herself and the case. He'd even given her a written commendation. But all that hadn't changed Henson's mind. If anything, he was worse, clearly angry that she'd succeeded so well, and all on her own. Her stomach burned. Anything more about Beverly had been lost in the bustle of preparations for her new assignment. Cleveland FBI had searched Beverly's apartment but found no hint of a safe house or other documents. Whatever additional information Polly had hoped to uncover had been lost when Beverly died. Twinges of guilt rippled through her, but she pushed them away. She'd done her job the best she could.

She walked to the newsstand and back. She checked the wall clock near the archway. Any second now.

A few minutes later a long whistle blurted the train's arrival.

She rushed to the platform, trying not to run.

The train lurched to a stop, then inched its way forward like some gigantic creeping dinosaur. A great billowing surge blasted from the engine as power released from the brakes.

Passengers began pouring from the six cars like ants from a jar, scurrying to their destinations. It seemed like everyone from the state of Ohio got off the train but Kalena. Then finally, she stood on the train steps, holding the rail with one hand, her suitcase in the other, searching the horde of people.

Polly nervously watched, anticipating the moment when Kalena would see her, their gazes would meet, and they would connect. When it happened, Polly momentarily lost her balance, as if someone in the crowd had shoved her.

Kalena smiled widely, her eyes vivid and intense as she hurried to her. She placed her suitcase beside Polly and hugged her, grasping her purse.

Polly fought the yearning to kiss her.

"Oh, how I've missed you," Kalena whispered, embracing her, engulfing her in pure emotion.

It entered Polly, filling her, then spilling out, washing over her. "You're here. You're here," she said, squeezing Kalena. "Come on." She broke their embrace and picked up Kalena's bag, locking their arms, leading her to the street. She hailed a taxi at the curb. "Statler Hotel," she told the driver.

The cabbie nodded.

Kalena sat quietly, close beside Polly, hands resting on her purse in her lap.

What was she thinking? Polly patted her arm. "How was the trip?"

"Long, but good." She smiled. "Aunt Berna, Richard, and Lionel send their love. Are we going to your cousin's?"

"Tomorrow." Polly gave her a crooked smile, hoping her meaning was clear.

Kalena licked her full, ripe lips and swallowed. She shifted, then crossed her legs, sliding her dress over her knee when it rode up.

Everything about her kept Polly's focus—her posture, her facial expression, her beautiful geometric print dress, her coat. Did she have any idea how captivating she was?

Kalena smiled demurely.

She knew. She had to know because Polly couldn't take her eyes off her.

They didn't speak, not because Polly didn't have anything to say, but she feared once she opened her mouth, the words of desire would tumble out, and the driver would hear.

They got out at the main entrance to the hotel, then made their way through the portico to the lobby, filled with festive lights and decorations in red, silver, and green. Poinsettia baskets and beautiful bouquets of red roses and other flowers adorned the room.

Polly registered.

The clerk lifted the room key and hit the bell on the counter. "Welcome to the Statler. We hope you have an enjoyable stay with us, Miss Sylvester."

"Thank you," Polly said.

"This is beautiful," Kalena said. "I feel like I've been given a gift."

"Charming," the clerk said, and smiled broadly at Kalena.

A bellhop appeared in a gray uniform and greeted them. He took the room key from the clerk, then Kalena's luggage, and escorted them to their suite on the fourth floor.

Polly tipped him as he left, then turned to Kalena, who stood by the window, looking out at the view.

"It's wonderful. Do they always decorate the city like this for the holidays?"

Polly stepped beside her and gazed out, seeing the multicolored lights below. "Washington seems to be particularly festive this year. I'm sure it has to do with what's happened."

Kalena turned toward her, her piercing gaze almost shocking. "The lights are lovely," she said, in a hushed response.

"We have to talk."

"I know." Kalena moved to her and wrapped her arms around her. "I died a little each day you weren't with me."

Polly stroked Kalena's face, then her hair, searching her eyes for confirmation that asking her to come to Washington had been the right thing to do. "I've asked myself a thousand times if it was a mistake for us to be together." Then she kissed her.

Kalena returned her kiss, sliding her hands down Polly's back and then to her waist. "It doesn't feel like a mistake."

But Kalena had nothing to compare her feelings to. She'd been with only Polly.

"I have to leave for God knows how long. How will that affect you if we continue? You haven't been with anyone else. Maybe—"

Kalena stepped away, grasping Polly's shoulders. "You think because you were the first woman I went to bed with that somehow what I feel for you is just a fleeting emotional attachment?"

Polly nodded. "I'm worried that it is."

"You're far from the first person I've had the opportunity to go to bed with, albeit most of the others have all been men, but nonetheless the decision was mine. You're everything I've ever hoped or dreamed of having. I've questioned if the situation and circumstances had any kind of influence on how I feel about you." She embraced Polly tenderly, as if she were made of spun gold. "I've waited for you all my life. If anything, the timing and the situation did more to pull us apart than bring us together. And in spite of it, we are together. That's how strongly I feel about you."

Polly took a half step away and clasped Kalena's hand. "Are you sure? Are you absolutely sure?"

Kalena leaned in and kissed her. "Yes. I wouldn't have made this trip if I didn't feel the way I do about you."

Polly responded viscerally, throbbing and aching to be with her, to feel her warmth against her, to caress and satisfy, and to surrender to her. Time was fleeting already, and she didn't want to waste another second.

❖

Kalena lay in Polly's arms, the night shadows dancing through the window. She traced the curve of Polly's hip with her fingertips. Polly moved closer.

Kalena's feelings were stronger now. She wanted Polly, but more than that, she needed her. Yes, the sex was wonderful and fulfilling, but the moment she saw her at the train station and stepped into her embrace, she felt like she was home, like she'd finally arrived at the place where she was complete and whole.

She kissed her neck and face, sliding up to her ear. "When do you have to go to work?"

Polly groaned. "The twenty-sixth for final paperwork. I'm taking the train to New York on the twenty-seventh, and then the ship."

Polly pulled the covers around them, then repositioned and moved on top of Kalena, showering her with soft, warm kisses. "When will you go back home?"

"I'm taking the last train on the twenty-seventh. I wanted to make sure I got to see you off."

"I can't believe you're here."

"I can't believe I left Aunt Berna alone on the holiday. It's a good thing she has lots of friends who want her to spend Christmas with them, or I'd feel so guilty it would ruin being with you."

"Let's go shopping tomorrow and get something really special for her," Polly said. "I owe her a big thank you."

"So do I." Kalena laughed, but the reality loomed over them. Polly was going away from her, an ocean separating them, and neither of them knew for how long. Could they endure the separation? Could Kalena hang on to her, or would Polly get caught up in the turmoil and intrigue of a world at war?

Kalena lived a simple life in a small town, surrounded by friends and neighbors she'd grown up with. Being in Washington was overwhelming. She'd panicked just getting off the train and seeing the mass of people. She didn't know anyone. But Polly was a woman of the world, an agent who lived an exciting life surrounded by interesting, intelligent people. She was sailing across the world to be involved in the war, something that felt far away from Ohio. After Polly left, would she remember the small-town woman she'd spent these few weeks with? Or would she forget her when other, more worldly women were around her?

Back home Kalena had only Lionel and Aunt Berna to share her feelings with, but they couldn't understand everything. Who could she turn to when Polly was no longer with her? How could she endure their separation? The thoughts pressed like a vise, wrenching, squeezing tighter with each passing hour. How would she do it?

CHAPTER TWENTY-EIGHT

Polly gripped the cab door as Kalena scooted out. The driver opened the trunk and set Kalena's suitcase beside her. He tipped his hat when Polly paid him, then drove away.

Elizabeth's home on Twenty-fifth Street, just north of New Hampshire, wasn't far from the Potomac. A three-story brick townhouse, it had originally been part of the estate of William M. Bradford, a prominent Washington lawyer who had sold the property to Elizabeth's family when he had retired and moved to Leesburg, Virginia.

They climbed the steps, and Polly held the front door open for Kalena.

Elizabeth's housekeeper met them in the foyer. "Good afternoon, Miss Sylvester," she said. "Miss Elizabeth is in the parlor with guests."

"Thank you, Anna," Polly said. "This is my friend, Kalena Mikloska. She'll be staying with us. Will you please make sure this gets up to my room?" She handed the luggage to her.

Anna smiled at Kalena. "Yes. Of course. Pleasure to meet you, miss."

"Thank you. It's nice to meet you also," Kalena said.

"If you need anything, please let me know," Anna said as she started up the stairs.

Polly escorted Kalena through the house. Almost every room was elaborately adorned with Christmas decorations. A large blue spruce Christmas tree, with homemade decorations and multicolored lights, towered majestically in the formal sitting room off to the left of the foyer.

"This is a magnificent home," Kalena said, eyeing the furnishings and edging slightly closer to Polly. "It's a little overwhelming."

"I know what you mean," Polly said. "I felt that way the first time I stayed with Elizabeth. And I'm family. No matter how many times I'm in this house, I can't help but admire the decor." She pointed to the custom moldings on the high ceilings. "Look at that. It reminds me of something you'd see in a king's private residence. Much of the interior is from different parts of the world."

Kalena gazed at the ceiling admiringly, then took in the rest of the room. "This is all so beautiful."

"As you can see, the house is enormous, so it's perfect for entertaining, which Elizabeth is known for." Polly laughed. "Her parties are legendary." She hid her smile, thinking about the surprise she and Elizabeth had in store for Kalena.

When they arrived in the parlor, Elizabeth set her delicate cup and saucer on the ornately carved end table and rose from her wingback chair. She smiled. Her graceful movement as she crossed the Persian carpet to greet them created an aura of dignity and regality. If America had royalty, Polly was sure Elizabeth would be somewhere in the upper echelon.

Elizabeth glanced at Polly but walked directly to Kalena. "Kalena, how wonderful you're here." She clasped both of Kalena's hands. "Look at you. You're as lovely as Polly said you were."

Kalena blushed.

Elizabeth spoke in French, telling Polly how she had understated Kalena's beauty.

Polly beamed, replying in the same language that she would never be able to describe Kalena's stunning features.

Kalena smiled. "I didn't know you spoke French," she said to Polly.

"I'm so sorry." The heat of a blush crept up Polly's neck. "How rude of us. Elizabeth and I have spoken French to one another since I was a young girl. It's just a habit. Please forgive us?"

Kalena grinned, a mischievous twinkle in her eye. "Thank you for the compliment, Elizabeth. You have a lovely home," she said in French.

Polly was flabbergasted and speechless.

Elizabeth laughed. "You are indeed a treasure."

Polly recognized the two women sitting on the sofa. Unfortunately, one of them was Margo Harrison, someone with whom Polly had shared occasional trysts.

Margo had called several times when Polly first got back to Washington. Polly had told her they wouldn't be seeing each other anymore because she was leaving town and had started seeing someone. But Margo had continued to pursue her. Now here she was. She hoped Margo would behave herself in front of Kalena.

The woman Margo had been sitting with rose. Polly noticed their physical familiarity. Obviously, Margo and whoever this woman was were intimately involved.

Polly gave Margo a side glance and half smile when they approached.

Margo eyed Kalena, then arched a brow at Polly. "We'll be going now," she said, directly to Polly. She gave her a sultry look, then stroked Polly's arm like she was petting her cat. "I'm sure I'll see you again soon."

Polly stiffened and stepped back.

"This is Kalena Mikloska, from Ohio," Elizabeth said. "Kalena, this is Margo Harrison and Charlette Callaway."

"Wonderful to meet you," Charlette said, smiling.

Charlette's posture, the clothes she wore, the carefully formed vowels of her speech all indicated her breeding and status in the social circles in Washington. She was Margo's pet, someone to show off when she needed a boost in her ego or a step up for someone or something she wanted. Polly felt sorry for Charlette because, judging by the way she occasionally gazed at Margo, it was clear she cared deeply for her.

Margo nodded and grinned, showing too many teeth. Polly wasn't sure if she intended to charm Kalena or tear her to shreds. "Yes. It's good to meet you. I do hope you enjoy your visit to our fair city. It would be natural to be somewhat intimidated. I'm sure you aren't used to the hustle and bustle of a big city being from…Ohio, was it?"

"Yes. It is a little intimidating," Kalena said. "But if seven presidents of the United States can get used to it, I'm sure I can. Besides, I know Polly will take good care of me."

Polly cheered silently as Kalena held her smile until Margo's vanished. She couldn't have been prouder of Kalena for standing her ground. She wanted to laugh out loud and tell Margo to go home and curl up on her sofa because she was totally outclassed.

When Elizabeth returned from seeing Margo and Charlette out, she slipped her arm around Kalena's waist and guided her to the sofa. "Come, sit beside me. I have a thousand questions to ask you."

❖

Kalena traced her finger on the detailed carving on the large poster bed. The room was spacious and elegant, unlike anything she'd ever stayed in. She was awestruck by the beauty that surrounded her. But she wasn't about to let her admiration show, especially around Margo Harrison. It was obvious Polly and Margo were more than acquaintances. The image of Polly in bed with her made Kalena's stomach churn. She was reminded once again of how very different their lives were, and how much more experienced Polly was in the ways of the world. How could she compare?

Margo seemed to be everywhere she and Polly went. When they were in Lafayette Park on Sunday afternoon, Margo and her friends were there. When they went to a restaurant in the downtown district later that evening, Margo and her cronies were there. And Monday morning, Margo stopped by Elizabeth's and wanted to speak with Polly, but Elizabeth told her she wasn't available.

Kalena knew Polly was trying to avoid Margo, but the situation grated on her. Obviously, they'd had sex more than once. How many other women had Polly bedded? The more she thought about it, the more uncomfortable she became. She wanted to discuss the subject with her, but between packing up Polly's apartment, shopping, meeting Polly's friends, sight-seeing, and attending social events, they hadn't had time.

Each night after they had made love, they were exhausted and fell asleep. The days were flying by too quickly. Kalena wanted to slow things down, but she didn't know how. She wanted to talk with Polly, but they were rarely alone, except at night, and who wanted to talk when they could make love.

Polly had told her about the formal dinner Elizabeth was having on Christmas Eve, tomorrow. Then she and Polly would be spending Christmas Day and Friday, the twenty-sixth, at the hotel once again. They had just four nights left.

A bolt of panic shot through her. She had only today to shop for a dress for the Christmas Eve dinner and to find other attire for the holiday activities. She couldn't wear what she'd brought with her. It wasn't nearly fancy enough for this group of people.

Elizabeth was gracious and attentive and cordial. Kalena could see why Polly held her in such high regard, but well-wishers, friends, and acquaintances were constantly going in and out of Elizabeth's house. Kalena had been introduced to at least a hundred people in the short time she'd been there. As much as she appreciated all Elizabeth had done to make her feel welcome, she wanted to be alone with Polly.

"Are you ready for some serious shopping?" Polly asked as she entered the bedroom. "When we're done, I need to stop by the apartment and get a few last things, lock up, and give the key to the landlord."

"Yes. I'm ready." Maybe they could be alone later tonight?

When they entered the boutique, Kalena was dazzled by the sight of the beautiful clothing—row after row of embroidered, sequined, laced gowns, and every kind of undergarments and shoes she could imagine. How would she choose? Then she eyed the price tags and took a step back.

Polly edged near her. "I have a charge account here, and I want to buy your gown for tomorrow's party."

Kalena shook her head slowly. "I couldn't let you. It's too much."

"No. It's not. Please. Let me do this. Consider it a Christmas present, or a going-away gift."

"But you're the one who's going away," Kalena whispered.

Polly smiled. "Please let me. It means more than you know."

Was she now someone's mistress? A kept woman? Would she end up with expensive gowns? Furs? Jewels for her fingers or to wear around her neck? Was this how it started? Would she become like Margo, chasing Polly, desperately reaching out for any kind of recognition or acknowledgment that they were once lovers?

Her mouth went dry. Her heart raced, and the room began to spin.

Polly grabbed her and guided her to a chair. She could faintly hear Polly ask for a glass of water from someone near them. She tried to catch her breath, but the more she gasped, the tighter her chest constricted.

"Deep breaths." She heard a female's calming voice with a slight Southern accent. "You'll be all right."

Kalena tried to see who was speaking to her, but she couldn't focus.

She breathed in a caustic ammonia odor and jerked unexpectedly.

Polly was kneeling beside the chair, stroking her arm, her face contorted with obvious concern.

That calming voice again was telling her to breathe. She drank the water that was offered, then took several deep breaths. She looked toward the sound of the voice.

A woman with silver hair, a beautiful smile, and the most perfect complexion Kalena had ever seen stood near her.

"Hi there." She touched Kalena's shoulder. "Darlin', you just sit for a few minutes and relax."

"Who are you?" Kalena asked.

The woman laughed. "I'm Adele Taylor, the owner of this boutique."

"Thank you," Kalena said, embarrassed, heat rising in her cheeks.

"Aren't you a dear? You sit there for as long as you want. No hurry." Adele walked away, leaving her and Polly alone.

"I want to go," Kalena said.

Polly rose. "All right. As soon as you're ready."

Kalena sipped more of the water and scanned the room. Two women stood in the corner by the undergarments staring at her. She rose from the chair and grabbed Polly's arm. "I want to leave right now."

Polly wrapped her arm in hers and led her to a taxi parked just outside the shop.

"I don't want to go back to Elizabeth's just yet," Kalena said.

Polly helped her into the taxi and told the driver to take them to an address.

Kalena didn't care where it was, as long as it wasn't around a lot of people.

Polly guided her out of the taxi and into a building.

Kalena recognized they were going to Polly's apartment.

Polly helped her onto the sofa and sat on the coffee table in front of her, watching her. She rose and went to the boxes, then dug through them until she held up two glasses and a pint of whiskey.

She brought the items and poured the drinks, handing one to Kalena. "You need this."

Kalena took a sip, then set the glass down. She breathed deeply but still couldn't control her emotions. "What am I to you? Am I just someone to have sex with?"

Polly leaned closer to her. "Is that what you think? That all you are to me is a fling?"

Kalena nodded. "Is that what Margo is?"

Polly grimaced. "Margo isn't anything to me. What we had was never important, and it's over now." She reached for Kalena.

Kalena pulled away. She didn't know why she rejected Polly's touch. If anything, she wanted to be in her arms and be reassured. Everything was confusing. She didn't know what was happening to her. She wanted to scream at Polly. No. She wanted to hold her. "But you were with Margo. And how many others?"

Polly bowed her head. "Several. But I can look back now and tell you that I never found what I was looking for." She met Kalena's eyes. Her gaze held hope. "I'm not proud of it, but the arrangement between me and Margo was strictly sex. She's married and sometimes wanted a woman."

"Should I be jealous of her?" Kalena searched her face.

"Absolutely not."

"Did you enjoy sex with her?"

Polly shifted and grazed her lower lip with her teeth, as if uncomfortable. "I don't really want to talk about this because I never want to hurt you, but if it's where you need the conversation to go, then I will."

"It is."

Polly nodded. "To be honest, it was purely physical, and that part was okay. But afterward, I felt empty and alone. I had no emotional involvement. And before you ask, *you're* so deeply embedded in my heart I couldn't get you out if I tried for a million years."

Her words went deep inside Kalena, filling her with the confidence to ask what she needed. "Did you ever love her?"

"No. We met each other's sexual needs, nothing more."

"How do you know I'm not more to you than a sexual need?"

"That's a topic I've wanted to talk with you about but didn't know how to bring up." Polly repositioned on the sofa and faced her. "I've experienced what it feels like to not be in love. Kalena, when I leave, I want you to go out with other women."

A wave of shock rippled through Kalena. "Why would you tell me that?"

Polly took Kalena's hands and held them when Kalena tried to pull away again. "You don't have a comparison. And you won't unless you have other experiences. Believe me, from a selfish perspective, I don't want to encourage you to go out with other women, but how will you know how you feel about me unless you have something to measure it against?"

Kalena glared at her. "Just because I haven't been with anyone else doesn't mean I don't know how I feel about you."

"Kalena, I'm not only your first experience with a woman, but I'm also your first sexual experience entirely. It's a powerful combination. How do you know what you feel for me isn't merely infatuation or, for that matter, extreme gratitude?"

Kalena recoiled, her anger flaring, heating her face. How dare Polly discount her feelings like that? She'd given everything to her, and now Polly wanted her to see other women? Polly had taken her like she was nothing. Taken her body and then used her like she was a piece of trash. She leapt to her feet. "So now you're done with me? That's all I am to you—someone to send running off to other women's beds? How could you? Why didn't you just leave me alone?"

Polly's eyes widened, and she stared up at her. "That's not what I mean. I don't want to be done with you. I don't *want* you to be with anyone else, but I think you need to so you can clarify your feelings about me."

She rose and inched closer. "I'm leaving. I have no idea how long I'll be gone or what will happen. We're entering a world war that none of us want to be in. But this much I do know. I love you, Kalena. And I will love you a thousand years from now. That's how sure I am about what I feel for you. I don't want you to choose to be with me because you don't know anything else. I want you to be with me because you can't imagine anything more. Do you understand what I'm saying?"

Kalena looked into Polly's eyes, and her heart began to soften. Polly had just told her she loved her. It was a shock, yet those were the most natural, comforting words she'd ever heard.

Polly brushed the back of her finger across Kalena's cheek. "I'm just saying if you want to date other women while I'm gone, do it. Don't feel guilty or like you're betraying me in some way. But please don't write me about it. I couldn't bear it."

Kalena leaned into Polly's touch. She wasn't sure she wanted to hear the answer to the next question, but she had to ask. "What about you? Will you date other women?"

"No. I already know how I feel about you. And that's my point. Date, so you'll know, so you'll have no doubt in your mind and in your heart. Just be safe and cautious and protect yourself." Polly slipped her arms around her.

Kalena sighed. "I've made a mess of things. I'm sorry. I don't know why I reacted this way."

Without releasing her, Polly eased her back down onto the sofa, holding her in a gentle embrace. "It's probably a culmination of everything that's happened. In just a few short weeks you acknowledged you're a lesbian. You had sex for the first time, and with a woman. You almost got yourself killed. You left your home and put yourself in a completely foreign environment, and on top of all of that, the country is at war, and who the hell knows what's going to happen next. You've earned the right to do whatever you want."

"Perhaps, but I'm still sorry for the things I said." She snuggled closer to Polly. "I'm confused most of the time about how I feel about all of this. I'm unsure about myself, and I don't like it." She wanted to tell Polly she was the love of her life, and she was everything she needed, but was Polly right? Did Kalena feel this way because she didn't have any other woman to compare her to?

"I think Elizabeth and I can help you with the confusion," Polly said, her breath warm against Kalena's ear. "We have a little surprise for you tomorrow evening. All the women who will be at the dinner party are lesbians. They're good friends of ours and will be a wonderful support group for you while I'm gone. I promise you'll have a great time tomorrow evening and meet some incredible women."

"Really? All of them are lesbians?"

Polly nodded, her excitement written on her face.

"Is Margo going to be there?"

"Absolutely not."

CHAPTER TWENTY-NINE

Kalena positioned the white linen napkin on her lap. The table sparkled with crystal goblets, intricately designed Christmas-themed china plates outlined in gold, and beautiful centerpieces arrayed with red flowers and candles. She was seated second right from Elizabeth. On Elizabeth's immediate right was Adele Taylor, the owner of the boutique where Polly and Kalena had bought their gowns.

Adele smiled. "You made a wonderful choice, Kalena. That dress looks perfect on you. The peach brings out your coloring."

"Thank you, Adele. Thank you for spending time with me and helping me pick out the perfect one. And thank you for your kindness." Kalena looked to her right at the end of the table. Each time Polly glanced at her, she smiled. She was talking with Angela Burrows. Kalena had been introduced to her when they had all gathered in the living room for drinks and socializing.

Angela was an assistant curator at the Washington Museum of Art. Her lover of ten years, Beatrice Renike, was seated at Kalena's immediate right. Beatrice worked in the State Department, specializing in interpretation of Italian documents. Across from Kalena was Margarette Simmons Pratt, whose family owned controlling interest in one of the largest oil companies in the United States. Next to Margarette was Sophie Wozniak, by far one of the most fascinating women at the party. She was a Polish artist whose family had moved to France when she was a teenager, and then had come to America in 1935. And like Kalena, she spoke both Polish and French, except Sophie had actually lived in France.

Kalena felt an immediate bond with her. Sophie had enthusiastically invited Kalena to come visit her on her parents' estate in Alexandria, Virginia.

The fourteen women seated at the table wore beautiful gowns or tailored tuxedos, each smiling and enjoying her individual conversations. Those in tuxedos had brought their formal clothes and dressed for the evening when they arrived. Once the party was over, they would change back into street clothes before leaving. Two of the guests would be staying overnight. Kalena was delighted that Sophie was one of them. The other was Olivia DeVore, a long-time friend and companion of Elizabeth, who was seated on Polly's left.

Kalena kept ogling the room, watching the women, fascinated that each one was a lesbian and that each seemed well adjusted. Despite all they had to go through to keep their preference hidden, they seemed genuinely happy, unlike the women she'd met in Cleveland. But these women and their accomplishments and family backgrounds made her uncomfortable when she compared herself to them. Would she ever be able to fit into Polly's circle? Did she belong here?

"Kalena, Polly told me you have boarders at your home," Elizabeth said. "Tell us what it's like in Ohio. How are you managing with all the changes? How are the women adjusting to working in the factories? What kinds of shortages are you experiencing in your area of the country?"

Elizabeth's gracious invitation to discuss topics Kalena was comfortable talking about eased her hesitation to join in. It was certainly a subject where Kalena could hold her own, and she entered the discussion enthusiastically. Between the delicious meal and the intriguing conversations, the hours flew. After all the guests had left, Polly and Kalena went upstairs.

"Can you unzip me," Polly asked.

"That's dangerous territory. Are you sure?" Kalena grinned.

"Oh, yes," Polly said, laughing.

Kalena slowly undid her gown and kissed her bare shoulders. "I've wanted to do that all night. You're stunning in that dress, and even more lovely out of it." She brushed her lips over Polly's soft skin. "I'm so sorry about yesterday afternoon."

Polly slid her gown down and laid it carefully over the loveseat, then made a twirling motion with her finger.

Kalena turned around, her back to Polly.

Polly tenderly undressed her, then nibbled Kalena's neck, sending desire raging.

Kalena tilted her head back and ran her fingers through Polly's hair.

"It's perfectly all right," Polly whispered. "I know this has been a very confusing time for you. I hope you feel better."

Kalena turned and wrapped her arms around her neck, pulling her gently to her. "Yes. It's been a wonderful evening."

Polly kissed her with lips full and soft, her tongue probing and demanding.

Kalena moaned.

They removed each other's remaining clothing and went to the bed and made love.

When they were both sated, Polly lay at Kalena's breasts as Kalena stroked her back.

"I can hardly believe we have only two days left," Kalena said. "Promise me we can spend Friday alone. I don't want to share you with anyone."

Polly kissed her breast. "Yes. Tomorrow, after Christmas breakfast together, we can leave for the hotel. Friday, after I go to work in the morning to pick up my paperwork, we'll have the rest of the day for just us. Elizabeth understands what our needs are. She won't intrude on our time in any way. And there are some more things we need to talk about," Polly said.

"More?"

Polly laughed. "When we write each other, we can't say anything about our relationship and our feelings for each other. The letters I write are subject to review and will be scrutinized, and any letters you write to me could be used against me."

"You mean I can't write how much I miss you or long to be with you?"

"Not directly. Just picture someone reading your letter to a group of men sitting around a smoke-filled room looking for something to discredit me or use against me."

"How on earth will we be able to communicate our feelings to each other? I'm already frustrated, and you haven't left yet." It wasn't fair to Polly, really, for her to feel that way, but she couldn't help it.

"Use your imagination. I'm sure we can come up with something," Polly said.

Kalena breathed deeply. "Can you tell me where you're going and what you'll be doing when you leave on Saturday?"

Polly raised onto her elbow and watched her, tracing her finger around her navel. "I can tell you I'm taking the train to New York and then a ship to London."

"That's it? That's all?"

"I'm sorry, but for now that's all I can say."

"How long do you think you'll be over there?"

Polly shifted and lay on the pillow, looking at the ceiling with a solemn expression. "Possibly the duration of the war."

"How long do you think that will be?"

Polly shook her head slowly, deliberately. "I hope no longer than a year, but no one knows. I heard a rumor at work the other day that it will be at least two to three years before we'll have enough trained troops, adequate supplies, equipment, and armaments to launch a full-scale attack in Europe, and no one seems to know how the war with Japan will go. That will be a naval war, fought on islands in the Pacific. Whoever controls those islands will control the entire Pacific. And it's going to take time to build up our naval fleet after the devastation at Pearl Harbor."

"*Two to three years*? Does that mean you'll be over there the entire time?"

"Most likely."

Kalena had no idea it could be that long. Her hopes sank. How would she be able to cope?

Soldiers were going to war. Sailors were sailing off to the Pacific, leaving their wives and families, their loved ones. Did she have a right to complain?

Her turmoil of the day before had returned, bringing with it more confusion, uncertainty, and despair. It hovered over her, waiting to descend. One minute she was coping, and the next she was falling off a cliff, dropping, knowing she would hit the ground any second. She sighed deeply.

Polly turned to her and slipped her hand over her waist. "Tomorrow's Christmas." She looked at her watch. "Actually, today is Christmas. Merry Christmas. We have two days, my love. Let's not waste a single moment worrying about something we can't change. Tell me who you enjoyed meeting at the dinner party."

Kalena looked into her eyes. Polly was right. They had two days left, and she didn't want to waste a moment of them. Her emotions were so up and down she felt like a teeter-totter in a school yard. She was exhausted from trying to control them. Maybe she should stop fighting them and accept that she was in turmoil right now. She wasn't the only one dealing with saying good-bye to the one she loved. There, she'd said it to herself, tried it on like a luxurious coat. It felt warm and soft and comforting. But how could she tell Polly she loved her, not knowing when or if she'd return? Was it fair to Polly? To her? Polly had told her she loved her, and the words brought strength and comfort and security to her. Didn't she owe Polly at least that before she left?

At this very moment, thousands of women across America were doing the same thing she was, except they were saying good-bye to their men. There was no difference in the feelings, just the gender. And the fact that she had to hide hers and they didn't. "Let's go downstairs and open our Christmas presents."

Polly laughed. "Now?"

"Yes. Now. Come on. We'll put on our nightclothes and go downstairs, make some hot chocolate and wake up everyone who's asleep, and we'll open presents and celebrate that we're together on Christmas Day. We'll stay up all night and watch the sunrise, then have breakfast. Then we'll go to the hotel and make love as long as we want, and sleep in each other's arms."

"That's a wonderful idea, but I don't think Elizabeth and Olivia would appreciate the disturbance. They haven't seen each other in over four months."

Kalena was shocked. "You mean they're with each other? Together?"

Polly chuckled. "Yes."

She hadn't had a clue, even though she'd been near them all night. It was a thought for another day. "They'll have plenty of time to sleep a few hours. Come on. Let's do it."

Polly checked her watch. "All right, but let's just keep it among Sophie, you, and me."

"No. Let's wake up Elizabeth and Olivia. Please."

Polly scrubbed her face, then smiled. "All right. Let's do it.

But if Elizabeth or Olivia is perturbed, you're the one who's taking responsibility."

"I will. It's totally my idea. Only you wake them."

"Thanks a lot."

Kalena's heart was light for the first time since she'd been in Washington. At this moment the dark clouds weren't looming over them. There was no tomorrow. Only now.

CHAPTER THIRTY

Polly sat crossed-legged on the floor near the Christmas tree, with Kalena beside her. Elizabeth and Olivia cuddled on the sofa, and Sophie stretched out in the overstuffed chair, her slippered feet on the ottoman.

Polly and Kalena tore open the packages they'd given each other. Kalena had told her she wanted them to open their presents at the same time because it might be years before they got to do it again. It made sense to Polly.

Kalena lifted the lid to the large box and yelled, "I don't believe it. Look at them." She held up one of the volumes of the *Encyclopedia Britannica* to Elizabeth.

Elizabeth and Olivia laughed.

"I think you'll find everything you need in those," Elizabeth said.

Polly was enjoying Kalena's excitement too much to finish opening her own gift.

Kalena caressed the leather cover of one of the books, then kissed it. "I love them. Thank you, Polly." She looked over at her. "You haven't opened yours. Hurry up."

Polly couldn't take her eyes off Kalena. She wanted to remember this moment—their first Christmas together. She wanted to burn it into her memory, hang on to it, and never let it go.

"Hurry," Kalena said again.

Polly finished ripping the paper off the box, then dug out the newspaper stuffed inside. At the bottom was a small, red velvet case. She glanced at Kalena, then slowly opened it. Inside was a delicate gold heart-shaped locket with a chain. On the back was engraved *To PS from KM Always*.

Polly fought the tears. Never had she gotten such an intimate and meaningful gift. It couldn't have been given at a more critical time.

Kalena leaned toward her. "Look inside," she whispered.

Polly snapped open the pendant. There, looking back with a beautiful smile, was a picture of Kalena. Polly's eyes welled with tears. "It's more than beautiful. It's perfect. I have no words. Would you put it on me?"

Kalena rose onto her knees and clasped the chain around Polly's neck. She looked into her eyes, then cupped her face. "I'm with you now, wherever you go." She kissed her quickly on the lips and sat down again.

Polly couldn't help but touch the heart every few minutes.

Everyone opened the rest of their presents.

"I'm glad you got us up, Kalena. I feel like I'm ten years old again," Olivia said.

Sophie raised her cup of hot chocolate. "Hear, hear."

"Yes. I feel like I'm ten, but my body has reminded me I'm not. We're going back to bed," Elizabeth said. She stood and reached for Olivia. "Come, darling. A big day tomorrow and dawn will be here soon enough."

Sophie also rose. "I'd love to stay up with you, but I have to leave at nine o'clock in the morning to visit my sister and her family, or they'll never forgive me. Polly, I wish you all the best. Send us your address as soon as you can. God bless you, dear one."

Polly pushed herself up from the floor and hugged her.

Sophie bent down and kissed Kalena on the cheek. "Merry Christmas, my loves. Thank you for this. It was sweet."

"Good night. Merry Christmas. I hope you enjoy your visit with your family," Kalena said.

"Merry Christmas, Sophie. Give my regards to your sister and her family," Polly said.

"I surely will. Good night." Sophie left the room.

"They're all wonderful," Kalena said.

"What?"

"You asked me who I enjoyed the most meeting at the dinner party. All of them." Kalena smiled. "I love my gift. I'll enjoy it every day."

Polly sat and touched her necklace once more. "If I told you this locket means more to me than anything I've ever gotten in my life, it still wouldn't convey to you how special it is."

They lay down on the floor among the ripped colorful paper, discarded ribbons and bows, the scent of the Christmas tree filling the room, the lights glowing.

Kalena reached up and brought Polly to her. "I love you. You are the love of my life. I know it."

They had no more words, only their love filling them to overflowing.

❖

Kalena sat across from Polly, their catered Christmas meal set up in their hotel room. She watched Polly, trying to see any indication of what she was thinking.

Polly tilted her head slightly and smiled.

Kalena pushed her food around her plate like a cat playing with a favorite toy.

"No appetite this evening?" Polly asked.

Kalena rose from the table and took Polly by the hand. "Lie with me."

They lay in bed, Kalena's arms wrapped around her. "I can't stop thinking about all the thousands of women here in the US who are right now doing the same thing I'm doing and feeling the same thing I'm feeling," Kalena said. "I think the tears and sorrow we're all feeling are raining down over the land. I saw the pain in their faces on the train, and I see it when we go places. Everywhere I look, it's as if we're in one big basin of gloom, and the only relief we get is when the sun momentarily breaks through the storm clouds. Is it going to be like this for the entire war, the entire time you're away from me?" Kalena buried her face in Polly's neck.

Polly stroked her hair, then lifted Kalena's chin and kissed her. "We'll have to fight more than Germany and Japan."

"What do you mean?"

"We'll have to fight despair, depression, and loneliness. The world is at war and in turmoil." Polly looked into her eyes. "You are a lighthouse to my soul. My love for you steadies me and keeps me anchored. I'll always have that. Like you said when you gave me my locket, you'll be with me wherever I go." Polly kissed her again. "Come on. Let's take a carriage ride down Constitution Avenue. It's Christmas, and the city is lit up and waiting for us."

They dressed warmly and walked to the row of horse-drawn buggies, the drivers dressed in colorful red tails, top hats, and leather gloves. An attendant directed them to the lead carriage, where the assistant helped Polly and Kalena into the plush open vehicle.

Kalena brushed her gloved hand over the red leather seat, then traced the design in the finely tooled door.

The attendant settled a soft wool checkered blanket over their laps. "Samuel is your driver. Enjoy the ride, ladies."

From the driver's seat, Samuel tipped his hat to them, then flicked the reins. "Step up," he said to the elegant bay horse.

Polly and Kalena held hands under the blanket.

The refreshing cool air brushed against Kalena's face as the carriage glided down the street, the colorfully decorated lampposts lighting their way. The clip-n-clop of the horse's hooves rhythmically announced their presence along the historic route. Samuel turned right, onto another street.

People strolled the sidewalks, couples arm in arm, children dashing about.

Polly slipped her hand from under the blanket and pointed. "Look. There's the back of the White House."

Kalena watched in awe as it came into full view. "It's magnificent."

The horse picked up its pace, as if sensing where they were.

"President Roosevelt and Prime Minister Churchill did the Christmas Tree Ceremonial Lighting yesterday," Polly said.

"Are they in the White House this evening?" Kalena asked, straining to get a glimpse, trying to see in through the windows.

Polly laughed. "I'm not sure if they're home tonight. I imagine they are."

"Polly." Kalena lowered her voice. "I heard last night that Mrs. Roosevelt is a lesbian. Is that true?"

Polly pressed her finger to her lips, then pointed to Samuel.

It was obvious Polly didn't want to discuss the subject right then. Kalena was sure it wasn't just a rumor. She made a mental note to bring it up again when they were alone.

They passed in full view of the White House. Crowds of people were milling around the gates and fencing, enjoying the festivities. A beautiful, fully decorated Christmas tree stood majestically at the corner of the south end of the grounds.

Samuel turned slightly toward Polly and Kalena. "This is the first year the Christmas tree has been on the south lawn. President Roosevelt said yesterday at the lighting ceremony that *'against enemies who preach the principles of hate and practice them, we set our faith in human love and in God's care for us and all men everywhere.'* That's a noble thought." He nodded and turned back in his seat.

The white lights illuminating the White House made it appear almost translucent as it shimmered in the darkness.

Kalena pulled the blanket tighter around them. "What a great idea to do this." How would she ever manage without Polly near her? Now that they had proclaimed their love for each other, what would their future hold? What was the point of their love if all they got to do with it was hold it for only a moment? Would it grow or diminish while they were separated?

Polly pointed to their right. "Over there is the Lafayette Building. That's where OAD headquarters is located. And over there is the War Department."

"Where do you work?" Kalena asked.

"When I'm not on assignment, I work over there." She pointed to a smaller structure west of the Lafayette Building.

Kalena clung tightly to Polly, continuing to watch the people and the sights as they rode back to the hotel.

Tonight, and then one more.

Chapter Thirty-one

Polly arranged the documents carefully, slipped them into her attaché case, locked it, then set it on the floor beside her.

"Well, Enigma, are you ready?" Assistant Director Williamson winked and sat in the chair opposite her.

She smiled and lightly brushed her wool skirt, then crossed her legs. "Yes, sir. I'm a little nervous, but I should adjust fairly quickly."

She was more than a little nervous but confident in her abilities. She looked around the room, remembering the last time she'd been in his office. It seemed like a lifetime ago. Everything had changed for her, and it was because of Kalena. Not her job. Not the assignment. Not what she did. It was Kalena. She'd made such a difference in her life.

Williamson leaned slightly toward her, as if to emphasize what he was about to say. "I want you to know before you leave, that I consider you one of our most competent agents. You're trustworthy and dedicated, and your reasoning skills are outstanding. I know you'll represent us with the utmost integrity and professionalism."

Polly's cheeks became hot. "Thank you, sir. I appreciate your confidence in me."

"You've certainly earned it." He handed her a folded sheet of paper from the inside pocket of his suit coat. "This is your written order. A copy of it is in your file. You are hereby officially assigned as a consultant to British headquarters for Special Operations Executive, SOE."

She tilted her head in question, having never heard of that branch.

"The SOE was organized last year to initiate resistance and disrupt enemy activities in occupied Europe." He shifted and looked more intently at her. "Help them interpret data, strategize, and support them in any way you can. You'll be fully updated after you arrive. You'll be under the direction of their bureau chief, not our military leadership."

Polly took the letter and read her orders. She was going to Europe, in the thick of war, with confidence in her skills and assignment. "I see I'm to remain under SOE jurisdiction until I receive orders from this office to return to the United States."

Williamson nodded. "That's correct. I don't know how long it will be, but I assure you we'll consider the needs of SOE and the benefits of your placement with them. Send me official reports monthly. And do send me a personal note occasionally about how you're doing. Direct all correspondence through special post at the United States embassy."

She nodded, her mind whirling with all the information and the adventure ahead.

"Now, Polly, can I do anything for you before you go?"

She pondered a moment, then grinned. "Send me some York Peppermint Patties now and again? I really like them."

He laughed and slapped his knee. "By God, I will. I surely will." He stood.

She rose and clasped her satchel.

His eyes were moist, but he had a broad smile. "Safe journey, Polly. Our prayers and hopes go with you."

She walked down the marble steps, her high heels making a tapping sound. She reached the main exit just as someone called to her.

"Polly. Hey, Polly."

She smiled and turned, immediately recognizing the voice of Jimmy Pendergast, her fellow agent.

He rushed to her and grabbed her in a bear hug. "Guess what?" He finally let go.

She couldn't help but laugh at his enthusiasm. "Um, from the look on your face and the sparkle in your eyes, it's certainly good news. Our work isn't something that would make you that happy, so it must be personal. Let's see—"

"Stop. I want to tell you before you figure it out."

Polly laughed. "Well, it's something very special."

He lifted his chin and laughed loudly. "Boy, is it ever. I'm going to be a dad."

She wrapped her arms around him. "That's wonderful news. Congratulations, Jimmy."

He took a step back and inspected her. "When are you leaving?"

"Tomorrow morning. The eight-fifteen to New York."

"Gee. I didn't realize it was that soon. It seems like you just got back into town. There's so much I want to talk to you about. Can we meet for drinks later this evening before I head home?"

She smiled. "I wish I could, but I have plans."

Jimmy scrunched his face. "Of course you do. It's your last night. I'm sorry." He hugged her again. "Give 'em hell for us."

"Good-bye, Jimmy. Take good care of your family. Write me?" she said.

"You bet I will. Be safe."

She went through the exit, out to the sidewalk, and hailed a cab. Then she looked back at the building. The huge United States flag, anchored on the façade, snapped in the crisp December breeze, reminding her that freedom was protected by sacrifice.

She drew in a deep breath. "Help me see it through no matter the cost." She turned and got into the taxi.

❖

Kalena threw her arms around her when she entered the hotel room. "I thought you'd never get back."

Polly laughed. "The meeting was an hour and a half too long." She kissed her, then set the attaché case by her suitcase.

The bright sunlight shone through the hotel window.

She caressed Kalena's cheek and looked deeply into her eyes. The pain was there, half hidden by the promise of a few more hours.

"What did you do while I was gone?" Polly asked.

"Absolutely nothing, except go downstairs and buy you something."

Polly chuckled. "I can't jam another thing into my luggage."

"You have to find room," Kalena insisted. She went to the bed and brought back a brown package, then handed it to her.

"What's this?" Polly asked, kissing her cheek. She tore open the wrapping and gazed at the leather-bound book.

"It's a journal. For you to write in," Kalena said.

"It's just what I need. Thank you. I'm sure it'll help me record my thoughts. Will you keep one also? For me? So I can read it when I get home?"

Kalena nodded. "Yes. We can pick out another later today. It'll be fun knowing you're writing in yours also."

During a long silence they looked at each other. The pain was there again, hovering, as if anxiously biding its time to take center stage. Polly shoved it back, unwilling to allow it to invade. Its moment would come soon enough. But not now.

A loud knock on the door startled her.

"Who on earth is that?" Kalena asked.

Polly smiled when she opened the door.

"Miss Sylvester?" the concierge asked. "When would you like it delivered and set up?"

"We'll be leaving in a little while. Please make sure it's ready by four this afternoon."

He nodded. "I'll see to it personally."

She tipped him.

He thanked her and left.

"What was that all about?" Kalena asked.

"A surprise for later," Polly said. "Let's have lunch at the Commodore, then go for a stroll in Lafayette Park?"

"All right. I'll get dressed."

After their meal, Polly hailed a taxi, which dropped them off at the park.

They strolled arm in arm along the path, then sat on a bench and watched the people enjoying their day. Polly lifted her face to the sun. "I don't think I've ever seen a more pleasant December afternoon. It's gorgeous out. Look at that vivid blue sky. Not a cloud to be found." She smiled as the sun warmed her.

Kalena closed her eyes and lifted her chin to the sky. "That is nice."

A petite woman with dark hair and holding a camera approached them. "Hi. I'm Eve Arnold, a freelance photographer. Would you allow me to snap a few photos of you two? I'd be happy to mail you a copy if you'd give me an address where I can send it."

"Yes, please," Kalena said. She slipped her arm in Polly's and leaned into her.

Eve laughed.

Polly stood. She couldn't permit anyone she didn't know to take a picture of her or give them any information. From Eve's confident expression and the way she projected herself, she was being honest, but Polly couldn't do what she asked. "How about some pictures of just her." She pointed to Kalena.

Eve lowered her camera. "If it's a problem, I understand."

"Just shots of her will be good," Polly said.

"That's perfect," Eve said. "Hold that pose for a moment." She moved around Kalena, snapping pictures from different angles. "Do you live here in Washington?" she asked her.

"We're visiting," Kalena said, looking at Polly and holding her gaze.

"That's a great shot," Eve said.

Polly couldn't take her eyes off Kalena. Did Eve see what was in her eyes? Love was looking back.

Eve slid the camera strap around her neck and pulled out a pen and pad from her shoulder case. "Who would you like me to send the copies to?"

"Please send them to me." Kalena spelled her name and gave her the address. "I'll be happy to pay the costs," Kalena said.

"Oh, no. That's not necessary. It's my pleasure to send them, although it may not be for several weeks." She stuffed the book and pen back into her bag. "Thank you again for allowing me to take the photographs. You have a lovely glow about you. I hope I was able to capture it on film. Happy New Year. Good day." Eve continued on her way.

"That was fun," Kalena said. "I wonder if she'll really send them."

"You'll know in a few weeks," Polly said. She checked her watch. "Let's go back to the hotel."

"Can we walk a little while longer?" Kalena asked. "It's so beautiful. Let's enjoy it until the sun goes down."

Polly rose and reached for Kalena's hand, tucking it into the crook of her arm. "I think it would be a sin to waste this beautiful sunny day inside."

Kalena held on to Polly's arm as they sauntered through the park.

When they reached the hotel and exited the elevator onto their floor, Kalena fast-walked through the hall, a couple of steps ahead. Polly vaulted in front of her at the last second. "Let me open the door."

Kalena laughed.

Polly hoped the items she'd requested were in the room as instructed. It was important the evening be perfect. She took a deep breath and held it as she opened the door, then beamed, exhaling in relief. Everything was set up exactly as she'd imagined.

Kalena walked past her and stopped mid-step, scanning the room.

On the dresser was a phonograph with a stack of records next to it. A small table was positioned off to the side, adorned with a bouquet of flowers and holding an ice bucket with a bottle of champagne and two glasses.

Kalena smelled the flowers, then touched the bottle. She turned to Polly.

Polly gazed at her. The expression of joy and pleasure on Kalena's face sent her heart soaring.

"Look at what you've done," Kalena said, clasping her cheeks.

They slipped their coats off and embraced.

Kalena held her in her arms. "How I wish we could stop time and freeze this moment."

"We'll hold this night in our hearts and never let it go," Polly said.

She searched the records. Among them were tunes from Artie Shaw, Jimmy and Tommy Dorsey, Glenn Miller, and several others.

Kalena turned off the lights.

Color from the city flooded in, giving the room a sultry, soulful appearance, taking on a personality of its own.

Polly selected a song to slow dance to and slipped it on the player. She reached for Kalena and guided her to her.

The music began.

Kalena stepped closer.

They held each other and swayed to the beat.

When the song was over, Kalena chose another record and slid into Polly's arms, pressing into her.

They danced. And in those precious moments the night was theirs.

Kalena led her to the bed.

They slowly undressed each other.

"I'll never let you go," Kalena whispered.

They moved as one, fulfilling each other. The intimate sounds of their lovemaking, the colors of the lingering Christmas lights softly illuminating the room, and the scent of the flowers created a euphoria that Polly swooned in. It was a memory lodged in her heart, one she could take with her for as long as the world was upside down, until she could return to Kalena once more.

They drank champagne in bed, ordered a meal from room service, and shared the remaining hours. And when sleep overtook them, they drifted off, encased in a cocoon of love.

❖

Kalena woke in a cold sweat, her heart racing. How long had they been asleep? How much time did they have left?

The lights still shone through the window but now cast a muted glow. Curious to see the cause, she slipped from the bed and gazed out. A thick fog had settled over the streetlamps, which seemed to wrestle with their capture, determined to fulfill their appointed duty to pierce the darkness.

She looked at Polly, barely able to see her silhouette. She went back to the bed and nestled next to her, engulfed in the warmth of her body. She tucked the covers around them and buried her face in her neck, breathing in her aroma. She kissed her breasts, then her shoulder.

Polly stirred. She folded her arms around Kalena and held her. "I love the scent of your hair." She kissed the top of Kalena's head.

"What time is it?" Kalena asked, not really wanting to know.

Polly rolled over and checked her watch on the nightstand. "It's five. We have a little time left before we have to get ready."

Kalena snuggled closer, kissing Polly's breasts again, the nipples firm and erect. She thought of making love one last time, to satisfy Polly, but she needed to lie with her, to be with her, entwined. She kissed her neck once more, feeling the softness of her skin against her lips, tasting the salt of her sweat from the night's passion. She licked her, then took in a deep breath.

Polly laughed. "What are you doing? That tickles!"

"I'm making a memory of your taste and scent."

Polly squeezed her. "I love your touch and fragrance. Sometimes you move so gracefully it's as if you defy gravity. The music of your voice fills me. And I adore the way you play with your hair when you get nervous or self-conscious."

Kalena nudged her cheek against her. "I love the way you try to please me." She scooted up to Polly, so close they shared the breath between them. But she could still see the expression of desperation and pain, which lingered in her eyes and was etched in her face. Was it Polly's or a reflection of her own? "One last kiss, my love," she whispered.

Polly's lips brushed against hers, and then she entered, her tongue slipping into Kalena's welcoming mouth. Every nerve, every tendon and sinew thrilled to the sensation. The kiss was unhurried and wet and probing, searching for Kalena's desire and need. And when Polly found it, she increased her demand for more, until in that last moment before she withdrew, she filled Kalena with her own need, her own longing and desire.

The lingering sensation radiated through Kalena's breasts and into her. This was their final kiss of passion and yearning. The realization of its loss consumed her. She forced back the emotion, knowing morning tears were the saddest of all, and, once released, the exquisite pain would seep into her soul.

They lay together, the morning's light announcing their imminent separation.

The phone rang. Their wake-up call.

They showered together in an unspoken masquerade of deception, avoiding each other's eyes, unwilling or unable to see each other's pain.

They dressed, then sat silently at the table and ate.

Finally, Polly broke the silence. "We need to either be this way the entire morning or deal with it."

Kalena placed her fork on her plate, unable to restrain her tears.

"We aren't the only ones," Polly said softly, her lip quivering.

They rose and embraced.

"We need to do everything we can to help each other through this separation," Polly said.

Kalena nodded. "I know."

"Are you sure you want to go to the station with me? You don't have to. It may be easier on both of us if you stay here until it's time for you to leave."

Kalena shook her head. "No. I want to. I need to see you get on that train."

They packed their remaining belongings and called for the bellhop.

He loaded their luggage onto a cart, then started to leave.

"We'll be there momentarily," Kalena told him.

He tipped his hat and closed the door.

She took Polly by the hand and kissed her, then wiped the smear of her lipstick. "Think of me often," she said, searching Polly's eyes and seeing a thousand years of last kisses and the sorrow of the ages.

Polly's face softened, and she smiled. "Only now and then. And in between."

They entered the cab, sliding in beside each other.

"Union Station," Polly said.

The mass of people shuffling in and out of the entrance created a deluge of confusion.

A gray-haired man, dressed in a blue uniform, tipped his hat to Kalena. "Eight-fifteen, miss?" he asked.

Polly held up her ticket.

"Ah," he said and nodded. He tagged her luggage, then loaded it onto a wagon. "I'll see it's taken care of. And yours, miss?" he asked Kalena.

Kalena rummaged through her clutch purse and pulled out her ticket, checking it. "Five thirty this evening to Cleveland."

He nodded and tagged her luggage. "It'll be stored and loaded, ma'am."

Polly gave him a gratuity and picked up her attaché case.

He touched his hat and left.

Kalena slipped her arm around Polly's. She wanted to tell her to make sure she wrote her, but it was silly. Of course, Polly would write. A bolt of panic surged through her. "You have my address?"

Polly laughed. "Yes."

"How long for the ship to cross?" The panic began to build, roiling in Kalena's stomach.

Polly patted her hand. "About five days. I promise I'll write as soon as I can."

The eight-fifteen train whistle blew its first warning.

Kalena tensed, the sound going through her like a stab to her heart.

The rumble of the engine vibrated the platform.

The press of the crowd surged forward. Good-byes were shouted. Women wept.

Kalena fought back the tears and tightened her grip on Polly's arm, pulling her closer.

The whistle blew another long blast.

"All aboard," the conductor yelled.

Passengers began to move, waving and lining up.

Polly slipped her arm from Kalena's.

Kalena locked eyes with hers. Desperation washed over her, choking her.

Polly cupped her face. "Keep busy and be safe until I come back." She pulled Kalena into her arms. "I love you."

Kalena wrapped her arms around her neck, forcing herself not to kiss her. "I love you, Polly Sylvester. I'll keep the light on in the window so you can find your way back to me." Tears streamed down her cheeks, mixing with Polly's.

Polly brushed her lips with her fingertips, searching her eyes.

"Be safe, my love. Be safe," Kalena said, then tore herself away from her.

Polly walked to the train, stepped up, turned, and waved. Then she entered, and the iron monster engulfed her.

Kalena frantically peered through the windows, trying to follow her through the car. She sat in the eighth seat from where she entered, on the platform side.

When Polly saw her, she waved again and blew her a kiss.

Kalena raised her hand and held it there, groping for her final drop of self-restraint.

The whistle blew a last farewell. The workers removed the portable steps. The train lunged forward, ripping Polly from her.

Kalena stood immobile, unable to leave, or breathe, or scream. She fixated on the train until the last remnants of its existence disappeared around the bend. The crowd dispersed, ebbing away from the platform, leaving her among the discarded ticket stubs and early morning newspapers.

Polly was gone.

The reality of her absence pulled Kalena down into a sea of despair. She was sinking, drowning, going under for the third time. With head lowered, she turned and trudged toward the waiting area.

She looked up and couldn't believe what she saw.

There, in the middle of the platform, locked arm in arm, were four smiling, waving women, tears trickling down their faces. Elizabeth, Olivia, Adele, and Sophie.

Kalena ran to them.

They gathered her in their arms, surrounding her.

"You missed her," Kalena cried. "She's already left."

Elizabeth kissed her wet cheek. "Oh, sweetheart, we didn't come to see Polly off. We said good-bye to her Christmas Day. We came to be with you."

Kalena wept. When she finally regained control, she gazed at the women gathered around her, trying to accept that she now had friends who understood her pain, and longing, and the deepest imaginations of her heart.

Polly would return to her. She was sure of it. She was counting on it. Someday they'd be together again, but until that day came, she'd hold on to her love at any cost.

EPILOGUE

Wednesday, December 20, 1944

Kalena hurried from Hurst Hall on campus and barely caught the bus, jumping on at the last moment before the driver closed the doors. "You're cutting it close again," he said, smiling.

"But today's the last day of classes before Christmas break. Had to make the most of it," she said, slipping the coins into the slot. She made her way to the center and sat next to an older woman clutching a bulky package on her lap.

Kalena smiled and said hello, sticking her bookbag between her feet.

Three more semesters and she'd graduate with her degree in Liberal Arts. Polly had been right about keeping busy. Kalena hadn't wasted her time. When she returned home to Ohio, she had immediately signed up for classes at the University of Akron. But when Aunt Berna passed away from pneumonia in March of 1943, Kalena sold the house and moved to Washington DC. She'd planned to get her own apartment, but Elizabeth had insisted she live with her. "Getting your own place is a waste of money," Elizabeth had said. "And besides, the company here will do you good."

She'd transferred her college credits to American University in DC and continued toward her degree.

It wasn't that big an adjustment to move in with Elizabeth, since she'd made the trip to visit her about twice a year after Polly had left. Even before Aunt Berna's death she'd considered moving to Washington, but she couldn't bear the idea of leaving her alone.

Since the Allied invasion of Normandy on June sixth, everyone was hopeful the war in Europe would end soon. The thought of another year without Polly was almost unbearable. How much longer before she came home? She almost wished she weren't on Christmas break for two weeks. The time dragged and seemed to slow to a crawl when she wasn't busy. But she had a paper to write and exams to study for, which would occupy her mind. And Elizabeth had planned a party for the twenty-third. Sophie would be there. She hadn't seen her in months. Their friendship had blossomed, and she was a comforting support. Sophie had finally met someone and was bringing her to the party.

Kalena was excited to meet her, but the familiar ache of Polly's absence tugged at her heart. It had been three years, almost to the day, since she'd said good-bye to her. Polly wrote when she could, but her letters were often vague and short. All Kalena knew about her work was that she was in London for a time, and then not. Polly couldn't say where, but for months afterward Kalena didn't receive mail. When she did get letters, they were always postmarked from London, and her address where Kalena sent her weekly mail was always the same. She missed her so desperately and still cried herself to sleep occasionally. Though she'd met plenty of women over the years, no one had come close to touching her heart, and she'd kept her love for Polly guarded and secure.

Kalena entered the house and started up the stairs to her bedroom to change.

Elizabeth came to the entryway, an odd expression on her face. "Kalena…you have a cable."

Kalena froze mid-step, gripping the handrail. She stared straight ahead, not turning. She noticed a deep scratch on the edge of the step in front of her, a piece of lint stuck in the corner. Anna must have missed it when she cleaned.

"Did you hear me?" Elizabeth asked.

Kalena continued to stare. "Who's it from?" she choked out.

"OAD, here in Washington." Elizabeth's voice cracked.

Kalena's knees buckled, and she wavered. She covered her mouth to muffle the gasp. She took a deep breath, then struggled down the steps, stopping in front of Elizabeth, dropping her bookbag on the floor.

"It might be good news," Elizabeth said. "Telegrams aren't always bad news." She abruptly stopped speaking and offered it to her.

Kalena reached for it with a trembling hand, then pressed it to her chest. "I can't open it."

"Come sit down." Elizabeth guided her into the living room and sat with her on the sofa.

Kalena continued to clutch the envelope to her breasts, Elizabeth beside her, her arm wrapped securely around her shoulder.

The only sound was the grandfather clock, ticking the seconds away.

"When was the last time you heard from her?" Elizabeth asked.

"Five weeks," she mumbled. Polly had to be all right. Nothing could have happened to her, not after all this time. It was a mistake. Perhaps the wrong address. That's what had happened. It came to Elizabeth's house by mistake, and she had misread who it was for. "I need to go to the dentist. It's been too long. Wouldn't want to get a cavity. And if I have one, it's better to catch it before it gets bad."

Elizabeth tightened her grip on Kalena's shoulder.

"I should wash that sweater out this evening and block it on a towel, so it'll be ready for the party." Kalena's fingers seemed to move by themselves, and before she became conscious of it, the message was a wadded, wrinkled mass against her breasts. Heavy tears dripped down her cheeks, sliding onto her arms.

Elizabeth offered a tissue.

Kalena shifted and glared at her, thrusting the telegram at her. "You open it."

Elizabeth nodded. She released Kalena's shoulder and clasped the envelope, smoothing it out on her lap, then opened it, starting at the top edge, then ripped it, and pulled the slip of paper out.

Kalena watched her eyes move back and forth as she read the words, seeing a smile begin to form.

Elizabeth patted Kalena's knee. "I'll read it to you."

All's well, stop.
Arrive 12-22, 5:45 p.m. Union Station, stop.
Polly.

Kalena collapsed into Elizabeth's arms.

❖

Kalena paced, barely noticing the crowd as they shuffled past. The platform at Union Station had emptied once more, then began to fill again. She checked her watch. Six more minutes. What would she be like? What would she look like? Had she lost weight? Would she still be the same? Had her feelings for her changed?

She couldn't tell by her letters.

More seconds and minutes passed.

The whistle blew. The platform vibrated as the train pulled into the station. Her heart beat so fast she could hardly catch her breath.

The engine brakes released with an eruption of noise when the train finally came to a full stop. Men rushed past her and stood by the exits to assist the travelers as they stepped down.

Kalena scanned the people leaving the six passenger cars. Each person. Men in suits. Men in uniform. More men. A woman with a baby. Seven more women. Not Polly. Where was she?

A woman stepped lithely onto the platform, smartly dressed, long hair, a Fedora hat partially obscuring the view of her face. Was it her? She couldn't see a full profile. *Look up. Look this way.*

The woman turned slightly, then smiled demurely with an engaging expression.

Kalena's heart skipped a beat. "Polly."

She ran to her.

Polly threw her arms around her and held her, kissing her face.

In that moment, unspeakable joy, relief, and comfort swept through Kalena, wiping out all the bitter sadness of their separation and the pain and turmoil of their years apart.

"I'm home, Kalena, my darling. I'm home. And I'll never leave you again."

BIBLIOGRAPHY

Books:

Atkinson, Wilmer, 1919, *How To Do Things,* Reference 917.7136, Washington Square, Philadelphia.

Barberton Public Library, *Barberton Directory 1941,* Reference Ohio R917.7136, Barberton, Ohio.

Faderman, Lillian, 1991, *Odd Girls and Twilight Lovers,* Columbia University Press, New York.

Kelleher, Stephen E., 2014, *A Pictorial History of Barberton, Ohio*, The Barberton Historical Society Press, Barberton, Ohio.

Koltnow, Ronald, 2018, *Barberton Fried Chicken—An Ohio Original,* American Palate, Charleston, S.C.

Legrand, Jacques, 1987, *Chronicle of the 20th Century,* Chronicle Publications, New York.

Life Magazine, June 1955, *Special Collector's Edition 1945.*

Norton, Mary Beth, Katzman, David, Escott, Paul, Chudacoff, Howard, Paterson, Thomas, Tuttle Jr., William, 1982, *A People & A Nation, A History Of The United States, Volume II: Since 1865,* Houghton Mifflin Company, Boston.

Pryor II, James I., 2014, *Images of Aviation Akron Aviation,* Arcadia Publishing, South Carolina.

Sommerville, Donald, 2008-2009, *The Ultimate Illustrated History of World War II*, Hermes House, London.

Trivisonno, Justin, *Collection-Barberton and Local Area, Vol. 3.,* Ohio 2013-012.032R779, Barberton Public Library, Barberton, Ohio.

Wilson, Jr., Vincent, 1992, *The Book of Distinguished American Women, Second Edition,* American History Research Associates, Maryland.

Online References:

Case Western Reserve University. *Encyclopedia of Cleveland History. Cleveland Union Terminal.* https://case.edu/ech/articles/c/cleveland-union-terminal

Encyclopedia of American History, BallotPedia. *Franklin D. Roosevelt's State of the Union Address, 1941.* https://ballotpedia.org/Franklin_D._Roosevelt%27s_State_of_the_Union_Address,_1941

Online Etymology Dictionary. https://www.etymonline.com

Rebels Market. *What Did Women Wear In The 1940s.* https://www.rebelsmarket.com/blog/posts/what-did-women-wear-in-1940s-women-s-fashion-and-clothing-from-the-1940s.html

RetroWaste. *1940s Fashion: Clothing Styles and Trends.* https://www.retrowaste.com/1940s/1940s-fashion/

UVA Miller Center. *September 11, 1941: Fireside 18: On The Greer Incident.*

https://millercenter.org/the-presidency/presidential-speeches/september-11-1941-fireside-chat-18-greer-incident

UVA Miller Center. *December 8, 1941: Address to Congress Requesting a Declaration of War.* https://millercenter.org/the-presidency/presidential-speeches/december-8-1941-address-congress-requesting-declaration-war

Victrola. *Jukebox History: Evolution of the Jukebox.* https://victrola.com/blogs/articles/jukebox-history-the-evolution-of-the-jukebox

About the Author

Suzie Clarke is a native of Northeast Ohio and has a medical and business background. Before her life as a writer, she specialized in public health, working with women in all aspects of their lives. When not writing, she can be found spending time with her family, backpacking, or out on the golf course.

Books Available From Bold Strokes Books

Almost Perfect by Tagan Shepard. A shared love of queer TV brings Olivia and Riley together, but can they keep their real-life love as picture perfect as their on-screen counterparts? (978-1-63679-322-1)

The Amaranthine Law by Gun Brooke. Tristan Kelly is being hunted for who she is and her incomprehensible past, and despite her overwhelming feelings for Olivia Bryce, she has to reject her to keep her safe. (978-1-63679-235-4)

Craving Cassie by Skye Rowan. Siobhan Carney and Cassie Townsend share an instant attraction, but are they brave enough to give up everything they have ever known to be together? (978-1-63679-062-6)

Drifting by Lyn Hemphill. When Tess jumps into the ocean after Jet, she thinks she's saving her life. Of course, she can't possibly know Jet is actually a mermaid desperate to fix her mistake before she causes her clan's demise. (978-1-63679-242-2)

Enigma by Suzie Clarke. Polly has taken an oath to protect and serve her country, but when the spy she's tasked with hunting becomes the love of her life, will she be the one to betray her country? (978-1-63555-999-6)

Finding Fault by Annie McDonald. Can environmental activist Dr. Evie O'Halloran and government investigator Merritt Shepherd set aside their conflicting ideas about saving the planet and risk their hearts enough to save their love? (978-1-63679-257-6)

The Forever Factor by Melissa Brayden. When Bethany and Reid confront their past, they give new meaning to letting go, forgiveness, and a future worth fighting for. (978-1-63679-357-3)

The Frenemy Zone by Yolanda Wallace. Ollie Smith-Nakamura thinks relocating from San Francisco to her dad's rural hometown is the worst idea in the world, but after she meets her new classmate Ariel Hall, she might have a change of heart. (978-1-63679-249-1)

Hot Keys by R.E. Ward. In 1920s New York City, Betty May Dewitt and her best friend, Jack Norval, are determined to make their Tin Pan

Alley dreams come true and discover they will have to fight—not only for their hearts and dreams, but for their lives. (978-1-63679-259-0)

Securing Ava by Anne Shade. Private investigator Paige Richards takes a case to locate and bring back runaway heiress Ava Prescott. But ignoring her attraction may prove impossible when their hearts and lives are at stake. (978-1-63679-297-2)

A Cutting Deceit by Cathy Dunnell. Undercover cop Athena takes a job at Valeria's hair salon to gather evidence to prove her husband's connections to organized crime. What starts as a tentative friendship quickly turns into a dangerous affair. (978-1-63679-208-8)

As Seen on TV! by CF Frizzell. Despite their objections, TV hosts Ronnie Sharp, a laid-back chef, and paranormal investigator Peyton Stanford have to work together. The public is watching. But joining forces is risky, contemptuous, unnerving, provocative—and ridiculously perfect. (978-1-63679-272-9)

Blood Memory by Sandra Barret. Can vampire Jade Murphy protect her friend from a human stalker and keep her dates with the gorgeous Beth Jenssen without revealing her secrets? (978-1-63679-307-8)

Foolproof by Leigh Hays. For Martine Roberts and Elliot Tillman, friends with benefits isn't a foolproof way to hide from the truth at the heart of an affair. (978-1-63679-184-5)

Hard Pressed by Aurora Rey. When rivals Mira Lavigne and Dylan Miller are tapped to co-chair Finger Lakes Cider Week, competition gives way to compromise. But will their sexual chemistry lead to love? (978-1-63679-210-1)

The Laws of Magic by M. Ullrich. Nothing is ever what it seems, especially not in the small town of Bender, Massachusetts, where a witch lives to save lives and avoid love. (978-1-63679-222-4)

The Lonely Hearts Rescue by Morgan Lee Miller, Nell Stark & Missouri Vaun. In this novella collection, a hurricane hits the Gulf Coast, and the animals at the Lonely Hearts Rescue Shelter need love—and so do the humans who adopt them. (978-1-63679-231-6)